Lucky Night

ALSO BY ELIZA KENNEDY

Do This for Me

I Take You

Lucky Night

A Novel

Eliza Kennedy

 CROWN
NEW YORK

Lucky Night is a work of fiction. Names, characters, places, and incidents either are the product of the author's imagination or are used fictitiously. Any resemblances to actual persons, living or dead, events, or locales is entirely coincidental.

CROWN
An imprint of the Crown Publishing Group
A division of Penguin Random House LLC
1745 Broadway,
New York, NY 10019
crownpublishing.com
penguinrandomhouse.com

Library of Congress Cataloging-in-Publication Data
Names: Kennedy, Eliza, 1974- author.
Title: Lucky night : a novel / Eliza Kennedy.
Description: First edition. | New York : Crown, 2025.
Identifiers: LCCN 2024024405 |
ISBN 9780593800836 (hardcover ; acid-free paper) |
ISBN 9780593800843 (epub)
Subjects: LCGFT: Novels.
Classification: LCC PS3611.E5585 L83 2025 | DDC 813/.6—dc23/eng/20240610
LC record available at https://lccn.loc.gov/2024024405

Hardcover ISBN 978-0-593-80083-6
International edition ISBN: 979-8-217-08732-7
Ebook ISBN 978-0-593-80084-3

Printed in the United States of America on acid-free paper

Editor: Amy Einhorn
Editorial assistants: Lori Kusatzky and Austin Parks
Production editor: Abby Oladipo
Text designer: Andrea Lau
Managing editor: Chris Tanigawa
Production managers: Phil Leung and Heather Williamson
Copy editor: Laurie McGee
Proofreaders: Robin Slutzky, Katy Miller, and Rita Madrigal
Publicist: Mary Moates
Marketer: Kimberly Lew

1 2 3 4 5 6 7 8 9

First Edition

The authorized representative in the EU for product safety and compliance is Penguin Random House Ireland, Morrison Chambers, 32 Nassau Street, Dublin D02 YH68, Ireland, https://eu-contact.penguin.ie.

Lucky Night

part one

the orgasm gong

one

Do you hear something?

Hmm?

Nick.

Hmm.

There. She turns her head toward the door. What is that?

He turns too, buries his nose in her hair and inhales.

Not too deeply. He doesn't want to be weird about it.

It's an alarm, she says.

What's that scent, grapefruit? Verbena? It's delicious.

Nick?

What is verbena, anyway? An herb. No. A flower.

Something to do with tea?

Do you hear it? she says. Sort of a faraway ringing?

Away. Far, far away. Like her voice, drifting toward him, loop-ing and weaving through the glow, the fuzzy-edged haze of animal contentment that descends on him in these moments, sprawled on this bed, any bed, various beds at various times, always with her, breathing hard, limbs splayed, the glow hovering over him like a . . . like a what?

Never mind. This isn't the time to strain for comparisons. A question has been posed, his attention sought on a vital point of acoustic interpretation. He rouses his wits. Come on, boys! Look alive! Letsgoletsgoletsgoletsgolets—

He raises his head. Listens.

The alarm stops.

He drops back on the pillow.

It's nothing, he says. And now it's over.

Stand down, men. The troops trudge back to their barracks, their card games, buffing their boots. His hand comes to life—just one, the rest of him still flattened, demolished by that astonishing, that really unbelievable—

He searches the folds of the duvet.

But what was it, do you think?

He finds her hand, lifts it to his line of sight. Nice hand. Lovely hand. *My roving hands.*

One of this joint's exclusive amenities, he says. An orgasm gong.

An orgasm gong, she says.

He feels the joints of her fingers. The rounded edges of her nails. It's the newest thing, he says. The staff ring it whenever two guests come simultaneously.

She laughs, her low, throaty chuckle, and the glow, which had thinned perilously as he was called upon to react, to think and speak, rolls over him again, thick and orangey-pink. Why orangey-pink? He doesn't know. He's just reporting here, okay? Just telling it like it is. Like how she's turning to him now, resting on her side so that her beautiful breasts stack vertically, decline beautifully, breastily bedward—thank you, oh thank you gravity, all hail the Earth's rotations!—and her face hoves into view, smiling at him. Jenny. It's been too long.

Now all he needs is her touch, the lightest, the least—

She drapes a leg over his.

Oh hail!

He can't bear it. Steady on, men! What a relief his thoughts in these moments are private, not broadcast to the world, or to her. *Whole joys.* He's an island, blissed out but well-fortified. Because happiness like this is asinine.

Who rings it?

Hmm?

Who rings the gong?

She's resting a hand on his hip. Tapping her fingers lightly. *To taste whole joys.* He feels each tiny tap. The weight of her hand. *Full nakedness, something something.*

The gong, he says. Right. Well, as you might expect, they don't assign this crucial task to any yahoo rolling in off the street. It's the responsibility of a special employee. Carefully recruited, meticulously trained. They call him Gong Boy.

She laughs again. That husky chuckle!

He is purely, stupidly content.

The online reviews rave about him, he says. You're going to start seeing copycat services in all the major hotels, but for now, this is the only gong in town. Hey, would you mind . . . ?

She knows what he wants, and no, she would not mind. She slips a hand under him to scratch the nape of his neck. He shudders the length of his body, down and up, and down.

Whole joys right here.

A whole shitload of whole glowing joys.

It didn't sound like a gong, she says.

True, but that's Gong Boy's genius. He shoves the pillow up to give her easier access to his neck. Always trying to be helpful. He interprets the intensity and essence of any given synchronous climax and translates it into sound compositions that accurately reflect the specific event.

Where does he come up with this shit? Honestly, it just flows out of him. Like his copious come into her glorious oh the scratching, the scratching, her nails on his skin!

It's heaven. He shudders here in heaven.

So ours was fiery, she says. Alarming. Sounds about right.

Opening the door to her an hour ago—what was it she'd said? And everything that came after. Now, their rituals. The scratching. The idle conversation, grandiose because he knows she loves it.

Has Gong Boy ever screwed up?

He cranes his neck, a fresh wave of goosebumps coursing down his arms. It's rare, he says, but he does occasionally misjudge the emanations.

What happens?

Well, it's a serious problem. This place only opened last week. They have a brand to build. When he botches one, management has no choice but to administer correctives.

Oh no! What do they do to Gong Boy?

They beat him with a giant dildo.

She laughs. Jenny laughs! He makes her laugh, not to mention come, fierily, alarmingly. He kisses her. *Souls unbodied,* or something about bodies, clothes, where the fuck are these lines coming from? It's on the tip of his . . .

Wait.

Something terrible is happening.

She's going away.

The weight of her leg across his legs, her fingers in his hair, her boob stack nudging his arm—all withdrawn. Why?

He opens his eyes. She's sitting up, feet on the floor.

No! No no no!

What—where are you going?

To the minibar. She's standing, stretching. I want to grab a drink.

He reaches out, but just misses her. She can't leave his side, not now. He needs her close, right after. He is lonely by himself in a still-warm bed. It's always been that way. He's never told anyone.

I brought champagne. He points to the ice bucket on the nightstand, the glasses, all within easy reach.

I'd love some sparkling water. She moves toward the lacquered cabinets lining one wall.

Would you? Funny thing. He scrambles up, propping himself against the headboard. Champagne is sparkling water. With bonus champagne flavor.

She pauses in the center of the room, taking it in. She moves to the window, which is huge, a wall of glass. They're on the forty-second floor. Manhattan blazes all around them. *Between above below.* Snow is falling. Beyond the river and New Jersey there's the faintest smudge of light in the February sky. The world's glow. Also disappearing.

God, she says. In her faint midwestern accent it comes out *Gad.* Can you believe this view?

He can't. Especially when she bends to scratch an ankle. Compensation for the loss of her proximity. One hand on the back of a chair for balance, one foot off the floor, hair spilling over her shoulder. Her ass, pale, rounded, slightly too large for her slender frame, and therefore perfect.

Gad, he thinks. Help me, Gad.

However many times you see it, she says, it never gets old.

Right you are, my lady. The shadowy cleft, the two deep dimples hovering above. The astonishing substantiality of it, its exquisite assness, which he gets to behold, to fondle, to (occasionally, if only superficially) probe.

Look at her. So at ease when she's naked. At home in herself, able to wander a room unashamed, baring her remarkable everything. No self-consciousness, no restraint.

He pulls the duvet over himself. It's chilly in here.

Jenny. Come back to bed.

Just a sec. She drifts to the wall of cabinets, opening one and poking around. Closing it and opening another. He's a patient man—well, no—but this is too much. She's wasting their precious time, frittering it away on views and beverages, when he needs her near him.

Which is why he sits up and announces:

We're not using the minibar.

She turns to him, puzzled. We always use the minibar.

Fuck, that's true.

Not anymore, he says. Twelve dollars for M&M's? Fifteen dollars for water? It's an outrage. It's extortionate.

She looks amused. You're only realizing this now?

Why won't she come back? It's a scam, Jenny. A convenience penalty. I'm not paying it.

She rolls her eyes. Relax, El Cheapo. I'll pay.

El Cheapo! The glow surges. He swoons. Internally. Externally he frowns and drops back onto the pillows. Nothing to see here.

But to feel. To feel! That's, well, that's all he needs.

It's going to be fine. Yes, she's still standing, her naked body still an unconscionable twelve to fifteen feet away from his. But she'll be back.

Relax, El Cheapo.

She opens the fridge and pulls out a small green bottle. Crack of the cap, a hiss. The sound of his hopes deflating. Don't be so dramatic, for Gad's sake. She's got her damn water, now she'll come back. She'll see how badly you want her, and she'll . . .

Trail a hand along the television console. Meander to the sofa, examine the bland art on the wall above it. Sip her water. Ask:

What time's your flight tomorrow?

Eight fifteen, he says. They just got here. Why is she already thinking about the end?

She gazes down at the tasteful magazines fanned across the coffee table. Where are you going again?

Houston.

She looks around the room, which is long, low-lit, cream and gold. This place is crazy, Nick.

It opened Friday. We're some of the first guests, he says. Probably the first people to use this bed.

Hint.

Fucking.

Hint.

Which she doesn't take. Instead, she roams back to the cabinets, picks up the minibar menu, a long, slim volume, bound no doubt in the skin of some sustainably slaughtered animal. What is she jonesing for now, Pringles? One of those triangular chocolate bars in the yellow wrapper? What are those called?

Oh hell, it doesn't matter! What matters is that the glow is shredding, it's in danger of disappearing completely.

Something that's not in danger of disappearing? The water she so desperately needed. She's taken a single sip.

This aggravates him. Intensely.

Not that he'll say so.

No. He won't say a thing.

How's that water? he says.

She takes another dainty taste, another siplet. It's delicious.

Oh good. Is it quenching your thirst adequately?

It is. She smiles at him from behind the lip of the bottle. She's on to him. Thank you for asking.

Well, I was worried. You've barely tasted it, after your great hue and cry for refreshment.

Hue and cry, she says. My great hue and cry.

I just mean you seemed really intent on hydration, blasting out of bed the way you did.

She holds the bottle out. Would you like some?

Oh no! He waves the very thought away. I wouldn't deprive you. You're obviously saving it for some emergency.

She beams at him now, her big, toothy grin. It's so good to see you, Nick.

Then get your ass back here, woman! He flips open the duvet. She moves toward him. The glow is gone, alas. It heaved its last while she traipsed around the room and he sniped and pouted. Doesn't matter. She's coming now, she's three steps away, two, setting down her precious water. It's been way too long. Sick kids, work trips, one obstacle after another. So many obstacles, he wondered . . . but no. They're here, he's got her, they have the whole night, and—

I have to pee, she says.

What? No. She can't—

He sits up, lunges. Wait!

But in a dozen quick steps she skirts the bed and rounds the corner. He hears the bathroom door slide on its track, the latch snap shut.

He falls back onto the pillows.

Well, hell.

The smoke detector blinks at him from the ceiling. The only ugly thing in this place, which, incidentally and for the record, is not cheap, because El Cheapo is not actually cheap, okay, does she have any idea how much this room cost? The room she just fled.

He'd been so close! But he'd lost her, lost the scent. All he can do now is paw the ground, circle the tree. Whine softly and wait.

Because what, you're a hunting dog, and she's your prey? Not entitled to leave your presence, even to perform necessary bodily functions, required instead to dance attendance as you recline on this bed, upon its many pillows, like a pasha?

No, not a pasha, not a hound. Just a man, thwarted despite so much privilege. Pillowed by privilege. There really are a ridiculous number of pillows on this bed. He replays her escape to the bathroom. He'd missed the finer points, intent as he'd been on finagling her back into a horizontal position. Now he recalls the high-stepping way she walked, on the balls of her feet. Her legs. Her lovely long back. Her ass.

Oh Gad, her ass.

He's not supposed to do this. Parcel her out, reduce her to her component parts. But what's the harm? Here, secretly, in his head and nowhere else, what's the harm? He'd love to take her in the ass someday. He dreams about it. How he would enter her slowly, consumed by her intense grip. He's never done it with anyone. He's proposed it to her once or twice, just casually suggested it. She's not enthusiastic.

Which is fine. Obviously.

A memory surfaces, floating up from out of nowhere. A yellow room, Jenny walking across it. An old room, high-ceilinged. Walls the color of butter. Where was that? Doesn't matter. Be here. Be content. Tall windows. She was walking away there, too, naked. And he was . . . they've never stayed in a room like that, have they? Six years now—Jesus, six years—meeting once or twice a month, in places like this, blandly luxurious. In the apartments of out-of-town friends. Once, memorably, in the Alonzo F. Bonsal Wildlife Preserve. Never in an old yellow room. *Where my hand is set.*

Toblerone. That's the name of the triangular chocolate in the yellow wrapper. Great. Glad we got that straightened out.

How could she bolt out of the room like that? Couldn't she tell he needed her? Did he have to spell it out? This is the problem with Jenny. She can be a little oblivious. A little obtuse. He lifts the sheet. His cock slouches against his thigh, squat and truculent. He reaches down and wiggles it loose from its sticky moorings. A few leg hairs cling, protesting. *Noooo! Don't go!*

Obtuse? Because she can't read your mind? It's not her job to minister to your moods. To guess at your unspoken needs. If only you weren't so reluctant to flat-out ask for what you want—stay close, keep touching me, I don't know why but I'm always sad after I come—if only you didn't choose to connive and harangue rather than—oh, horror!—*express vulnerability,* you'd be content right now, not sprawled here bitching about what you don't have. When you have so much. Gifts. Achievements. Virtues? Let's say qualities. Success, as it's conventionally understood. Gobs of it.

Was it a dream, the yellow room? Dark polished floors. Jenny padding away from the bed, toward—whoa, hey, hang on. Not *padding.* Walking. Don't get fancy. She's the writer, okay? You're the boring one. The one who gave up his shining dreams.

He's going dark. He doesn't want to go dark.

Jenny! he shouts.

Just a sec! she shouts back.

He doesn't get why she won't even entertain the notion. She likes his finger up there just fine. Still, he doesn't nag. He's not a Neanderthal. Although he thinks she'd love it. It could be their thing, the sex they have with each other and no one else. The idea captivates him. The shamefulness of it, the basic physical wrongness. Not that anyone else seems to see it that way, sodomy being all the rage nowadays, to the point that it feels like at any given time half the world is penetrating the other half anally. And all parties are perfectly content about it.

You wouldn't be. Not even if you got it. Listen to you now. Carping and complaining, when you have so much. He plucks at the crisp sheet, rubbing it between his fingers. *How blessed am I in something something.* He's going to kill himself if he doesn't figure out where these lines are coming from. Happens all the time now, fragments of poetry, skittering in from the old life. Erased and corrupted, recorded over, but not lost entirely. Golden boy. So much promise. Don't go dark. Remember the blessings, the gifts. He has the whole world. Just not Jenny, who prefers dithering in the john to diddling him in this wide, white, brand-new bed.

He hears the distant alarm again. A short burst, three or four seconds. Must be faulty. New building, new systems. Or another couple has in fact scored a mutual O. There should be a prize. It's hard work, holding back when he knows she's close. Her body tenses. Her expression becomes concentrated. She looks so young. How she must have looked before he knew her. Tom knew her then. They met in college.

A prize. What would it be? An engraved platter. Kudos on Completing the Sexual Response Cycle in Tandem! A pair of etched goblets: Thank You for Coming! It's an accomplishment. It happens rarely. How could she disappear right after?

It comes to him now, all at once:

Full nakedness! All joys are due to thee.
As souls unbodied, bodies uncloth'd must be,
To taste whole joys.

And the glow bursts over him, a rushing, tumbling torrent. Whole joys! They have the whole night. He's on his way to Texas for a deposition. She's returning from being on set. Her family thinks she's coming home tomorrow. His thinks he's already gone. They're both supposed to be somewhere else, but they're here. In a few hours they'll fall asleep together. He'll wake at three, as he does most nights, but instead of hating the clock, rolling over and forcing himself back to sleep, he'll reach out and find her warm and willing. He'll have her again at dawn, and, if his cock hasn't fallen off by that point, once more after breakfast, among the room-service crumbs, before he heads to the airport and she to the train.

He is giddy. El Cheapo. He rolls around in the sheets, back and forth, a happy hound. No more evasions and maneuvers. No more baroque veiling talk. Him and her, *bodies uncloth'd. Before behind between above below.* She can have all the water she wants.

Convenience penalty.

You really are an asshole.

He hollers for her again. Jenny!

Rightrightrightrightright. She just needs one more look. Feet apart on the cold marble, she twists, peering over her shoulder. The mirror is one of those big jobbies, wall to wall to ceiling to sink, with a magnifying insert, which . . . which we will not discuss. No, we will pass over the magnifying insert. We've got troubles enough. She tightens her butt, then relaxes it. The results are dismaying. When she's not clenching, her bottom is smooth, if plentiful. When she clenches, it shrinks up nicely, but those nasty little divots appear.

She looks over her other shoulder. Maybe a different angle . . .

Nope.

Junior year abroad, that was her downfall. It was twenty years ago, but nothing's been the same since, asswise. Florence. The pizza. The ice cream. Wine in cheap student bars. She and Daphne, her blond bouncing roommate, used to huddle at the kitchen table clutching their coffee, the oven door wide open, blasting heat. Laughing like maniacs because the apartment was *still so fricking cold.*

They were in Italy! Nobody told them there was winter there! God they were dumb.

Henrik lived upstairs. He was Swedish, a philosophy student. She couldn't believe it the first time she saw his tight turquoise briefs, so at odds with his Nordic solemnity. They were about to have sex, but she couldn't stop giggling.

Which didn't go over well.

Clench. Release. Clench. All the food on set didn't help. Craft services, they called it. She kept picturing women hunched over in one of the trailers, assembling junk food with glue guns and glitter paint. She'd tried to make a joke about it to Juan Pablo, but he didn't understand. She'd been bored all week. It was supposed to be exciting, being *on set*, but she was always in the way, with nothing to do except amble around and admire how faithfully they'd re-created Wilderkill. How they'd *realized her vision*, as the production designer kept saying. *Wouldn't you agree the house is essentially a character in your novels?* She'd nodded, oh yeah, totally, but she didn't agree. A house is a setting, not a character, duh. Still, she didn't want to be rude. So she listened and nodded as various intense and possibly highly medicated movie people explained her books to her. Nodded, snacked and avoided Juan Pablo's increasingly loaded looks.

European men. They think they can get away with anything.

Seduction. Tiny underwear.

She shivers. Chilly in here. She touches a folded washcloth, a tiny round soap wrapped in pleated tissue. Whatever happened to Henrik? And Daphne. They were so important to her back then. People disappear if you don't keep up with them. Especially the friends of your youth. Sometimes they disappear right in front of you, changing so much they become unrecognizable. The way Tom says she's become don't think about Tom right now. Tom is fine. You're fine. Somewhere in the world, Daphne and Henrik are fine.

She could look them up on Facebook. She should.

She probably won't.

There's another mirror above the tub, offering another dispiriting view of the old stern. The old tailpiece. She wonders what Nick thinks. She knows what he says he thinks—he never stops saying what he thinks. But is what he says he thinks what he really thinks? Could he be secretly repulsed by her abundant flesh and its numerous small indentations? No, dummy. He wants you. Think about how he looked when he opened the door—that wasn't politeness, okay? That wasn't suppressed horror. She remembers what she said when she saw him, and she cringes. He didn't seem to catch it, thank God. His hands were already on her.

She looks over her shoulder again. Alas, my vast Florentine ass. She watches it in the mirror. Clench. *Uhnnh.* Release. *Ahhh.*

She grunts absurdly, like a weightlifter.

Uhnnh. Ahhh.

Woman! he yells. Have you fallen in?

She jumps, startled. Moves to the sink. There's a man waiting for you, dingbat. She splashes water on her face, pats it dry. What you needed, what you lacked and longed for—you have it, and you're in here goofing off in front of the mirror! She smooths her eyebrows. She has to make an effort to appear comfortable when she's naked with him. He said something once, praised her for her unselfconsciousness. And so with him she is the Jenny who is loose-limbed and carefree. Not a mass of quivering female insecurity. She combs her bangs with her fingers. Then it's not really you he's waiting for, is it? And if he knew the real you, he might not be so eager oh stop. You're in this to please yourself, not him. That's what you've always said. Still, he probably wishes you were a tiny bit less bottom heavy oh my God *stop.*

That is one ginormous bathtub, boy. They could have a bath later. She should go back out. Surely his neediness has abated by now. She hadn't really wanted water, or to pee. She'd just needed a little distance. From the bed, and from the look in his eye. Right after, that's when he clings—the only time. She has learned to flee it, to harden herself against it. Otherwise . . .

The toilet! She said she had to pee—she better make some relevant noises, or he'll be sure to comment. *What, no flush? Letting it mellow?* She lifts the lid and squats. Her belly fold smiles up at her. Hello, doll. You're looking stop with the body stuff, honestly. The criticism. It's boring. It is what it is.

It is what it is, she says. What it is, what it is.

What. It. Is.

There's a phone on the wall beside her. A man put it there. Must have been a man. And men look at it—or will look at it, Nick said this place is brand-new—men will look and be pleased that they can wheel their deals and master their universes while ensconced on the old throne.

Not that they'll ever use it. No man likes to talk while shitting.

But every man likes options.

She flushes. Lordy that's a roar! At the tail end of it, she hears . . . is that another alarm? They should leave. Run downstairs, have a drink. There was that awful fire in the Bronx a few years ago. How many dead? And that Orthodox family in Midwood. They'd left their hot plate on for the Sabbath. The children burned up in their beds. Was it four of them, five? The mother jumped out a window and survived. But did she? Could she? Jesus. You follow the rules, the weird rules to worship your God the way you're told he demands it, and he just . . . he fucks you. Fucks you and takes your babies.

She pinches the towel hanging above the toilet. It's warm. Holy global warming! This place is literally gleaming. A far cry from the bathrooms at home. Even with Trini coming once a week now, they're gross. The entire house is grubby. Her house, her car, her body, which hasn't been her own for years. Even now, somebody is always hanging on her, making her sticky. Ben and Natey come into her office and take her Scotch tape. Leave balled-up socks on the dining room table. She lives in a world of boy. She makes half-hearted gestures to assert her femininity, or at least create some sort of balance. Polka-dotted canisters in the kitchen. A flower-shaped pillow on the living room sofa. They take turns farting into it, shrieking with laughter.

Beasts!

Still, it's going to be awful when they become teenagers. All surliness and excess hair. She needs to enjoy these last few years of sweetness. Eyes lighting up when they see her. Hard hugs from thin, bath-smelling arms.

She misses them suddenly. She's pierced by it. She should have gone straight home from upstate. But Nick was so intent on having the whole night. They've never had a whole night before. She was surprised he wanted one.

She should text Tom. Love you, hug the boys for me, see you tomorrow. Her bag is on the floor, tossed in here during the madness of her arrival. She digs through her notebooks and magazines and finds her phone, swipes it awake, only to be shamed by a screen full of notifications. She owes calls, emails, texts to everyone. Little pieces of her attention, which she's hoarding for herself right now. Here's something from Charles. The subject line is all caps, that's never good. She'll quickly write back and say . . . what? Hey, Charles! So I'm crouched naked in the bathroom of a luxury hotel in Midtown, but I thought I'd respond to your question about the paperback cover.

She drops the phone back in her bag.

The madness of her arrival. Had Nick heard what she said? Surely not. He would have stopped everything to pick it apart in his relentless Nick way.

There's a cluster of toiletries by the sink. Hand soap, lotion. A tiny sewing kit. Natey loves this kind of junk. The labels are sleek and expensive-looking, but they don't identify the hotel. Perfect. She sweeps everything into her bag.

She wants to be out there, she meant it when she said how good it was to see him. She'd missed him. They've never had a whole night. She splashes water on her face before she remembers she already did that.

Scattered!

He hollers for her again, and she swells with happiness. Six years, and he's still bellowing for you. Six years and he still looks at you the way he does. Despite the ass-divots. Despite the stupid thing you said when you saw him. Did he hear it? Surely not.

She slides open the door and steps out.

There he is, stretched out on the rumpled bed, sipping champagne, looking excessively pleased with himself. Is he handsome, in the conventional sense? In any sense? Probably not. But God, does he do it for her. He just does. The way his mouth moves when he talks. His expressive hands. How had she thought of giving him up, the time she almost gave him up? Lunacy! She loves how worked up he gets about things. How he fumes. He is passionate, enthusiastic. He has an opinion about everything.

Is he good-looking? She can't tell. He's simply the man she desires.

He sets his champagne glass next to her rings, which are heaped on the bedside table. He peers up at her, head cocked.

Were you renovating in there, or—

I didn't come, she says.

two

She blurts it, really. A notch too loud.

Excuse me?

I didn't come. Before, when we . . . you know, when you did.

He opens his mouth to speak. Closes it. Frowns.

Yes you did.

No, she says. I didn't.

What is she talking about? He pulls himself up, pushing the damn pillows out of the way.

You came, he says. You definitely came.

I didn't. Hopeful smile. But I'd love to try again.

She moves toward the bed. He raises a hand to stop her.

All that noise. All that hooting and hollering and *oh God, oh Nick*ing! What was that?

It felt so good. I just didn't quite, you know. Get there.

You faked it.

A little. Can I get back in bed?

No, he says. You never fake it. You told me that once. It was a real point of pride.

She glances away, her eyes going vague. I know, I just . . . it felt wonderful, and I could tell you were about to come, which is always so exciting, almost as good as . . . so, I guess I joined in.

Except you didn't, he says.

Well, no, but—

Have you ever faked it before?

Nope, she says.

Nope. Nope! He knows what she's doing. She's in retreat, resorting to her midwesternisms, her jeezes and cripes, hiding behind a bogus aw-shucks simplicity until the storm passes and it's safe to come out of the cellar.

Good luck with that, cookie.

I loved it, she insists. Like always. So what if I didn't, you know, reach the pinnacle? Let's give it another chance.

She's close to him now. She pulls the duvet down, brushes his cock with her fingertips. It stirs. Traitor. She kneels beside the bed and kisses it. She takes it between her lips and sucks, gently. Maybe she's right. It's not a big deal. He shouldn't give her such a hard time that she has to come over here and play handmaiden to his wounded ego. Isn't it a little hypocritical to ding one's affair partner for dishonesty? Plus, he could extract all sorts of concessions in round two. Punish her for her grievous infraction. His cock likes the sound of that. Yes, we have a seconding of that motion, we have an enthusiastic—

The problem isn't that you didn't come, he says. It's that you pretended you did.

The delicious pressure ceases. It's possible she sighs, even with his cock in her mouth. She releases him, sits back on her heels and waits, inscrutable.

That's not totally accurate, he concedes. The faking is an issue. But also? I love making you come, Jenny! You know this. Being inside you, feeling you around me, feeling you chase it, and overtake it?

The faraway alarm rings again.

And then, you're so beautifully helpless, in the grip of it. That's not polite to say, I know, I'm a Neanderthal, but I don't mean helpless as in my prey or anything.

The alarm stops.

Something's wrong, she says.

Your orgasms are the best, Jenny. They're a splash of color in a drab, shitty world. If you could see them, feel them the way I do, you'd understand.

The alarm starts ringing again.

She stands.

And the thing is, I make them happen. I—

Nick, could you—

I know, he says. Trust me, I know what that sounds like. The arrogant male, the preening baboon, beating his chest and roaring about his vaginal prowess. I get it. Why do women fake orgasms? Because it's such a big goddamn deal to their baboon-partners that they come, even though most of them have no clue how to make it happen! But I do, Jenny. I've done the homework, okay? Put the time in, sorted out all those complicated folds—

Nick, stop! I'm trying to count!

The alarm is still ringing.

It's a million miles away, he says. It's nothing.

It stops.

See?

But she doesn't see.

That was at least twenty seconds. She moves toward the door.

Jenny, what are you—Jesus, don't open the door.

I won't. She places both hands on it, palms flat. She's feeling the door for heat! Their clothes are heaped beside her in the vestibule. He'd stripped her right there and dragged her to the bed, both of them frantic and laughing. It had been so long.

I think I smell smoke, she says. Will you call down?

Call down?

To the front desk. Ask them what's going on.

This is a new hotel, he says. They're testing the system or some-thing. It's not—what are you doing now?

She's bending, nose to the doorjamb, ass high in the air.

She sniffs.

Well now. This is interesting. She's distracted. He could go over there, grabbing the baby oil on the way. She squats farther, hands on her knees. He's brought the same small bottle to every meet-ing, in case he finds her in a receptive mood. The thing's like a holy relic by now.

She's pressing her ear against the door. I can hear people in the hallway.

I don't doubt it. He's out of bed and rummaging through his roller bag. They were probably drawn by the sound of your fraudu-lent orgasms.

Oh my God, Nick, will you drop it? It doesn't matter!

Doesn't matter. He pulls out his Dopp kit. Doesn't matter. Right. Hey, none of this matters. Their thing—never did, never could. Where the hell is the baby oil? This has always been a purely physical arrangement. Sure, there were moments, early on, when he was bowled over by her. She was beautiful, she was smart. You open a door, and your arms, and she's there. What was it she'd said when she came in? Something surprising. Anyway yes, early on, blown away, overglowed, he would look at her and consider the possibility. Love? he'd think, as they caught their breath on various beds, in various rooms. When she let loose with her rau-cous laugh at something he said, or launched into one of her ram-bling stories. Could I? Could we? Could this?

He searches the outside pocket of his suitcase. He didn't leave the baby oil on the bathroom vanity, did he? Because Jesus that's going to be a whole conversation with Caroline when he gets home.

She inhales audibly. He sees her shoulders rise with the effort.

Hey, he says. McGruff the Crime Dog. There's no smoke.

Could we? Could this? No, he decided, every time. It's the glow. Lust plus like. Plenty of like. Even now, when she's acting like a nutjob. She's great company. She's charming and funny. It's been immense fun to watch her transformation from harried homemaker into successful author. Massively successful. Who would have thought? Young adult novels, of the paranormal ro-mance variety. Two so far. Sold millions of copies.

So, no. Love has never been on the table. But so much else is.

The table is groaning, it's a feast of delights. He has so much. This night, this room, this woman.

Who's feeling the door again, trying to gauge the heat of the imaginary inferno raging on the other side.

Enough.

He abandons his search for the baby oil—please Christ don't let him have left it on the vanity!—and joins her at the door, which he unlocks and flings open.

The hallway is empty.

Stretching into the distance in both directions, the carpet spotless, the lighting expensively dim. No dazed and panicked guests. No shouts or running footsteps. No smoke.

All this he displays to her, throwing an arm wide, the way he does in front of juries. See? Do you see, people? Do you *see*?

She nods. She sees. Outstanding.

He closes the door. Now they can get back to the serious business of their mutual—

I still think we should go, she says.

She scoops up their clothes and walks back into the room. She drops everything on the bed and starts sorting through it.

He leans against the door. Lowers his head.

And laughs to himself.

Because it's all very comical, when you think about it.

This exorbitant room, a whole night, which required so much planning, created so much anticipation. Of course the universe would test them with something as small-bore and stupid as a fire alarm on the fritz. Test them, and try to thwart them.

But fail.

Because there's no way, okay? There's *no way* they're going to get dressed, trudge down the hall, into the elevator, through the lobby and out into the mercilessly cold dark and joyless winter night to stand around on an icy sidewalk scuffing their feet and waiting for some mythical all clear, carving precious time out of this, their first and only full night together.

Sorry, universe! Ain't gonna happen.

He pushes off from the door with his shoulders and wanders toward the bed. She's plucking up garments, examining them like a washerwoman. He should bend her over right there, kick her feet apart, and—

Down, boy.

He passes her, heading for the window.

We'll just run downstairs, she says, turning her blouse right side out. Make sure everything's all right, then come back. Okay?

He doesn't respond. It really is a hell of a view. People will never give up on this city, no matter how impossible it becomes. Not as long as you can stand at a window over all of Manhattan like this, like a—like a what?

Don't get fancy, golden boy.

Or we could get a drink, she says. So we don't use the extortionate minibar.

He can hear the smile in her voice. He knows she's watching him, trying to placate him.

We could even stop by Herve's party, she says.

Herve's party, he thinks. Herve's party.

Said so offhandedly, as if he should know what it means.

He turns from the window. Herve?

My hairstylist. She's buttoning her blouse.

Herve, your hairstylist, he says.

Yep. She buttons the last button, only to find an extra buttonhole at the bottom. Defeat. She starts unbuttoning. He's having a going-away party. Didn't I mention it?

Herve, your hairstylist, having a going-away party? No, I don't recall you mentioning that. Where's he going?

To medical school, she says.

He is silent. She looks up from her buttons. What's wrong?

What's wrong? Where should he start? There's her sudden and irrational need to flee the room. Her suggestion that they attend a party for a hairstylist-slash-medical student.

Whose name, Herve, she pronounces *Hurv*.

She's making it all up.

She must be.

But why? What's her plan, what's her angle?

He takes a seat on the sofa, throws an arm across the back. His penis flops down against his balls.

Patience, men.

Your hairstylist is having a going-away party, he says. And you want us to attend.

Blouse successfully buttoned, she spots her bra at the foot of the bed. Her shoulders sag. She begins unbuttoning again.

Jenny?

I don't *want* us to, I'm just saying we could. Stop by. Why not, if we're going out anyway? He's cut my hair for fifteen years. We've been through a lot together.

He nods. Thinks:

Bullshit.

This is such bullshit!

Why did the fake orgasm throw him? This is what she does. Tells little lies. To avoid conflict, to smooth over hurt feelings. He props his feet on the coffee table, ready to suss out her game. She'll never admit that she's lying. He'll have to force her to spin out her absurdities until they collapse. Then she'll shrug, and start laughing, and they'll finally go back to bed.

You've been through a lot together? he says. You and Hurv?

We have. She shakes out her balled-up tights.

That's interesting. You know, I've been going to the same barber since I moved here after law school. In all that time, all that togetherness, I've learned one thing about him: his name. It's Raul. And I only know that because it's stitched on his shirt.

Why is he harping on her about this? And what on earth happened to these tights? Are you sure that's his name? she says. Are you sure it's even his shirt?

Good point. Maybe his name is Aloysius and he stole Raul's workwear in order to fulfill a lifetime dream of being a barber in Midtown. But tell me this. Why must women become intimately familiar with every single person they interact with? Why must you always *go through a lot together*? Why must you share, and re-late, and confide?

We, she says. We women. Because here I am! She waves to him. All women. Ready to explain us to you.

I wish you would. Why can't you have a simple, impersonal exchange of services for money?

Abandoning her hopelessly tangled tights, she steps into her skirt and wiggles it up over her hips. Whether Herve and I can or can't enjoy one of your little, whatever, sterile capitalist transac-tions, she says, we don't. We like each other. He cuts my hair, we chat about our families, our problems. He's read both my books.

Something you've never bothered to do, she thinks. Snob.

We're friends, she concludes, reaching for a boot that somehow ended up under the bed.

Are you sure about that? What if he's not really going to medi-cal school? What if he's just switching salons and wants to shed some clients?

This is a ridiculous conversation, she says.

You're telling me.

She hears the skepticism in his voice. She looks up from the boot she's struggling to zip. Does he think she's lying about Herve?

He showed me his acceptance letter, she says.

So you've been through a lot of mail together as well?

She bites back a smile. He's going to school in Topeka.

Topeka! he cries. Of course. Our boy is heading to Kansas, that wellspring of excellence in medical training, to become an MD.

Yes! she says. Actually, no. He's going to be a DO.

His story is changing already.

It's the same thing! She's trying so hard not to laugh. He's going to whatchamacallit. Osteopathy school. He'll be able to do every-thing an MD can do.

Plus cut and color, he says.

Why are you making fun of Herve?

Hurv again. He can't let it pass. That's not how you pronounce that name.

That's how Herve pronounces it.

It's French. You pronounce it *Airv*.

Yeah, well, I'll be sure to let *Airv* know he's been saying his own name wrong for thirty-five years.

You're making this up, he says.

I am not!

You are lying! He jumps up from the sofa, pointing at her. There's no party! There's probably not even an *Hurv*! Admit it— you're using random and ridiculous inventions to lure me out of this room.

She's laughing now, helplessly. Why would I lie about that?

Sweetheart? he says. That is the mystery of all fucking mysteries.

She's fully dressed. She strides to the bathroom and returns with her phone. She taps and scrolls and holds it out to him, magnificent in her anticipatory vindication.

You're going to feel very bad that you doubted me, she says.

Get over here, Jenny.

Read the email, Nick.

Take off your clothes, he says, and climb onto my cock. Right now.

Read the fricking email!

He takes her phone. Reads.

Well well. It looks like Herve McIntyre (*O my America!*) is in fact having a going-away party at a wine bar a few blocks away. He'd love to see you before he leaves for Kansas, so please stop by between six and nine.

He hands the phone back to her.

Apology accepted, she says.

He grabs her wrist and yanks her onto the sofa. She is laughing, slapping at him.

You asshole! Leave me alone!

Impossible. Not being able to leave her alone—one of the prevailing conditions of his life for the past six years. He gathers her and stands up, staggering a little (oh the old bones!), lurches over to the bed and throws her on it.

He's got her now, caught her whole. He crouches on top of her, pinning her arms down, kissing her neck, biting and sucking. He's naked, she's fully dressed. This is unusual. She's almost always naked before he is, the removal of her clothing being his utmost priority. But he likes this reversal. The feeling of her fabrics on his bare skin. He is lesser. An animal. Savage.

And yet, away you must go, Jenny's clothes. Off and away, you, you what? *Gown and girdle.* You *spangled breastplate.* Amazing how the lines come back to him.

He called her sweetheart. That made her melt a little, even though he was teasing when he said it. Has he ever called her sweetheart before? Honey, a few times, offhand. Lady mine, when he's in his mock-heroic mode. Also sweet queen, which is a quote, she doesn't remember from what. He's not big on endearments. Not with her, anyway. Though sometimes, the way he says her name, whispers it right in her ear when he's on top of her, like he is now—

Jennyjennyjennyjennyjennymyjenny

Well, that's plenty. If not too much. But pet names, any sort of lovey-dovey cuddly smoochykins business? That's not Nick. He has affection for her, she knows, but his mode of expressing it is rougher. He banters. He mocks. God, does it make her wet. Submission to his harangues. Domination by his merciless wit. She shouldn't love it so much.

Oh well. It is what it is.

He does occasionally call her by her married name, just to annoy her. Tom's awful name. She's never used it—professionally she's Jennifer Parrish, the name she was born with. Because what insane Polish person ever thought that made sense as a fricking *last name*? It's pure poetry, Nick says. Poetry on the tongue. He can be so irritating sometimes.

Not now. He's holding her wrists over her head with one hand, undoing her buttons with the other. Good luck, Nicky boy—those are some slippery little bitches. She twists under him like she wants to escape. Tries to bite the unbuttoning hand. He holds her face, his thumb deep in her mouth. Presses himself down on her and bites her ear.

No faking this time, he says.

No faking, she agrees.

None of your thrashing and yodeling. Unless you mean it.

I don't think that's going to be a problem, she says.

He busies himself with the buttons. She wishes, not for the first time, that she hadn't told him she'd faked it earlier.

Because that was a lie.

She came—of course she came! He'd obliterated her, swept her away as he always does. The lie was spontaneous. *I didn't come.* Such a mistake! What did she think, he was going to shrug it off? This is Nick we're dealing with. Analytical Man. The Great Interrogator. She reaches between his legs and strokes him.

Oh yes please, he says, pushing himself into her hand. Yes, that's—ow, too much! Jesus, woman, you're not milking a cow!

It was seeing her rings, on the table beside the bed. Coming out of the bathroom, about to rejoin him, and there they were, wedding on top of engagement band, reminding her of what happened earlier, when she took them off.

They'd made it to the bed from the door, they were naked, kissing, she was straddling him, he was biting at her hand, catching a finger, sucking on it. Her left hand. He'd held it up, the gold glinting.

I need you to take these off, he'd said.

And she'd obliged, twisting them loose, leaning over and placing them on the nightstand. He'd watched it all with a peculiar gleam in his eye.

She smiled down at him. Better?

Yes and no, he said. Part of me wants you to put them back on so I can watch you take them off again.

Oh, she said. So, you . . . didn't want them off. You wanted to watch me take them off?

Desperately, he said, kissing her palm. I always do.

And she was mortified. Because she'd misunderstood. For a flash, an instant during the twisting and tugging, she thought the sight of her rings bothered him. Reminded him that she was married to someone else, maybe kicked up, who knows, some possessive instinct.

She thought he wanted them off because he didn't like seeing them on her. Wrong. He wanted them off because he did like them. Her being married to someone else arouses him. He's turned on by the transgression, the—to him—delicious violation of morals and manners that brought them here.

Where they would never be together otherwise.

And, look—she knows this about him, okay, almost from the very beginning she's known it. But when he said it, his voice gone low and a little hoarse, when he caught her hand and said, *I need you to take these off*, her mind tilted sideways and that knowledge slipped out. She misread him, and—this is the worst part, the absolute worst!—she liked it. She thought he was jealous, and that pleased her.

So when she realized she was wrong, he was the opposite of jealous? She was mortified. How could she think that? She knows, *knows* that's not what this is about.

She'd gotten over it, obviously, she'd forgotten all about it, but when she came out of the bathroom and saw him sipping his champagne, propped up like a smug king, her rings stacked beside him, taunting her—silly Jenny, you were wrong wrong wrong, oh and by the way, you're married, so you're also doing wrong wrong wrong!—she hated herself all over again. Stupid! This thing you have is ideal, it works *so well*, you want to risk it, spoil it with greed for more?

You have a great life. Such good fortune. Be satisfied.

And so she toppled into a pit of shame and recrimination, all over a misunderstanding that nobody in the world would ever know about but her. Still, she had to blot it out, stop thinking about it. Which is why she lied and said she hadn't come, prompting a whole big . . .

I didn't even see you put this on, he says now, tugging at her camisole. Why so many layers?

It's freezing out, in case you hadn't noticed.

Right, he says. Thus the need for an additional tissue-thin top.

She bats his hand away. They tussle. The camisole rips.

Stop thinking about it. You're both over it. He is, anyway. Easy. Everything rolls right off him. He doesn't seem to feel a shred of guilt about what they do. Still, she wishes he wasn't so obvious about his pervy little cheating kink. He loves that she's Catholic, too. She's sinning, cardinally, mortally, breaking commandments, risking hellfire, for him and his atheist cock.

She arches her back so he can reach under and get at her bra.

Happy busk, he murmurs.

What?

He unhooks the clasp. Never mind.

Never mind. Which mind? She has so many. She's scattered, pieces of her everywhere. Many Jennys. He only knows this one, the partner in crime, side piece, suburban seductress. He doesn't know how she goofs with Natey and Ben. Her singing and dancing in the kitchen, her silliness. How she takes care of—cares for— Tom. How serious she is about her writing, what it means to her. How could he? He won't even read her books! They are a key part of her charmed life, a life she has to marvel at. Because she's never lost. Not anything she truly wanted, not anyone she loved. Parents still alive, boys thriving. She does what she loves, and she's made buckets of money. She has wonderful friends, she's in her prime (*these years are the years of my prime, girls, you must always recognize the years of your prime*). She has suffered so little.

Which means it's coming for her. That alarm. They should have gone down. Or called. He wouldn't even call! But why didn't she call, instead of asking him to do it? Why is she always so passive?

I want to be on top, she says.

She pushes him off and climbs onto him, hiking her skirt up. He thrusts up against her, but she rises, evading him until he grabs her and pulls her down.

Oh yes, he says. Can you move back and forth, like—yes, like that. You still have your panties on? We're going to need to remedy that. Good God, Jenny, you have the most fantastic breasts I ever—slow down, you're moving too fast.

She thrusts against him faster. Since when do you get to tell me what to do?

Since . . . oh God, do that again. Kiss me. I swear your mouth is . . . oh goddammit, Jenny.

A charmed life. Only one truly awful thing has ever happened to her. The Tom thing. Which really was miserable. Though she has a hard time accessing the pain now. It's like the agony of labor—once it passes, you can never fully recall what made you scream so loud and hate the world. Thus does a species survive. And a marriage.

Though speaking of labor. She still can't get over that he did it when she was pregnant. Could he be more of a cliché? She'd quit her job, she had a maniac toddler, a belly like a fricking whale . . . there were scenes. Tears. How could yous. Though even amid the worst of it, while she was ranting and raving, she had the oddest feeling. That none of it was real. Or rather it was, but the Jenny participating in it—Betrayed Wife Jenny, sobbing and reaching for throwables—wasn't her. She was playing a part, performing horror and heartbreak while some other Jenny was lodged deep inside, arms wrapped around her knees, waiting for the drama to subside.

What does that mean? Is she a fraud, a sociopath, does she not really feel? Impossible. Her love is immense. For her family, her work, the world. But she's felt that strange dislocation a few times since. Mostly with Tom, big arguments where she's lost it, she's just going nuts, but part of her stands aside, head cocked, like, *Yeah, I'm not buying this. Are you buying this?*

She's on her back again somehow, he's gotten her skirt off, he's kneeling over her.

Where's that thing you had on? He feels around on the bed and finds her camisole. I want you to wrap it around my cock. I want you to stroke me with it.

Like this?

Oh God yes, don't stop.

So okay, she's a schizo and a cuckoobird, fine. This relates to lying to Nick how? Unclear. But now she's faked a fake orgasm, and he's going to be intent on making her come. She might not be able to pull it off a second time so soon. Meaning that she might have to fake it for real.

Faking It for Real: The Jenny Parrish Story.

Funny how he believed the lie about the fake orgasm, but didn't believe the truth about Herve's party. Not that she blames him. She does lie to him from time to time. Whether she's eaten at a particular restaurant, read a particular book. She's knocked a couple of years off her age, too. Stupid stuff, but crucial. Because she realized, around year two, that he couldn't be the only person she tells the truth to. If she's going to betray everyone she loves, she can't not betray him. That would be fatal. 'Twould be fatal, as Nick would say, in his mock-heroic mode. Or Julian, her main character.

He enters her at last. God, that's . . . maybe she will be able to come again. Poor Herve. She promised him she'd stop by, but then the thing with Nick came up, and it had been so long. Yet another person she's letting down. Line forms to the left. Single file, please. No cutting.

Stop. Be here. Where he's thrusting away, growling in her ear. The sweetness of it, the perfect fit. The absurdity. Sex is so ridiculous, so easy to mock from the outside, but when you're in it, when you're doing it? It's . . . God, it's life. It's the whole world. The only thing worth doing. How could she have thought of giving this up, the time she almost gave it up? Her secret. The thing in her life that's all hers. Even if it's completely wrong.

I want you from behind, he whispers, close to her ear. Jenny. Can I have you from behind?

I'll think about it, she says.

Completely wrong. Here it comes—guilt, her constant companion. The affair adds plenty to the running total—*you're a cheater, you're a liar, selfish, so selfish*—but even without it she'd be full up. Do the boys get enough of her attention, what about Tom, are her parents okay, why is she surfing cat adoption sites when she should be reviewing copyedits? She is faulty, inadequate, a personal project in constant disarray.

Will you focus? Be here, with him, in this room. Where your luck may have run out. Did that alarm ring three times? Four? They should have called down. She knows too much about fires. She did a lot of research when she was writing the fire that destroys Wilderkill at the end of the trilogy. (Suck it, weirdo production designer!) Immersed herself in it, in fact, ending up with far more knowledge than she needed to torch a crumbling mansion.

Ten Famous Buildings Destroyed by Fire.

Notable Infernos Through the Ages.

The Twenty Deadliest Building Fires. Click to view slideshow!

Now she remembers something. You aren't supposed to evacuate a high-rise during a fire. Not if it's a new building. Hey, there's a useful tidbit plucked from the rabbit hole! Fire codes are so strict now, buildings so well-made, you're safer sheltering in place.

Okay! So they're right where they should be. That's reassuring.

Unless she's wrong, and they should have left. The alarm a warning, part of a grand plan. Her bill's come due, and it's time, at long last, for her to know what it means to suffer.

The Lord does love a fire.

Hey. He's stopped moving. Where are you?

What?

He brushes her hair back from her face. Where are you, Jenny? Where'd you go?

Said so gently. So kindly! She can't help it—her eyes fill with tears.

Oh, honey! he says. What's wrong?

Honey. She can't bear it. She wipes away the tears. I'm okay. I'm fine.

He doesn't believe her. He waits. Face so close to hers she can't look away.

I'm sorry, she says. It's just . . . I'm afraid of fire. Really afraid.

He nods. He kisses her.

Then let's get the hell out of here.

She feels him leave her. He sits up, starts looking around for his clothes. Not aggrieved, not reluctant in the least. Willing to set aside what he wants in order to soothe her fears instead.

Who is this generous, easy man?

You don't mind? she says.

He shrugs. I'd rather stay, but so what? It's early. We can get something to eat, then come back and resume normal operations.

She feels a rush of gratitude. She wants to take it all back—we can stay, it's no big deal, I'm being a ninny. She's been given what she wants, so of course now she has to try to thrust it back to the giver with both hands.

What about sushi? he says. I could go for sushi.

Let him do this for you. You'll feel better if you know, if you run down and check.

We'll eat, then we'll stop by the party. He's pulling on his pants. You can introduce me to Herve. We'll tell him I'm your cousin. Or your close personal manicurist.

She searches for her bra among the bedding. They'll check with the front desk, be reassured that it's a system test, a glitch in the wiring, and she'll stop thinking about God and guilt and Jewish children in Brooklyn.

Even better, he says. You go into the bar on your own, start hanging with the Herve coterie, talking about, whatever, split ends, the Hippocratic oath, and I'll slink in later, in my trench coat, and leer at you from the bar.

She reaches for her blouse. You sure know how to make a girl feel sexy.

What can I say? It's a gift. So I leer, you join me—drawn by my oily charm—I buy you a drink and put a hand up your skirt, we sidle out to the alley, where I rip off your clothes—

He is interrupted by a short, piercing chirp.

They look up.

The smoke detector above the bed chirps again.
They hear a faint, buzzing static.
Then:

> *May I have your attention, please. May I have your
> attention.*

A statement, not a request.
The voice is a man's. Bronx-accented. Calm, yet firm.

> *This is your fire safety director speaking. An alarm has
> been triggered on the fifth floor of the building. The New
> York City Fire Department is currently en route to
> investigate the incident.*

Oh no, she whispers. No no no.
It's fine, Jenny, it's—

> *There is no need to evacuate at this time. We ask that
> guests remain in their rooms to facilitate access of fire
> personnel to stairwells and hallways. We apologize for
> any inconvenience. Further announcements will be
> made shortly.*

Another chirp.
Then silence.

part two

criminal conversation

three

The voice stops, the smoke detector lets off another weird little chirp, and he's already halfway around the bed, reaching for the phone.

I'm sure it's nothing, he says. I'll just call down and ask for a few details.

She watches him, heart in her throat. She tries to avoid canned phrases like that when she writes, clichés and tired flourishes, but you know what, this one works, it pretty much exactly describes how her heart feels right now, stuffed way up in a space too small for it, hammering wildly, desperate to escape.

And go where, heart?

What's the plan?

Hello, he says into the phone, this is . . . yes, I'll hold.

He rolls his eyes at her like, *these people.* He must not be the only guest who, while sure it's nothing, decided to call down for a few details. In dozens—hundreds?—of rooms like this one, up and down and all around, they stand at identical bedside tables, hold identical receivers, not nervous, not fricking *saturated* with apprehension, oh no. These chill information seekers are simply exercising their right as paying guests to ask questions, and to have those questions—

Yes, he says. This is Nicholas Holloway in room . . . that's right. I'm not bad, thanks, but I am a little curious about . . . exactly.

Look at him. Phone to his ear, brow furrowed. Listening, nodding.

Mm-hmm, he says. Hmm. Mm-hmm.

This must be what he does every day. Standing in his office, astride the world, making calls, assessing the evidence. Asserting his prerogatives. Not shirtless and barefoot with his fly undone, but otherwise? Exactly like this.

I understand, he says, but surely . . . no no, you go ahead.

She makes fun of such men all the time. Makes fun, or rages against them. The supremely, oh-so-naturally entitled males of the species, with their brimming confidence, their—look at that wide stance, the fist on his hip!—power poses. Presented with a general announcement, anything preceded by a *May I have your attention* or, especially, any kind of chime or bell? Forget it. Those are for plebes, darling. No, these exalted beings will call down by God, they will insist on bespoke replies to their, let's face it, probably pretty basic questions. They take their outsize portion as their due without a thought, a qualm. They're infuriating.

But she can't deny they're handy to have around sometimes.

They execute.

And how long do you expect that to take? he asks.

Yes, he executes. And what does she do? She cedes. She asked him to call down earlier, when she'd rushed to the door like a loon. Why hadn't she called? Reached for the phone, taking action to calm her own spastic worries, instead of deferring to, relying on, him? You can't say *spastic* anymore. She had no idea until Charles's assistant corrected her one day. *It's just, I have a cousin with cerebral palsy? And that word is really triggering.* She was mortified! She never wants to be unkind. Though compared to some of the things they used to call each other when she was a kid . . . but of course, times change. For the better, mostly.

Well, maybe not mostly. Somewhat.

Somewhat for the better.

All right, he says. We'll wait to hear more.

He hangs up. It's a false alarm.

It is? They're positive?

She can breathe again. They're safe. Everything's fine!

Almost positive, he says. False alarms have been popping up on different floors since they opened last week—an electrical glitch of some kind. They thought the problem had been fixed, but apparently not.

Almost? Apparently? She doesn't like these words. They're wishy-washy. Invertebrate.

They're checking it out though, right? Investigating?

Absolutely, he says. But the woman I just spoke with said there's no need to worry.

He comes back around the bed and takes her hands. Not a master of the universe, not an entitled jerk—he's still the patient, generous guy who showed up a few minutes ago. Who clasped her head and kissed her and said, *Where are you, Jenny? Where'd you go?* Who chose to indulge her worries over his own pleasure.

It's okay, he says.

He brushes her hair back, tucks a lock of it behind her ear, and she feels the pull. She wants to bite his hand, grab his ass and press herself against him, feel his tongue in her mouth. She's fritzing with anxiety but still wants him to bend her over the arm of the sofa and—

Did the alarm come from inside a room or from a hallway? she asks.

The desk clerk didn't say. Does it matter?

It might. A fire inside a room would be behind a door made to withstand heat and flames, I forget for how long. It's in the fire code, the, you know, rules for building buildings? Are there even guest rooms on the fifth floor, or is it something else, like a parking garage? In bigger spaces a fire would have more oxygen to feed on, which would make it—

Hey. He puts a hand on her shoulder, gives her a little shake. Fireman Phil. We're safe. Whatever the configuration of the fifth floor is, it's thirty-seven stories below us. The typical floor height of a high-rise is, what, nine feet? That means this nonexistent problem is at least three hundred and thirty-three feet away.

Did you just multiply that in your head? That fast?

I'm a genius, what can I say? So you can trust me and quit worrying.

Wait, she says. The fifth floor? We heard the alarms earlier. We couldn't have if they were all the way down on the fifth floor.

Jenny . . .

But she's moved away. She picks her skirt up from the floor.

We need to leave, Nick.

Look at her, taking her due. Executing. It feels good!

They asked us to sit tight, he points out. They wouldn't have done that if there was a real problem.

What if they don't know? she says. What if they're wrong?

She wishes she didn't sound so pleading and pathetic. Execute, woman! Power pose!

We were about to leave, she adds. You were ready to leave.

Because we didn't know what was going on. Now we do. Jenny. Come on.

She sighs. Still holding her skirt, she moves to the window. *Come on, Jenny.* Snow swirls on the other side of the glass. *Be cool, Jenny. Get with the program.* She doesn't see any flashing lights. The street is too far down, even when she presses her forehead against the glass.

Comeoncomeoncomeon.

That fire in Midwood happened in winter, too. Imagine plunging from such heat into the freezing cold. Imagine choosing to do it, willingly leaving your no. That mother couldn't have left all those babies. She must have been dragged out. Rescued.

Yeah, right. Rescued straight to hell.

Nick isn't budging. Well you know what? She'll go without him. Yes. She'll run down and make sure everything's all right. They usually leave separately anyway. She hates that part. It makes her feel . . . doesn't matter. This is different. Let him stay and wait for the all-clear, passing his time however he likes. Drinking champagne. Doing lightning math.

Go. Do it.

Just go.

She frowns at the snow. Bounces her forehead against the glass. She won't go, not alone. She knows this even as she marshals all the reasons why she should. This is their night, their one whole lucky and long-awaited night together. To leave early, and without him, would feel consequential in some way she can't put her finger on. It would be, what? A renunciation. Something she could never undo.

God, listen to her. A renunciation? She's overwrought. Fraught and overwrought. The entire situation is so minor. Why is she flipping out?

This happens at the firm all the time, he says.

She turns from the window. He's sitting on the edge of the bed, dropping a few slivers of ice from the bucket into his champagne.

Fires? she says.

False alarms. One of the security guys comes over the intercom and tells us to stay put while they check out an alarm on the ninth floor, or the thirtieth, or what have you. A few minutes later he comes back to say everything's fine. Some jackass burned their leftovers in an office microwave, or snuck a joint in a stairwell. It's life in big buildings, you know?

He sets down his glass and holds out a hand. She walks over. He pulls her close so that she's standing between his knees.

This is nothing, Jenny. And if it is something, it's a very minor and faraway something, being dealt with by professionals. If we leave, we'll have to take the stairs, since they've shut down the elevators—which is standard procedure, the woman told me. So we'd be schlepping down forty-two flights.

She nods. True. All true.

Here's a final consideration, he says. I checked the weather for Houston tomorrow, and when I saw it was going to be seventy degrees, I left my winter coat at the office. Which means that if you make me go down and kick around on the sidewalk, I'll freeze my balls off. Think of my balls, Jenny. Won't you pity my poor testicles?

He points at his crotch, making a sad face, and she marvels at him. She really does. Imagine going through life, through this perilous world, with such ease! Reaching for the phone. Joking about his balls. Confident that everything will work out for him, because everything always has.

Must be nice.

Well, maybe it's not just nice. Maybe it's the key. Maybe she should take her due, she should execute, not by insisting they scurry down a skyscraper, but by following his supremely rational lead. By setting her fears aside and choosing—that's it, *choosing*—to treat this situation as the mere inconvenience it almost certainly is. She's a grown woman—you're a grown-ass woman, Jennifer!—who shouldn't spoil a long-anticipated evening because of some dumb superstition.

Because yeah, God's really coming for you. And he's going to get you by burning down a huge building.

You're that important.

She takes a deep breath. Exhales.

You're right, she says. We should stay.

He pours her a glass of champagne. She takes a sip.

Oh, it's good. So cold.

Okay, but those alarms earlier, they must have been much closer than the fifth—

You sure? he asks.

Yes, she says. And she is. This is life in big buildings, in a big city. So she's going to stop being a big baby, she's going to drink more of this delicious fizzy water with bonus champagne flavor, and as soon as they're given the all clear, they'll—what was his phrase? Resume normal operations. He's got such good phrases, all the witty words, he should be the writer not seriously *that's* where you're going right now? There?

Knock it off.

He finds two bathrobes in a closet, pristine and impossibly soft, sleeves tucked into their tightly furled belts. They shed the clothing they'd managed to put on before the announcement, swaddle themselves in the robes and return to bed, sitting up side by side against the headboard.

She sips her champagne. What should we do now?

Nothing strenuous, he says. Maybe a little light fellatio?

Nick!

He grins at her. She bursts out laughing.

Jenny laughs!

She's fine. Thank Christ.

They don't have to leave.

I think it could do both of us some good, he says.

Both of us, huh?

He'd never seen her like that. Poor girl. Welling up—her tears, then his tenderness. A new feeling, wanting to protect her. So he got on the horn, asking for an explanation, a timeline. Stern, but not yelling. Not even close. He yells at work. Acts the Big Boss. Partnerman. People must think he's overcompensating, he's wearing a mink thong and being regularly pissed on by a dominatrix in a Hell's Kitchen dungeon or something, but no, sorry, he's not that interesting. He's just a dickhead lawyer.

Why not? he says. You love doing it.

She laughs again. Look at her! Totally at ease, she's lost that hunted look. Now all he needs to do is keep her amused until those clowns downstairs get their shit together.

Love? she repeats. Let me tell you something. No woman on earth loves giving blow jobs.

No woman, he says. Not a single woman, in the history of human copulation, has ever been aroused by sucking a man's dick.

Correct, she says.

Why did he go hunting for robes? She's bundled up when he needs her naked. Even if he can't touch her. Yet. It kills him when she's so definite—*correct*, with that prim little smile, and earlier, her forceful *We need to leave, Nick.* He wanted to toss her onto the bed and—

But he restrained himself. He's not a monster, he wouldn't dream of trying to fuck her fears away.

Okay, he might dream of it, but he would never do it. Unless she was game.

Is she game? Might she . . .

No. It's too soon.

Give her time.

He would have gone downstairs if she'd insisted. He never would have made her leave the room alone. It's bad enough watching her go at the end of an ordinary evening. To have it happen tonight, after all his planning and anticipation, would have felt . . .

Never mind. Because it didn't happen.

Still, she was spooked. He would have only made it worse if he'd shared a small correction the desk clerk had made. The alarm wasn't triggered on the fifth floor, as the fire safety director had announced, but on the fifteenth. Which is nothing. Completely irrelevant, as far as they're concerned. But telling Jenny would have complicated things, when it doesn't matter. They're still so far away.

From nothing. That's the main point. There's nothing down there.

So. Back to blow jobs.

Oral sex is fine, she's saying. It can even be kind of fun, if the man we're giving it to is super into it. But the act itself? Not a turn-on.

Speaking for all women now? he teases. Explaining yourselves? I thought you didn't do that.

Yeah, well, this one's a no-brainer, she says.

Is it? Because several women have told me that sucking cock is one of the great pleasures of their life.

Several, she says. Wow.

Three at least. Possibly four.

Were they assembled in a group when they announced this to you? she asks. Like a chorus? Chanting, or . . .

She's mocking him! They're bantering. She's fine. Leaving would have been a waste of precious time, it would have been . . . oh, but they could have fucked in the stairwell. Glaring lights, the possibility of exposure. Her on the step above him, pinned against the wall, skirt rucked up, her cries echoing as he savagely—

Settle down.

Separate conversations, he says. They assured me. Swore up and down. How do you explain that?

They were lying to you. She holds out her glass. May I have more champagne?

He reaches for the bottle. Yes, my reluctant fellator.

She laughs. Right, I'm such a reluctant . . . whoa, that's plenty. Thank you.

My pleasure. He eases the bottle back into the bucket. Now. Why would they lie?

Who, your harem of cocksuckers?

It's his turn to laugh. Yes. My harem. Why would they lie about loving blow jobs?

She shrugs. To reassure you, maybe. To make you feel less ashamed about what you want.

I'm not ashamed about what I want.

Sure you are, she says. Deep down. We're all ashamed, all the time, about everything. She sips her champagne. Though maybe they weren't deliberately lying. Maybe they genuinely believe that giving head turns them on.

But they're wrong?

Yes. They've been brainwashed.

To enjoy dicks in their mouths?

To please men, Nick.

Ah, right. He tops off his own glass. Because women are systematically indoctrinated, they've internalized misogyny, been warped by sexist propaganda, yadda yadda.

She stares at him. Yadda . . . yadda?

Danger zone!

Let me rephrase, he says. You're referring to the indisputable fact that women in our culture are conditioned to serve the interests of men.

In all cultures, she says, and yes.

Meaning that any male-benefiting desire a woman expresses, such as for the aforementioned dick in the aforementioned mouth, is more likely the result of that woman being trained to want what men want her to want, than it is some inherent desire of her own.

Exactly, she says.

Okay, but why does that make her enjoyment of blow jobs less legitimate?

Why? Because, I mean, it's literally not legitimate. It doesn't arise naturally from her own inclination. Her innate self.

Her innate self, he says. What's that?

Oh my God. You don't believe in the self now?

Just hear me out.

She smiles, shaking her head. Just Hear Me Out: The Nick Holloway Story.

He refills their glasses. Good thing he brought two bottles. The way she's shaking her head, resisting him. She'd resist him in the stairwell, too. *Nick, no, someone might see!* But she'd be playing. She's as game as he is, as hungry, downright lascivious, a quality that shocked him when he first encountered it. Shocked and delighted him. So yes, she'd play, she'd sigh and succumb, he'd pin her against the railing, one hand on her lovely throat, his thumb pressing—lightly! lightly!—into the gorgeous hollow at its base while the other slides between her legs—

I'm just saying women aren't the only ones who are brainwashed, he says. We all are. There is no innate, no *natural* human, quote-unquote. We're each nothing more than the sum of the influences and norms and taboos that have been hammered into us since birth, most of which we're completely unaware of, and all of which we're powerless to change.

You don't think people can change?

Nah, he says.

Why am I surprised? I'm talking to Mr. Negativity here.

How is that negative?

She chuckles. Gee, Nick. Let me think.

It's realistic, he insists. We can become aware of what's driving us, the conditioning, the brainwashing, we can wake up to it— some of us can, anyway. And that moment of recognition feels great. Oh my God, I get it now, forces are controlling me, and they're inside me, they're inside the building! Epiphanies like that are a blast. But they rarely cause people to alter their behavior. We're too lazy, too . . . where are you going?

She's out of bed, reaching for her sparkling water, abandoned on the coffee table.

Listening to all these deep thoughts is making me parched, she says.

He watches her wander to the window. Is she done with the chitchat? Can he drop the philosophical patter and seduce her, re-seduce her, taking immense care, making sure she comes this time? He would have kept trying if he'd known. Didn't she realize that? He's a selfish son of a bitch, no question, but to her he wants to give. And give and give. Which is why it bothered him that she lied. She'd led him to believe he'd satisfied her, only to later reveal—ha ha asshole, gotcha!—he'd failed. Golden boy. So much promise. Turns out you can't even make a woman—

Oh let it go! She faked it and didn't tell you, you got sad after coming and didn't tell her. Everybody's hiding something. What did she say? Everybody's ashamed. He doesn't know about that. Lonely after an orgasm—it's ridiculous, but not shameful. Is she ashamed? She does have the whole religious thing to deal with. The Catholic guilt. Though how she can believe in, let alone continue to pay dues to, what's basically a global crime syndicate . . . it's baffling. He has zero spiritual leanings himself. Old-school WASP, church on Christmas and Easter, that's it. Sometimes he wishes it were otherwise. All those strictures against carnal transgression must add a certain zest to life. He'd probably enjoy masturbating even more than he does if he'd been taught since childhood to find it filthy and wrong.

Oh well. Like Jesus, we all have our cross to bear.

She's leaning close to the window, looking down. Then up. Then down again.

Jenny?

She returns, slipping into bed beside him.

So we're stuck with ourselves, she says. We're these, whatever, constructions, and we can't change, and that's not totally grim and defeating to you?

Not at all. Because it means we can relax. Quit lamenting how we've been warped and perverted, quit trying to parse out what aspects of our personalities are quote-unquote natural and quote-unquote authentic, and accept ourselves. Hapless, a little clueless, lacking free will, but alive.

Wait—we lack free will now, too?

Of course. And it's wonderfully liberating. For example. Let's say you feel the impulse to give a man a blow job. Some near-at-hand, compelling, deeply deserving man.

Don't you dare, Nick.

My point is, you don't have to interrogate that desire, worry about where it comes from, whether it's real or some sexist construct. He loosens the belt of his robe. You just own it, you accept the urge, and—

She pushes at him, laughing. Put that thing away!

I can't, Jenny. Like I said, I'm not in control here either.

Oh my God, stop waggling it at me!

That's not me, he says. It's the patriarchy. The patriarchy is waggling my dick at you.

Yeah, well, the patriarchy can kiss my ass, she says.

That'll work too. Roll over and . . . where are you going now?

Because she's out of bed once more, reaching for something on the sofa.

four

She holds up her phone. Just want to check on the boys.

He heads for the bathroom, leaving her to it. She drifts toward the window, tapping and swiping.

But as soon as she hears the door slide shut, she walks back across the plush carpeting. She doesn't tiptoe, she's not absurd, but she does walk . . . carefully.

To the door of the room.

Where she leans in, close to the doorjamb, and sniffs.

Very quietly.

No smoke. Good. That's excellent.

But let's just confirm . . .

She sniffs again. A big old inhale, low and slow.

Nothing. Great!

That's what she expected, of course, but great.

She sneaks past the bathroom again, eyes on her—whoops, she loses her balance, wobbles a little. What's that about? Too much champagne. Maybe slow it down with the drinking? She skirts the bed and takes a seat on the sofa.

Her first search—nyc fire tonight?—yields no results. How about:

fire midtown nyc now?

Nothing. Good. Now she'll just skim Twitter. And Facebook. And a few of the firebug subreddits where she's lurked in the past, for research purposes.

r/wildfire

r/arson

r/nationalfirenews

Some of those weirdos have police scanners. If there's a problem downstairs, a sexy Manhattan high-rise fire, someone will be talking about it.

That's all she needs—news, or preferably, the absence of news. Then she'll be able to continue mistressing the universe, beating back the flickers of unease that kept popping up while they chatted and sipped their champagne. It wasn't constant, she forgot about the alarms and stern instructions for long stretches, thanks to Nick and his barrage of hoo-ha. Reluctant fellator. How does he come up with this stuff? She sits at the desk and grinds it out sometimes, it can be excruciating to write one line that isn't total garbage. Meanwhile it just pours out of him.

Oh, good—this is good: according to @nycfirewire, the FDNY is battling active fires at an office building in Staten Island, a townhouse in Brooklyn and a small warehouse in Queens. Good? None of that is *good*, but there's nothing burning in Manhattan. That's a relief. Though still cool it with the drinking. And no sex, obviously. Sex would be wrong right now. Unlike sex all the other times you have sex with him, which is fine, totally moral and aboveboard and stop.

She walks to the window. She still can't see any flashing lights, not even reflected on the building opposite. But maybe they aren't on the street-facing side? Which way is north?

She's all turned around.

Nick doesn't believe in the self? Or free will? He certainly has a free willy. The way he keeps eyeing her, playing with the tassel on her belt. And he doesn't think people can change? She should have pushed back at his smooth certainties. She tried—she always tries—but he's too quick for her. He's like a speed skater, gliding effortlessly through points and counterpoints, while she feels like a duck who woke up to find its legs frozen into the ice of the pond.

Weird comparison, but okay.

The point is she feels dumb next to him, which she hates. But also kind of loves. He makes her think. Challenges her opinions, prods and teases. It's maddening. And so hot. God, she wants him again. Maybe they could no. You have to wait. It won't be long now.

She hears the roar of the toilet, the blast of the tap. A muffled exclamation. His head appears around the corner.

Can you believe there's no soap in this dump?

There is, she says. I mean, there was. I took it for Natey. He loves hotel toiletries. The little bottles and sewing kits and whatnot?

So you swiped them? You've sold millions of those vampire books of yours—you can't afford to buy the kid a few trial-size bottles?

Ghosts. My books are about ghosts. She smiles at him. And you're right. I've sold millions.

Congratulations. He nods at the phone in her hand. Everything okay?

What?

You were checking on the boys.

Oh. Yeah, they're fine. The soap is in my bag.

He disappears again. Checking on the boys, right . . . she opens her messages. She's gotten nothing from Tom since a text that morning: what did you do with the good spatula? She hasn't responded. She doesn't care for his accusatory tone. She also doesn't want to admit that she used the good spatula to scrape ice off her windshield, which is why it's currently in the back seat of her car. In pieces. So she types: I sold it to a passing Eskimo. That's what her father always said when she was a kid and couldn't find something. The stapler? Oh, an Eskimo came to the door looking for one and I gave it to him. Your tennis shoes? Sold 'em to an Eskimo!

Why an Eskimo? She never asked. Her dad is a good, kind man, a wonderful man, but the Eskimo thing . . . is it racist? Singling them out, mocking their, what? Nomadic lifestyle? Historical deprivations?

Can you even use the word *Eskimo* anymore?

She deletes her text without sending.

She checks Twitter, checks Google, checks Reddit. Checks into a mental hospital. Because honestly—what is she afraid of? Well, that's easy. She's afraid to die. More accurately, she finds it unfathomable. Nonexistence? Sorry—can't picture it! And she doubts there's anything waiting for her afterward, despite her half-hearted faith, which isn't founded on a belief in some higher power so much as on a gut skepticism that this excessively complicated world could have sprung into being from atoms and chaos. Bat sonar, and babies' perfect ears, and the convoluted reproductive systems of kangaroos—these things just kind of happened? She knows evolution is more sophisticated than that, it occurred over a span of time greater than her puny brain can grasp, there's hard evidence, something about geologic strata . . . still.

Kangaroos have two uteruses. And three vaginas.

They must be exhausted.

In short, it's all improbable. But if the alternative is true, she's facing eternal torment for her flagrant sins. Either way, she's screwed.

Thus the fear.

Flagrant sins. Does Nick feel guilty? She's never asked. The question falls squarely within the realm of That Which They Do Not Discuss. They scrupulously avoid talking about their marriages, their spouses. Caroline seems to adore him. The way she smiles at him at parties. Touches his hair. Jenny feels awful when she sees them together. Stabs of guilt, which she welcomes. Because if she won't stop doing what she's doing with Caroline's husband—and while she did consider stopping once, she hasn't—it's only right that she feel like a monster from time to time.

But she's curious, too. Do they still sleep together? Do they have nicknames? In-jokes? What do they fight about? Laugh about? She knows he's a good father. He dotes on Jill.

But what else is he? What kind of husband?

She moves to the window, then back to the sofa. Circling, circling. The way Nick talks circles around her. People don't change? What a cynic, what a . . . of course people change! She changed. She had an epiphany, decided to correct course, and it was daunting, agonizing even, but she did it. She—hey, she executed! God, it felt like an execution at the time. She can't tell him about it, absolutely not, but it happened. She changed.

So ha ha, Nick—you're wrong! You're completely—

There it is.

In the midst of berating herself she refreshed Twitter, and with a clutch at her heart now reads @nycfirewire's latest post:

MANHATTAN 10-41 code 1

Park & 50. Alarm reported 6.19 pm

Park and Fiftieth. That's them. What's a 10-41 code 1? She googles it and finds a site listing FDNY radio codes. She scrolls, scrolls, there are so many fricking codes . . .

10-41 SUSPICIOUS FIRE

Fire Marshall investigation is required.

CODE 1 Occupied Structure or Vehicle. A structure

(commercial, residential, public), or vehicle (car,

bus or train) that is occupied at the time of the fire.

So there is a fire. A suspicious one. Or does the code just mean an alarm has been triggered? Fire Marshall investigation is *required*. How could they know there's a suspicious fire if it still requires investigation?

Shouldn't a radio code be a little bit less ambiguous?

She checks a few other sites. Nothing. Good. She won't let this rattle her. She'll just—

What are you doing on the sofa? he demands.

He's standing in the bathroom doorway, watching her.

What's wrong with the sofa?

It's not the bed. Get over here, woman!

She rolls her eyes but she rises, smiling. Jenny's coming! She's on her way. His heart soars, as does his cock. Can a cock soar? It can certainly perk the fuck up, as his always does for her, this woman who quickens his blood. Who pushes him to lyricism, to think in ludicrous phrases like *quickens his blood*. Idiot thoughts. But so what? She's returning to bed.

Come, madam, come. Phone in one hand, glancing down at it, other hand plucking at her belt. That's right, my lady, loosen that encumbrance, that vexing . . . he could tie her up. Lash her wrists to those sleek and handy bedposts and lavish all his attention on her, for as long as it takes. Drive her mad, multiple times. Be driven mad by her in turn. Is she ready? Futzing with her phone—she's bored. He can cure that. He can—

It's been a while, she says. Should we call down?

The desk clerk said they'd make an announcement. Let's give them a few more minutes.

She slides into bed, and he adjusts his robe over his tormented genitalia. She's not ready. Which is fine. Though, to have her inches away, semirecumbent yet unattainable—it's torture. When they're apart he manages, barely. He has his rules, his bulkheads. His own hand, when necessary.

It's frequently necessary.

He crosses his ankles, tucks his cock under the belt of his robe so it doesn't whang out into the open. He settles back into the pillows.

So, he says. We were talking about your books.

Were we?

We were. Your millions of ghost books. I understand they're quite sexy.

They're romantic, she says. It's YA. I can't, you know, write pornography.

But there is boning, correct?

There is boning, she concedes. Very vague, and very hazily described.

He empties the last of the champagne into their glasses. So how does that work? he says. How do ghosts and humans screw?

Oh my God, Nick. Are you seriously asking me about this again?

You've never given me a clear answer! As a purveyor of this kind of literature, this spectral smut—

Smut! she cries. That's me. A big old smut slinger!

I just think you should be able to explain the mechanics.

She whaps him with the end of her belt. If you're so curious, why don't you read one of them?

He wrinkles his nose. I'm not really your target audience, am I?

Oh no, she says. You're too exalted. Too busy reading your, whatever. Dead Russians. Translations of obscure Austrian novelists.

Whoa, hey. Why the vicious attack on obscure Austrian novelists? What have obscure Austrians ever done to you?

They've bored me. She flops back against the pillows. They're so fricking boring! Reading is supposed to be fun.

Yes, it is. And her books are fun. Unquestionably. He knows because he has read them. She thinks he hasn't because, well, that's what he tells her. Or strongly implies, whenever he teases her about them, pretending he wouldn't lower himself to that kind of trash, et cetera. And normally he wouldn't. He bought the first one for Jill when it came out. Caroline gave him such hell—*Our daughter is twelve, Nick! This is for teenagers!*—so he never gave it to her. One night he flipped it open, to check out her author photo, glance at the acknowledgments—of course he wasn't in there, why would he be?—and he skimmed the first page, to see what all the fuss was about.

He stayed up until dawn reading it.

He keeps her second book at the office. A paralegal came across it one day. *Bought that for my daughter,* he said. Which didn't explain the cracked spine, but the paralegal was too intimidated by him to inquire further. They're well written, her books. Moderately engrossing, if you like that sort of thing. Millions do, as noted. They're a phenomenon. The second book ended with a twist that was truly breathtaking. Usually he sees that sort of thing coming. He was impressed. It must have been hard to pull off.

So yes, her books are fine. Probably good, given the genre. Again, he doesn't have much of a point of reference.

Is there penetration? he asks. Phantom jizz?

My characters are teenagers, Nick. I can't exactly douse them with jizz.

Well, one of them is four hundred years old or something, right?

She sets her glass on the nightstand. I'm going to explain this to you one more time. Then we're never going to talk about it again. My ghosts, my main ghost, really, the protagonist—

JoJo, he says.

Julian, she says, making a visible effort not to slap him, can assume a form, become, you know, a body, thanks to having studied certain . . . oh God. She covers her face. This is awful.

What?

When I have to explain it like this I feel so dumb! Of course, it's all dumb, it's—

It's not dumb, he says. Now he feels bad. JoJo. He knows her hero's name is Julian. He also knows how ghost-human banging works, since it's described in detail in the second book. Which he's read twice.

Yet here he is, giving her a hard time.

Keep going, he says.

Okay, let me just . . . she glances at her phone, then sets it face down on the nightstand. Right. So, Julian discovered an ancient book in the library of the estate he haunts. He was alone there for decades while the house was vacant, so he studied, and practiced, and when the moon is in a certain phase, and he feels a lot of desire . . .

He's motivated, he says.

Exactly. Meaning that when Sophie shows up—that's my human heroine—and they fall in love, this overwhelming and passionate love, he can become corporeal and, you know, do the deed. Though I focus on the kissing, the touching. The feelings. I kind of blur over the act itself.

The slipping of the ghostly p into the corporeal v, he says.

Nicely put. The film version will be a lot more explicit. And sensual. Juan Pablo wants to create a whole atmosphere of decadence and—

Juan Pablo?

The director, she says. Juan Pablo Torres.

She gets out of bed, picking up her phone on the way. He watches her move to the window, typing.

Juan Pablo? You can't just call him Juan?

That's his whole first name, so . . .

You met this guy last week?

But she's gone, lost in her screen. She twirls a lock of hair while she scrolls, twisting it into a little knot. Then she releases it and starts twisting it again.

Jenny?

Hmm? Oh. Yeah. She's still scrolling. We've been on a bunch of Zooms throughout the whole development process, but this was the first time I met him in person. He seems . . . nice. Friendly. He's smart, and—

He hit on you, he says.

She looks up, startled. What? No!

Holy shit, you're blushing! He came on to you, didn't he?

Of course not!

He waits.

Maybe a little, she confesses.

Ha! She's so easy to read sometimes.

I don't know! she cries. Maybe he's just really affectionate. I'm terrible at reading romantic signals.

I'm not. Tell me how he acted, and I'll tell you whether he wants to fuck you.

Fine, she says. All week he kept coming up to me—

He definitely wants to fuck you, he says.

You're so funny.

I need to see what this guy looks like. He reaches across the nightstand for his own phone. He's picturing a bear of a man, in one of those cargo vests directors seem to love. He types the title of her first book, and Juan Pablo . . .

What's his last name?

Nick, don't.

I just want to see him!

She sighs. Torres.

Torres, he murmurs as he types. Grizzled, probably. Always squinting into the distance, framing things with his thumbs and forefingers. Not without a certain amount of Latin machismo, which can be compelling, but between the salt-and-pepper stubble and the big gut, there's no way Jenny would—

His search returns photos of a sultry young god.

He turns the phone to show her. Is that him?

She comes back to the bed, leans in. Yep.

This guy's a director? How old is he?

He turned thirty last week. We had a party for him on set.

She helped throw a party for the birthday boy. How jolly. He swipes to enlarge a photo of Juan Pablo on a red carpet. This looks retouched, he says.

She leans closer. No, it's pretty accurate.

Those shining teeth. Those cheekbones. There's no way the guy actually looks like this. Where's he from, he says, Mexico?

Spain.

Barely speaks English, I suppose.

No, he's fluent. He studied at Oxford.

Oxford. The bastard! Did she sleep with him?

Don't ask. None of your business.

He taps on another image. Juan Pablo is so young. No hair on his chest. Low testosterone, probably. Honestly, what serious director allows shirtless photos of himself to show up on the internet? Frolicking in the surf!

It's unprofessional.

He tosses his phone and stretches out, hands behind his head.

Well well well, he says. Looks like our Mrs. Gryzb snagged herself a hottie.

She's twirling her hair again. She looks up from her phone and frowns. Don't call me that.

Did she sleep with him?

Do.

Not.

Ask.

Yes, he says, Mrs. Gryzb is doing very well for herself out in Hollywood.

She grabs a pillow from the bed and whacks him with it. That's Tom's name, not mine!

It's poetry, he says. Such poetry.

She whacks him again, and he catches the pillow, pulling her with it onto the bed. Film sets are very sexy. Rampant coitus, if you believe the gossip sites, which he doesn't because he doesn't read them.

He tickles her. She squeals and squirms out of reach. No, he's not jealous. He's curious.

She can do what she wants.

I hate my name too, he says.

Why? Holloway is a great name.

Holloway is fine. It's Nick I hate. Nick is a crook. A shyster. He's the guy who stands on a street corner with slicked-back hair, ready to show you some nice watches he's got on special.

You might be overthinking this, she says.

Who, me?

They both laugh. She picks up her phone and looks at it again. Sets it down.

Shouldn't they have made an announcement by now?

It hasn't been that long, he says. I'll call in ten minutes if we haven't heard.

She said it was ambiguous whether Juan Pablo hit on her. But she could be lying. Did she suck Juan Pablo's cock—not for her own sake of course, ha ha we know *that* wouldn't happen, meaning if she did, it would have been to please him, some jerkoff Iberian? Short, no doubt. Small-dicked. He could google how tall he is.

No, he could not, because that's pathetic.

You're not drinking your champagne, he says.

Trying to get me drunk? But she takes a sip.

Did Juan Pablo come to her room late at night, needing some rewrites? Did he engineer a tryst, with wine, perhaps some chorizo? Did he take her in a four-poster bed, part of the set dressing, of his *atmosphere of decadence,* surrounded by candelabra and—

This is killing him. It's also turning him on a little. Why should he care? She can do what she wants.

You don't think people can change? she says.

What's that?

What you said earlier. That we can't free ourselves from the norms and the brainwashing and so forth.

Oh. Yeah, no. Maybe a little around the margins, but major transformation? That's rare.

She nods, thinking that over. Then:

Has this changed you?

This? he says.

You know. She waves a hand at the space between them. This. Our . . . thing.

Ah. He nods. Right. This.

five

He knew what she meant right away. Playing dumb—*huh, this, whuh?*—was a stalling tactic. Because while he's happy to bullshit all night about books and blow jobs, delving into their *this*? Their *thing*? No thanks. Why should they? They're so good at not talking about it, at reveling in it without wrestling with its murky implications. Its *this*ness.

They've managed to avoid most conversations about it for six years. So why is she bringing it up now, and why in God's name is she asking whether it's changed him?

Has it changed me, he says, as if he's mulling it over, really considering it. *Has it changed me, hmm, let me feign contemplation . . .*

Where the hell is the all clear? He should call down.

We've been doing this for a while now, she adds. Six years.

That long? he says, stalling, stalling. They've always been on the same page about what *this* is. A fun—more than fun, a joyful—escape, a release valve from the limited and the humdrum. Since they realized how compatible they were in certain key respects, since they assured themselves that nobody was going to get hurt, that they would be careful, careful, *so careful*—since that time, how great has this been? If, you know, essentially unimportant.

Just over six, she says. It was New Year's Eve, six years ago . . .

When I abased myself before you in the Parks' kitchen, he says.

Essentially unimportant? That's not fair. He'd needed this, or something like it. Though in the privacy of his own mind, in the story he tells himself about his life—easy, pal, she's the storyteller, not you—he has tended to minimize its importance. Her importance. Because not everything has to be momentous, okay? Not everything has to be Something. Still—to call it unimportant because it's physical, because it's sex—that's not right, either. That diminishes sex, when it should be celebrated. Glorified. Especially sex with her. It's delirious, their connection. Alchemical. The things she does to him. The things she lets him do to her! She laughs— laughs while they're fucking! They're free with each other, they play. He asks her for things, says outrageous, filthy things to her, with no filter, no fear that she'll misunderstand or get offended. It's such a relief, so liberating, compared to . . . well, to the rest of life. They don't have to worry about consequences, judgments, even what the other thinks of them, outside of rooms like this.

That's what they have, and it's always been enough. For both of them. Though it's true that one time, early on, swept away, overglowed, he had suggested they meet more often, once a week instead of once a month. She'd shot that down quick. And rightly so. Better to keep their *this* limited. Reduce the chance of complications.

And so they've had six supremely uncomplicated years—he knew it was six, of course he knew—free of heartfelt protestations and fraught exchanges. She can tell her little lies. They can both fuck other people. He hasn't, but he could. Has she? Look at her, glued to her phone. Is she texting the baby Spaniard? Sending him erotic emojis, thanking him for the scores of simultaneous orgasms they enjoyed this week, his—

Your phone is a real source of fascination tonight, he says.

Sorry, I'm . . . she sighs. Bites her lip.

What is it?

I'm looking at news about the fire, she says.

There's news?

Not much. I found one tweet, and now there are a few more,

but all they say is that the fire department is investigating. I can't even tell if there's actually a fire, or if they're just responding to the alarms. It seems like there's something, though. They just issued a new radio code, a 10-76, which is a notification of an incident in a high-rise, which—

Jenny, he says. It's fine. They're doing their job.

I know. It just makes me feel better to check.

There's way too much information on the internet. Radio codes? Where are you even finding this shit?

From social media accounts that follow the FDNY. She's scrolling again. I came across them last year, when I was doing research. At the end of my trilogy, a fire destroys the house at the center of the story. I wanted it to be authentic, and—

Wilderkill burns down? he says.

Yes, it . . . she looks up. How do you know its name?

Hmm? Oh. Well. He reaches for his champagne. Takes a long sip. Jill read your books. She loves them.

She does? Jenny looks so pleased. I had no idea.

Yeah, she never shuts up about them. I must have heard it from her. Listen, stop stressing about the alarm. And don't look at the internet. It's a cesspool.

Right. You're right. She sets the phone down. Adjusts the pillows behind her. Picks up her champagne and takes a sip.

So, she says. Us. You. Change.

She's really not letting this go.

You said early on that you'd never, you know. Done anything like this before.

Had an affair, he says. Cheated on my wife.

Because if they must talk about it, they should stop mincing around and use the correct terminology.

Adultery. Voluntary sexual activity between a married person and someone other than that person's spouse.

From the Latin, *adulterare*, to pollute or defile.

Synonyms: infidelity, two-timing, fornication, inconstancy, entanglement, liaison. Faithlessness. Criminal conversation.

I guess I'm just curious whether it's made any sort of a difference in your life, she says.

I'm happier, for sure. He takes her hand and kisses it. We've talked about this—how I was in a dark place. Suffering my predictable midlife crisis.

Your malaise, she says.

Exactly. Which is gone now, thanks mostly to you. But has this changed me fundamentally? I would say no. He turns her hand over and kisses her palm. If only, right? If only knowing you could wash away all my flaws and failings.

He bites her thumb. Hears the sharp intake of her breath. He takes hold of her wrist, pulling her toward him.

Hey. Why don't we . . .

But she's drawing away.

I'll be right back.

And she's gone again. He picks up his glass. Empty. He goes to the fridge to collect the second bottle of champagne. She's still nervous. Should he have offered to go downstairs and check out the situation? God no. He tears the foil off the cork, untwists its wire cage. He could have called, though. He just doesn't want to break the spell of the night. There's something intimate about being confined in here with her. Insulated from the outside world. Even placing a phone call would be reaching out to that world. Acknowledging that it matters. He aims the bottle at the bland collage above the sofa—a dent could only improve the thing—and eases the cork free with his thumbs. Still, she shouldn't have to turn to the internet for information. He'll call down when she comes back.

Why is she so fixated on change—has he changed, can't people change? She hasn't. For all that's happened, her massive success, her glamorous new career, she's exactly the same as she was when they met. At a toddler birthday party, of all places, in one of those soul-murdering kiddie torture gyms. They chatted among the balance beams and brightly colored mats. Other people were there, he doesn't remember who. She'd just moved to town, another Brooklyn refugee. She had a messy ponytail. And a poppyseed stuck in her teeth. He would have said something, but he didn't want to embarrass her. She was so wonderfully unselfconscious, with her big guffaws. Her sexy weariness. He found himself thinking about her the rest of that day. She'd snagged in his mind.

He began to see her occasionally around town. At social events, when he was running errands, dropping Jill at the town pool. He would notice her and instantly feel awkward. Because, to be clear, he was *not* that guy. The married perv, the creepo dad, ogling and lurking—that was the last guy he wanted to be! It was disgusting. Of course he wouldn't *do* anything, would never approach her or signal his interest. But it felt wrong to even think about her. So he remained polite, but aloof. At the park, the bookstore. The occasional neighborhood party.

Settling the new bottle into the ice bucket, he notices her heap of rings, and his cock gives a valedictory twitch. Engagement ring, wedding band. He loves to watch her remove them. The way she thrusts her elbows out, twists and tugs, lips pursed, a crease between her brows. The effort makes her breasts shimmy gloriously. Until off the rings come, and she leans over to place them on the nightstand. *Where my hand is set.* She is naked then, shorn of any reminder of her other attachments, her full life of relationships and associations that could cause him a pang of . . .

What? Nothing. He doesn't feel pangs. That's part of what's so fantastic about her, and this. It's blissfully pang free.

He prefers her completely naked, that's all.

Mrs. Gryzb! he yells. Your presence is required in the bed-chamber!

This time she really did have to pee. Sweet relief! She flushes just as he hollers from the other room. Some variation of get your butt in here, no doubt.

But she's taking a minute. Doing a little check-in. A self-check, like you're supposed to do after hiking. Except instead of deer ticks, she's checking for latent terror.

She doesn't find much. Disquiet, sure. Why haven't they made another announcement? It seems like a bad sign. But this worry is fighting for brain space with a fresh source of agita: her cringing embarrassment at the turn their conversation just took, entirely at her instigation.

Has this changed you? Where did that come from? From what he said earlier, obviously, she was belatedly pushing back, waddling after him on webbed feet, but why did she make it about them? What kind of response was she expecting?

He hadn't even known it had been six years!

So, yeah. With that recent horror uppermost, her fears about the fire aren't getting much oxygen.

Ha ha. Aren't you clever?

Pull it together.

The toilet seat is warm. It wasn't warm the last time she was in here. Is it one of those fancy . . . why yes. Look at that control panel. He must have switched it on. He'd have been all over the option for ass-toasting, ready as he is to deploy every available amenity. Including her.

She moves to the sink. *Has this changed you?* He handled the question well. Answered without lobbing it back at her, or demanding to know why she was asking. He's so patient tonight. Since that first moment of tenderness—*where are you, Jenny, where'd you go?*—he's been so gentle. Who knew?

She plucks a hand towel from the stack under the sink. Everybody, maybe. Maybe everybody knows him. Patient, kind—that could be who he really is. And lustful, caustic Nick, handsy and horny, mocking and profane—that could be the version he shows only to her. Shady, street corner Nick. Because with her he doesn't have to be good.

You know what, though? No. She's seen him out in the world. They keep a careful distance, of course, but she can observe. Enough to know that his personality, his essential Nickness, is the same out there as it is in here. In their little sex pod. Their fuck bubble.

Six Years in a Fuck Bubble: The Parrish and Holloway Story.

She wanders back to the toilet, wipes a few drops off the seat.

Has this changed me fundamentally? I would say no. All righty, then. That's fine!

No it isn't. If she's being completely honest, it isn't. She would like to think she has some importance to him, aside from being a semiregular receptacle for his copious ejaculate.

A Semiregular Receptacle for His

Enough with the book titles. Honestly.

But yes. If she'd had some effect on him, however small, she wouldn't mind the imbalance. Because he has affected her, profoundly.

The man who can't even be bothered to read her books.

She examines the toilet's many buttons and blinking lights. What can it do other than warm your butt? Suggest some firming exercises? Slim it down with a little lipo? She presses a button and jumps when a little arm whizzes out from under the seat, spraying water.

Why does it sting that he's never read her books? She should be glad. Immensely relieved, in fact. Because if he had cracked one open, Mr. Super-Genius, Analytical Man, surely he would have noticed certain, let's say, essential similarities, between himself and her hero. He couldn't have failed to observe that Julian Blackwell is the eighteenth-century teenage ghost version of him, Nick Holloway. Romanticized, superficially altered, but undeniably him: his intelligence and intensity, his caustic wit, his quick gestures. The sound of his voice. The way he kisses.

It's all Nick. Nobody knows, but he would know, instantly.

She tried to disguise him at the time. She really did. But she was writing in a fever. Not in control of herself or what was pouring onto the page.

How could she be? She was so desperately, uncontrollably in love.

She moves to the door, but hesitates. She needs another minute. Maybe they'll make an announcement soon, and she can saunter back into the room free and easy, instead of skittering around, constantly checking her phone. Fritzy Jenny is getting tiresome.

It happened maybe six months into their little arrangement.

Everything was going great, it was low-key, casual. Exactly what it should have been. Until they had plans to meet one night, she was getting on the train, and he texted her. A work emergency had come up, and he was sorry, but he couldn't make it.

She read it and fell to pieces.

This is it it's over he's tired of you he's making an excuse, it's over it's over it's

Harpies, clawing at her.

When she recovered, she couldn't deny what it meant.

She was in love.

It was a catastrophe!

All that summer and into the fall she was full of it—full to the ears. The sensation was intoxicating. Her behavior was ridiculous. She spent hours concocting gemlike texts and emails, and waiting in agony until he responded. He would travel for work, and she found herself googling the weather for whatever city he was in. Every sugary pop song was rich with meaning. She soared. She crashed and burned. She couldn't come without wanting to shout it at him. She managed to restrain herself. Barely.

He is in my bones, she thought once, driving to see him, hands gripping the steering wheel. He is in my bones!

Ridiculous. Teenagerly. But true.

And all the while, the beloved? The object of her passionate devotion?

He didn't have a clue.

All that scorching mental rigor, and he never saw it. True, she did everything she could to hide how she felt, because when she wasn't exalted she was mortified. The first new man she sleeps with in ten years, and she immediately goes gaga? Real original. Way to go, hon.

Regardless, he didn't know, and she sure as hell wasn't going to tell him. But it was torture to keep it bottled up. So she started writing again. Her abandoned dream, her young self's obsession. She'd spent her childhood filling notebooks with stories, fairy tales, poems and plays. She was going to be A Writer. Then she got to college and was refused a spot in an undergraduate fiction work-shop. Such a minor thing. But she was so soft and eager—God, she was young! Too uncertain to withstand rejection, all too willing to accept any criticism as the unassailable truth about herself. She surveyed her sad scribblings, her lofty hopes, and was filled with shame. Hating herself for thinking that she might be good, that someday she might . . .

No. The world said no.

And she listened.

But now, saturated with dangerous feelings, desperate for an outlet, she fell back into writing as if she'd never been away, pick-ing up an idea she'd sketched out years ago. It was a teen romance, the perfect receptacle for her volcanic emotion, allowing her to re-veal and conceal her own heart. Because it's not quite true that Ju-lian is all Nick—he's her, too. She is both of her characters, two very different people falling in impossible, forbidden love.

Her love lasted eight months. Then she ended it. She decided, she changed. It sounds like a lie, like she's deluding herself, she must love him still. But she doesn't. Confident about so little, she is certain of this.

And he never knew. About her great love. How she turned it into books that changed her life. Then, how she triumphed over it. No, to him she was and still is pretty, pliant Mrs. Gryzb, the married woman he gets a kick out of secretly screwing.

She makes a face at herself in the mirror. He knows that name bugs her. The teasing about her books, too. *Tell me about ghost jizz, har har.* He loves to make her feel dumb about her big dumb best-sellers. Yes, she laughed at the time. But did he not notice how she was fidgeting around the room, how she couldn't stop checking her phone? Even when she confessed what she was doing, he dismissed it. *It's fine. They're doing their job.* Yes, okay, probably, but did it not occur to him that she might need a little more reassurance than that?

He can be so obtuse sometimes.

Why haven't they gotten the all clear? What is going on down there?

No. What is going on up here? Here is where the problem is. She means so little to him that he can't be bothered to console her, he means so much to her that she has to hide her need for consolation. It's not love, of course, that's well and truly over. But it's something, some power he has over her still.

Power. Of course. His power, which she gave him, which she has, historically, given to any man who's shown the least bit of interest in or approval of her. Why did she listen to him—*pity my poor testicles*—when she could have left? Why did she trust him? Why do women trust men? When has that ever worked out?

No. Don't generalize. This isn't about Women and Men. It's about him and her. And six years of so little importance that he hasn't even bothered to keep track of them.

Oh, she's tired.

She's exhausted suddenly.

And she's pissed off.

She slides the bathroom door open and steps out.

There she is! He's refilling his glass. I opened the second bottle. Let's—

Are you seriously not worried?

Worried?

Yes, Nick. Worried. About the total, she flings a hand at the smoke detector, lack of information about the fire?

There's no fire. Jenny, come to—

Why haven't we heard anything? It's been over an hour.

They said it would take time. Honey. Are you still scared?

Of course I'm still scared, she says. *Honey.*

The emphasis there, that dark and loaded *honey*, that's not good. She's planted at the foot of the bed, scowling at him. Did something happen while she was in the bathroom?

He sets the bottle on the nightstand and goes to her.

You seemed fine, he says. You said you were okay. I wish you'd told me you were still nervous.

Yeah, well, honesty isn't really our thing, is it, Nick?

Okay, so something definitely happened in the bathroom. Did

she get an upsetting text from Tom? He knows he hasn't done anything. He's been nothing but patient.

He moves toward the phone. How about I call down?

She follows him. The alarms, the announcement, she says. The
fact that we're trapped. None of that bothers you?

I wouldn't say we're trapped.

Don't quibble.

Jenny, I don't think you're being very—

Does anything bother you? she says. Ever?

Why is he being attacked?

He hasn't done anything!

Plenty of things bother me, he says carefully.

Has anything ever not gone your way? Have you ever been disappointed?

He wants to laugh, but that would only make things worse.
Still. *Have you ever been disappointed?* She has no idea.

Jenny, I understand you're anxious, and I'm sorry I didn't—

Answer the question, Nick.

Have I been disappointed? he says. Of course I have.

Yeah? Tell me about it.

Look, I don't know what happened in the bathroom, but I
haven't done any—

Oh, no. You're great! Her voice rises. You've been *super.* But it's
easy, isn't it? I mean, it must be easy to be you. On top of the world.
Better than me, smarter than me—

Jenny, what the hell are you—

Don't interrupt! She jabs a finger at his chest. You're always in-
terrupting me! Because you're the boss, right? You know best,
you're in charge, you get to talk, to—

The smoke detector chirps.

They look up.

It emits another short, piercing chirp. Then buzzing static. Then:

May I have your attention. May I have your attention,
please.

It's the voice they know, with its Bronx-accented mildness. Its calm authority.

This is your fire safety director speaking.

There's a long pause.
Why? Don't pause, fire safety director! Keep talking!
She can't breathe. She can't bear it. She's going to faint, or—

The previous alarm has been investigated by fire department personnel and has been resolved. I repeat, the situation has been resolved.

Resolved.
That's . . .

We are in the process of restoring functionality to the guest elevators, which we anticipate will take approximately thirty minutes.

It's okay.
They're okay!
Oh thank God. Thank God.
She keeps her eyes fixed on the smoke detector. She doesn't look at Nick.
He must be so annoyed with her.

We appreciate your patience, and we apologize for any inconvenience. Thank you.

The smoke detector chirps again.
Then silence.

six

She drops onto the bed.

She falls backward, closing her eyes.

She's going to take a minute. Take a minute and just . . . unclench.

They're fine. It's nothing.

It was always nothing!

He must be so annoyed with her right now.

She's not going to think about that. No. She's going to lie here and enjoy the relief spreading through her, rinsing through her veins, warm and velvety. Velvet doesn't rinse. So what? She can mix her metaphors. Because it was always nothing!

Oh thank you. Thank you, God. Thank you, fire safety director.

She keeps her eyes closed. It conveys a pleasant illusion of concealment. She's just going to lie here and . . .

She feels the mattress move.

He's sitting down.

He's close to her, he's even . . . is he . . .

Yes. He's stretching out beside her.

Is that a good sign, or is he better positioning himself to strangle her? Getting the right angle to . . . oh. No.

He's stroking her head.

She feels his fingers combing through her hair. One traces the curve of an ear.

The last remnants of tension leave her. She opens her eyes.

He's propped on one elbow, gazing down at her.

She gazes up at him.

A long moment passes.

I told you there was nothing to worry about, she says.

You did, he says. You assured me it was a false alarm. I wonder why I didn't listen.

Probably because you're a dingbat. You should have told me how freaked out you were.

Maybe, he says. But then, honesty isn't really our thing, is it?

That makes her wince. I'm sorry, Nick.

It's okay.

It's not. I shouldn't have lashed out at you when—

Jenny, it's fine. Let's forget about it, okay?

Really?

Well, no, he says. I'm going to store this up to throw back in your face years from now, when you're pissed at me about something.

Years from now. Years!

They're fine. They have years.

God isn't teaching her a lesson, and there's no fire.

But as far as tonight goes, he adds, we're good.

We're great! she cries. Let's have sex!

She tears open her robe and they have at each other. He bites her breast and she pulls his hair. He's on top of her now, forcing her legs open, sucking and biting her, that's going to leave a mark but who cares! She needs him inside her, she's clutching at him, won't he please—

He lifts his head.

What's wrong? she says.

Nothing. But I think I'll call down.

She blinks, dazed. Why?

He's already rolling off her.

Just to confirm that everything's squared away, he says. I'm sure it is, but why not double-check?

He picks up the receiver. He's calling down now, after refusing for so long? Is he teasing her? They can have each other again, so he's making her wait? What a contrarian.

But you know what? Fine. They've waited this long. She smiles up at the smoke detector. Good smoke detector, noble smoke detector. Bearer of glad tidings. Of good joy.

Let him call. She knows how to tease him, too.

Hi, he says. This is . . . sure.

She turns her head so she can see him. They put you on hold again?

Yes, damn them. He switches the receiver to his other hand and reaches for his cell phone. She watches him flick through his email.

Don't they know who they're dealing with? Nobody keeps Slick Nick waiting.

He glances up from his screen.

No, sir, she says. The King of the Street Corner doesn't take this kind of crap from anyone.

You better be careful, he says.

What are you going to do? Sell me a fake Rolex?

No, I'm going to drag you into the stairwell, tie you to the railing and fuck the living oh, hi! Yes, I'm here. We heard the announcement, and . . . go ahead.

She shakes with supressed laughter, watching him listen, his eyes on her like, *You are in such big trouble.*

So it was a false alarm after all, he says. Good. And the specific floor where the alarm . . . okay.

His robe is hanging open. She slides across the bed and reaches inside and takes his cock in her mouth. He inhales sharply, pushing himself toward her. She tastes herself on him, that odd metallic tang he claims to love. He's only half hard, so she can take all of him into her mouth.

Oh my *fucking* . . . no, he says, sorry, I wasn't . . . go ahead.

The person on the other end of the line keeps talking, and she keeps sucking his cock. A thing she loves to do. Of course she does! She denied it because, well, she has to deny him sometimes. Him and his certainties, his proclamations on human nature, on women. He's fully hard now. His hand grips the back of her head, his fingers tangled in her hair. How could she not get turned on by this? By how he responds, how he comes all undone.

She's wasted so much time tonight! Fretting and jabbering, tapping and swiping, when she could have simply wrapped her lips around his cock and blown her fears away. All her thoughts of punishment and mortality, God and Jewish mothers, she could have let it all go and—

So the alarm was . . . ahhh, he says. That's why . . . mm-hmm. And so the elevators oh goddamn, that's . . . no, I, I'm fine, I just . . . I have to go thanks bye.

He drops the phone and pulls her to her knees and they're kissing. Her hair is in his mouth. Her mouth tastes like champagne. They fall onto the bed, they're struggling and somehow she's on top of him, which suits him just fine. He slips his hands under her robe, reaching around for, yes, thank you Jesus, thank you fire safety director and all relevant saints, thank you for these two heaping palmfuls of splendid buttockry.

Have you ever been disappointed? She has *no idea.* Never mind, though, because this ass. He grazes the cleft with his fingers as they kiss. If only, if only. Here he goes, once again plotting his conquest of her mythic asshole. He won't suggest it now. Unless she seems game. She might be, flush as she is with a sense of reprieve.

And it comes upon him, all in a rush. The glow, the glow is back! Early this time, a premature glowification, but he'll take it. This is what they're meant for, made for, not conversations about disappointment, or humanity's capacity for—oh her skin, her teeth. Her tongue. Jenny! Lovely funny warm real, a flesh and blood woman who fucks him with abandon, who snorts when she laughs sometimes, who does dirty things willingly. Most of them, anyway. A woman of *infinite variety. Age cannot* what? *Wither her, nor—*

Here we go again with the goddamn poetry.

Forget it. The point, the bottom line:

She.

Wants.

Him.

Him! A man no longer young, not falling apart but let's face it, no Adonis either. Him, with his body that has begun to complain, to creak and pop, foreshadowing the inevitable: age decay decline decrepitude loss death the end goodbye. Fewer tomorrows than yesterdays. But there's still today. Tonight. He opened the door, and his arms, and she was there. What was it she'd said when she came in?

To him! Not to anyone else, not to Tom or Juan Pablo, that little fucker, with his elite education and his atmosphere of decadence. He doesn't matter. Only she does. Jenny. Who *makes defect perfection*. Who *makes hungry where most she satisfies*. Who may not have changed him, but who saved him. Who obliterated his persistent, crushing, yearslong malaise.

Did we ever stay in a yellow room? he asks her.

A yellow room?

An old room. With yellow walls, and a dark floor? Maybe at an inn?

I don't think so. Oh, Nick, do that again, with your . . . oh God.

Gad. He does it again.

And again.

You were so mean to me earlier, he says.

I know. She's bending over him, her mouth close to his ear. I was such a fucking bitch.

I think I deserve a reward for putting up with you.

We both deserve a reward. I was so scared. I was trying to play it cool, but I was out of my fucking mind with . . . what are you smirking at?

You, he says. You never swear this much.

What? I swear all the time.

Oh God, what she's doing now, pressing down on him, rocking against him, it's—

You don't, he says. It's always fricking and jeez and shoot with you.

I guess I need guidance. Her lips are on his throat. Can you teach me?

Is she—oh, she is, she's biting him, it's unbearable! And the way she's moving, is she ready, isn't it time for her to reach down and with two dainty fingers raise the head of his cock and lower herself to receive it, slowly, gently taking him—

I'll try, he says. Say, I want you to fuck me, Nick.

I want you to fuck me, Nick.

Not bad. Now say, I want you to fuck my pussy, Nick.

I want you to fuck my pussy, Nick.

Good, he says. Now say, I want you to fuck me in the ass.

But she doesn't.

She bursts out laughing instead.

What? he says.

You and my ass! she cries.

Me and . . . sorry, what?

She sits back, shaking her head at him and smiling. You never shut up about it. You're always trying to stick your dick in it. You're obsessed.

I am not!

She gives him a sly sideways look. She slaps his cheek lightly. Then his other cheek.

You. Slap.

Are. Another slap.

Obsessed.

She tries to slap him again but he grabs her hand and bites it. Grabs her other hand and pulls her back down. Kisses her laughing mouth.

So she knows about his devious anal scheming. And he thought he was being so subtle.

Why can't we try it?

We have!

Don't stop moving. Oh Jesus, Jenny, that's . . . I think you want it more than you realize.

She only laughs.

I'm serious. Your asshole is always so clean. Isn't that sending mixed signals?

No, Nick. It's sending the unmixed signal that I know how to clean my own asshole.

Okay, but—

Fine, she says. We'll do it. But you go first. I'll fuck you in the ass, then you can fuck me.

He's not one hundred percent opposed. What would you use?

We'll find something. She looks around the room. What about the bottle of baby oil you always bring with you?

She knows about the baby oil!

He pulls her down again and kisses her irresistible, teasing mouth. You're really something, you know that?

I do know that, she says. And you're really—

The smoke detector shrieks.

She gasps.

There's a blast of static, then a screech that makes them cover their ears.

She looks down at him, eyes wide. What the—

There's another explosion of static. A garble of voices.

Stand by! says a voice. *This is*—

They're both sitting up now, staring at the ceiling.

More screeching. Then a voice cries: *That ain't right!*

They gotta know—not cool, man! Not—

There's a final, earsplitting blast of static.

Then silence.

Nick, she whispers.

Right. He jumps off the bed. Let's go.

She's already scrambling for her clothes. They dress quickly, neither of them bothering with underwear. They are silent and businesslike. In no time they're ready.

As they head out, she scoops her coat off the floor. He opens the door.

The hallway is low-lit, immaculate. As it was before.

Empty, as it was before.

And smoke free.

Of course it is. The place is run by a bunch of cretins who should be taken out back and shot, but there's no danger. Still, they're out of here. He takes her hand.

As they move down the hall muted bursts of static come at them from behind the doors of the rooms they pass. They reach the elevator bank, a dozen sets of doors on either side of a black marble expanse. In the center, a table topped with a vase of tall lilies. He hits the down button, just to check. The screen above each set of doors blinks two red dashes.

So be it. Now where is—

There! Jenny points. Stairwell A.

He pushes at the door, which barely budges. There's a weight against it, like someone on the other side is pushing back. He puts his shoulder into it and heaves. The door opens and they practically tumble into the glaring white stairwell.

And the unmistakable tang of smoke.

seven

Jesus fucking Christ.

There really is a fire.

A fire, in this building. An honest-to-God . . .

We'll go slow, okay? he says. Hold the handrail.

Those boots of hers, those heels. Hot, but suboptimal. He starts down first. He hears the sound of feet, of voices echoing above and below them. A man is calling out somewhere, his words inaudible. So they weren't the only fools who stayed put until now.

They reach a half landing, turn, head down another set of steps. He looks back at her. You okay?

I'm fine, she says. You can go faster.

They reach another landing, passing a door marked Forty-One. The smoke is mild, barely a haze. Not even as bad as the Canadian wildfires last summer. Now that was smoke.

From fires that were thousands of miles away, though. Not hundreds of feet. If that.

Another short flight, a turn, down down down. Fortieth floor. He's a fool. Why this hotel? Why a whole night? Why did he insist, why . . . he glances back at her. She's moving steadily, eyes on her feet. Is the smoke . . . no, it's not thicker. Maybe it's slightly thicker. Like bar smoke, back when you could smoke in bars.

They should have brought towels. He didn't think this through. They have their clothes they can breathe through if it gets to that point.

But it won't. It can't. That woman at the front desk assured him, all but promised him. *It was a false alarm. Nothing to worry about, sir. Absolutely nothing.* Was she clueless, was she lying?

Doesn't matter. He needs to think. Work through the possibilities. Because this could be a real problem.

Possibility one: they go downstairs and wait out whatever's happening. Then they come back to the room, grab a few hours' sleep, he heads to Houston in the morning, she heads home, they're exhausted, more so even than usual, but their lives remain intact.

Thirty-ninth floor, turn, another flight.

Possibility two: they can't get back in the room. Fire department regulations, safety checks, whatever. Does he still go to Houston? He could buy clothes when he gets there. Borrow Marty's laptop for the deposition. But if he goes, and they find his bag in the room here—is their home number on his luggage tag? Fucking hell it might be. How does he explain that, if someone calls the house, saying they have his roller bag in a Manhattan hotel where he was never supposed to be? And what does he do with Jenny if they can't get back in the room—shove her on a train, good luck showing up at home in the clothes you're wearing and nothing more, not your bag, not even your fucking underwear?

Thirty-eighth floor.

Fine. If they can't get back in the room he'll postpone the depo. He won't go to Houston, instead he'll . . . what? Pretend to Caroline he's in Texas when really he's lurking in the city, waiting to collect his luggage, his possibly smoky suitcase?

This is a mess. A fucking mess.

Thirty-seventh floor. Their descent is twelve percent complete. Eleven point nine, specifically, good job, genius, too bad you didn't use your big brain to predict that you might need something to breathe through, because it's definitely smokier down here.

Jenny stumbles around the turn. He reaches back to steady her.

These stupid boots, she mutters. Keep going.

Half flight, turn, half flight. Thirty-six. *In vain thou kindlest all thy smoky*—no. No fucking poetry right now. Plus, that one is really not helpful. But then, none of what he's doing is helpful. He's catastrophizing. This is a nothing fire. No billows of smoke, no jets of flame spurting up the stairwell. They'll have it cleared up in an hour. Fallout will be minor, and he can handle it. Offer some explanation to Caroline. Does she suspect already? At times he's wondered. Thought maybe she suspects—and doesn't particularly care.

As he rounds the landing on thirty-five he glimpses a man disappearing around the turn below them. A bent bald head, a hand on the banister. The stairwell is full of the sound of tramping feet. He has been careful. He is a good husband. Things were difficult for a while, true, he got dark, wrestling the black dog, but then he found Jenny. He's a better man now. A better husband. Thirty-four.

Are you serious? Lauding your marital excellence while fleeing a burning hotel with your—whatever she is. They've avoided the words, always, the crass yet accurate designations. Girlfriend, lover, mistress. Shack job, fuck buddy. Criminal conversationalist.

The person whose very existence means you are not a good husband. At all.

Step step step. Down down down.

Thirty-three.

Jenny is coughing. They're going to reek when they get out of here. Okay, so possibility one, amended: if they can get back in the room, they take a long, hot shower. Sorry, Natey, I need those cute soaps to clean your mom! Even better: they leave. Grab their shit and find another hotel. Start the night over with a bath. A fresh white bed.

Thirty-two. Nearly a third of the way now, just—

Stop!

He stops, and she crashes into him. He braces himself against the banister, keeping both of them upright.

I need you to stop!

There's no one in sight. The voice is far away, echoing up to them. Leaning over the well, he sees only the backs of other heads, other people craning to see. Beyond, a gray haze.

Go back to your rooms. Now. This is—

There's a distant sound of raised voices, argument.

No. No, ma'am. You should not—the other stairwells are restricted as well.

He feels Jenny's hand on his shoulder.

You are interfering. We are working to contain this fire, and you are—

There's a squawk. Then the voice booms, amplified.

Listen up, people! The stairwells are CLOSED. Return to your rooms. For your OWN SAFETY, do not, repeat, DO NOT attempt to evacuate the building at this time. Return to your rooms, continue to shelter in place with your doors CLOSED, and await further instructions.

Another squawk.
Then silence.
He turns to her. She's on the step above him. For once they're exactly the same height.
I'm going to keep going, he says. A little farther, to . . . no, Jenny. You stay here. I just want to check. I'll come right back, I promise.
Down he goes, much faster without her to worry about. One

flight, then another, and another, skipping the last few steps of each, grabbing the banister and swinging around the turns, the way he flew down the big staircase at his grandmother's house when he was a boy.

He doesn't make it far. After four or five flights the smoke is too thick, even when he breathes through his shirt.

They could die here. Isn't that how most people die in fires? Panicking, bolting for safety, plunging instead into killing smoke?

They're better off upstairs. Firefighters are here. They're on top of the situation.

She's hovering on the landing of thirty-two when he returns. I heard you coughing, she says.

It's smokier down there, he admits. Not terrible, but we should get back to the room.

They trudge up the stairs. They pass other guests taking a breather on a landing, glimpse a few disappearing onto their floors. Still others pass them going down, intent on giving it a go, apparently. They exchange nods, quick grimaces, then carry on. Nobody's pausing to commiserate here. Nobody's banding together.

They exit on forty-two. The hallway is still clear. They reach their room. She sees the small black panel above the door handle and grabs his arm.

Oh no! Nick! We—

He pulls the keycard from his pocket. She sags against the wall. Thank God.

Inside, the door falls shut behind them, and they embrace. In the foyer of their low-lit, stupidly opulent hideaway, where they met, what, three hours ago, four? He'd opened the door and she was there. She said something surprising. Then she was in his arms.

Well that was a bust, he says, and she chuckles into his shoulder. Still responding to his easy ironies, that's a good sign. His nose is in her hair. There's that scent again. Lemon? Grapefruit? Smoky now. What her hair must have smelled like after a night out, back when you could smoke in bars.

He pulls back so he can get a look at her. How are you?

I'm, you know. She exhales shakily. Terrorized. But also weirdly calm?

Weird is right. She's said some nutty things tonight. *Has anything ever not gone your way?* What the hell? But she seems okay now. Unless she's just stunned.

Well, stunned will have to do.

He reaches for the door. I want you to notice something.

Nick, don't!

It's fine. We were just out there, remember? He cracks it about six inches. Take hold of it. He guides her hand to the edge of the door, above the handle. Feel that?

What am I feeling?

How heavy it is. Now let go. See how fast it closes? That's a solid door, Jenny. Probably steel. Now come with me.

He leads her to the bed and sits her down. He is a man of action now, of purpose. He knows what to do, he's in charge, he's on . . .

No. Bad cliché. Don't go there.

He's in his element, let's leave it at that.

You have your phone? he says. Good. Google New York City fire code. Or building code, city of New York. Try a few different combinations until you find it.

Why?

You said you did a lot of research into fire, right? I thought you could do a little more. Find out exactly how fire-resistant this building is. Doors, walls, building materials. Then you'll understand how safe we are. That we're perfectly safe waiting here while they put out the fire.

He reaches for the room phone. While you're doing that, I'm going to call down and tear that desk clerk an extremely capacious new—why hello there! This is . . . no, no I will *not* fucking—

He stares at the receiver. She put me on hold again.

He's outraged. And impressed. That took balls. Though it's not like he can storm down there and do anything about it.

Jenny is hunched over her phone, scrolling.

How's the research coming along?

She doesn't answer. She grabs the remote from the table under the television. The screen blinks to life, and she starts flipping. CNN. Fox. Some old movie.

Jenny. What are you doing?

She reaches NY1. A pretty, dark-haired reporter, bundled in a heavy coat, is standing on the sidewalk outside their hotel.

Behind her, firefighters are swarming through the lobby doors.

> *As you can see, Ron, dozens of firefighters have descended on the building here at Fiftieth and Park, the location of a newly opened luxury hotel.*

He ends the call. He'll try again later.

> *The fire is believed to have started approximately three hours ago in a laundry room on the twenty-first floor.*

Not the fifteenth? he says.

She turns from the television. Fifteenth?

Fucking hell. He blurted that out, he didn't . . . now she's staring at him.

Nick? Why did you say not the fifteenth?

The screen splits to show a pair of news anchors listening as the reporter speaks. Firefighters haul equipment into the building behind her.

Look at all those firemen, he says. They'll have this under control in no time.

Not the fifteenth, you said. Like you expected it to be the fifteenth.

Her eyes are boring into him. Goddammit. This is going to complicate things.

When I called down the first time, the desk clerk mentioned

there was a minor error in the original announcement, he says. The alarm hadn't been triggered on the fifth floor, but the fifteenth.

And you didn't tell me?

Does she really need to look so outraged? What does it matter? he says. Apparently it wasn't on the fifteenth, either.

You knew it was ten floors closer to us. You let me think it was farther away.

I didn't want you to worry, Jenny. I'm sorry, but . . .

He trails off, riveted by the television. She turns to see what's distracted him.

The camera has panned upward. About twenty stories above the ground, smoke is pouring out of the building.

Thick black sheets of it, billowing up the side of the building and rippling into the sky.

> *What you're seeing now is smoke escaping from the building's exhaust vents, which are just above the location of the fire.*

They watch in silence. Until:

Is there anything else you were told that you didn't want me to worry about?

No, Jenny. I . . .

The camera has cut back to the lobby doors. People are emerging, some of them assisted by firefighters. Evacuated guests. They look tense and dazed. Some are wearing white bathrobes.

The camera zooms in. You can see their faces, very clearly.

Oh, this . . . this is not good, he says.

She snorts. You think?

He grabs his phone. I'm going to email Caroline. You need to write to Tom.

She turns to him again. What?

We're not supposed to be here, Jenny. And when we get out, we might show up there, he points at the television, for the whole world to see. It's only NY1, but if someone we know catches it, or it goes online . . . look at that asshole, he's giving a thumbs-up to the camera! The point is, we could get caught, unless we lay a little groundwork to explain what we're doing here.

That's what you're freaking out about? she says. Getting caught?

He really wishes she would get with the program. This is not an ideal situation, he says, but we're safe. The fire department is on top of it, hell, they're in the stairwell chatting with guests, which suggests they aren't battling some *Towering Inferno*–type situation. It's just—

Chatting with guests? she says. Chatting, Nick?

> *The hotel has not disclosed how many people remain on the upper floors.*

I'm going to text Caroline and tell her . . . something, I'll figure it out. You need to text Tom, or email him, however you guys tend to communicate. Tell him . . . he snaps his fingers. I know—tell him this. You had to come back to the city early. For a last-minute meeting. And your publisher put you up at this hotel, which is why—

That fireman was not chatting with guests, Nick. He was yelling at us to get out of the way. So they can fight the fucking *fire*.

Jenny, I'm trying to help you. I'm trying to protect both of us.

Protect us! She laughs harshly. But not from the fire, right? From being exposed as cheating pieces of shit.

The newscast cuts to a commercial. He sets his phone down and walks to the window.

He gazes out, hands in his pockets. Watches the wind whip snow past the glass. It must be freezing out. The kind of bitter winter night they don't get many of anymore. They could be out there right now, shivering but at liberty. If only he'd—

Jenny, he says.

She doesn't answer.

*If you're just joining us, we're reporting live from the site
of a significant fire in Midtown Manhattan, which
we're told started shortly after six p.m. on the twenty-
first floor. Reporter Juliana Gonzalez is on the scene.*

She's still hunched at the foot of the bed, dividing her attention between her phone and the television.

He walks to her and crouches down. He touches her knee.

Jenny. Hey.

She looks at him.

We're not pieces of shit.

Yes, we are, she says. And soon we're going to be charbroiled pieces of shit, and it's your fault.

She's glaring at him.

I wanted to leave, she says, practically spitting the words. Twice I wanted to leave, and you said we should stay. Marshaled all your, she waves her hands, rational arguments, your reasons why it was fine, even while you weren't telling me everything you knew!

I didn't refuse to leave, he says. I was ready to go if you insisted, but you agreed to—

Bullshit! she cries. That is such bullshit! You persuaded me to stay because you thought you were right. You knew best. But you were wrong. We should have left, we could have left, and it's your fault we didn't.

He's been crouching at her level. Now he rises.

Let's take a break, okay? This has been intense, and we could both use a little space to—

She gets up, pushing past him, grabbing a corner of the duvet and dragging it with her as she crosses the room and plops down on the sofa. She wraps the duvet around her.

Right, he says. I'll stay here, you stay over there. We'll take a minute and cool off.

She rolls her eyes and turns away.

Fine. If she wants to act like a petulant child, that's her business. He's trying to help her, but he can only do so much. She's not
well. That tranquility of hers when they got back to the room was a
front. Like all her other fronts.

In addition to complications from the weather,
firefighters initially encountered a problem with the
building's standpipe system, which caused delays in—

He mutes the television. Enough with the yabbering news.
Enough with tending to Jenny. He needs to focus on what he's
going to tell Caroline. What minor lie will be sufficient to cover up
the much bigger one. He despises this part, the blatant falsehoods—
or rather, he despises himself when telling them. They're so mean.
So low. She deserves so much better.

He finds his phone. Taking Jenny's spot at the end of the bed,
he starts typing.

Hey. You're probably asleep, just wanted to let you know my flight
got canceled and I decided to put up at a hotel rather than come
home. I hope to leave first thing tomorrow but I'm on standby right
now, so who knows when—

Is he joking with all those clicks and clacks? Has he not . . . oh,
wow. He hasn't turned off keyboard sounds on his phone! What
kind of a monster . . . how is she supposed to *cool off* when he's tap-
dancing with his fingers over there?

Typical. Thinks of nobody but himself. Of nothing but his own
convenience.

She should call out to him, guide him through the process.
Hey, asshole! Go to Settings, Sounds and Haptics, Keyboard
Sounds, and *switch it the fuck off.*

But she's not going to be the one to break the silence. No sir.
Jesus, he's a fast typer. Cooking up a lengthy lie for his poor wife,

no doubt. One of his persuasive spiels, his three-dollar-word-studded mountains of horseshit.

How in God's name did she ever fall in love with this clown?

Not the first time she's asked herself this question.

She is dimly aware that her fury at him is preventing worse feelings from gaining purchase. Horror, overwhelming fear, et cetera. Sorry, guys, try again later. Right now I'm focused on the numerous shortcomings of Mr. Lacks Basic Phone Etiquette over there.

Including the fact that the only thing he seems to fear about their predicament, the only thing that mildly troubles him, is the possibility that they're going to get busted.

And she's the irrational one?

Though she shouldn't be surprised. He's always been excessively cautious. Proposing they meet in quiet bars, out-of-the-way restaurants. But mostly in hotel rooms. They arrive separately and reunite inside the doors of rooms like this one, away from the nosy, noticing world. And she understands—she doesn't want to get caught either. But couldn't he be a little less obvious about it? Not always fidgeting and glancing at the door when they're having a drink, not scanning the lobby on the rare occasion they enter a hotel at the same time. In private he loves that they're sinning—*part of me wants you to put them back on so I can watch you take them off again*—but in public he's eager to distance himself. Like she's some sort of crime.

Which she is. They are.

She gets it, she does.

Still. It's infuriating.

She separates out a lock of hair and twirls it until it coils up on itself close to her scalp, like a little horn. She lets it unspool, then coils it up again. Herve hates this habit of hers. *You're cruising for breakage, my dear.* But it's comforting. She lets the lock unspool again, then pulls it in front of her face, against her forehead, against her . . .

Her hair smells of smoke.

She plucks at the shoulder of her blouse—they're still dressed from their attempted flight, it's strange to be clothed in a room with him—and brings it to her nose. It smells of smoke, too.

Breathe now. Breathe. Think more about what a shithead Nick is. Deceiving her, ordering her around, assigning her research tasks like she's one of his minions, dictating a lie to tell Tom. A ridiculous one. No publishing company in the world would put her up at a hotel this nice. She's made hers millions of dollars, and still she's lucky if they book her into a fucking Ramada!

Whatever. She doesn't need his facts and reasonableness. She's not a puddle, okay? She's not pinballing around the room in a state of derangement. There is a fire. Professionals are handling it. She gets it. She doesn't need to be managed.

Where is her phone? Lost somewhere in the duvet. Doesn't matter. She'll check the news in a minute. See? She can hold off on that, too.

Though her stomach is fluttering. Her mouth is dry. She closes her eyes and focuses on her breathing. If only she knew how to meditate. She doesn't have the patience. For meditation, or yoga, or any sort of calming, mindful hobby. Tom and the boys love to tease her about it, how she takes up enthusiasms—knitting, the piano—only to discard them after a few half-hearted weeks. *Hey, guess what? Mom gave up on pottery. Ha ha!*

Did that mother in Brooklyn get teased by her children? Did they hang on her and make her sticky, fart into her decorative pillows? How did she survive when they weren't around to aggravate her anymore? Has she survived? God isn't enough, faith doesn't fill the days. You still have to brush your teeth and parallel park, take shits and do the laundry. All the while your brain is working, drumming it into you: *you left, you left them, you jumped out the window, you lived and you left them to die.*

A mother, separated from her children. Who chose to leave them behind. She doesn't want to judge the woman, but what she did is inconceivable. Unnatural.

Okay, but haven't you left your children?

You're here, after all. Here, and not home with the boys you claim to love above all things.

You jumped out your window six years ago.

You chose this fire over them.

eight

And with that . . . she needs to go away for a little while.

So she does.

She lowers her face into the duvet.

She stops struggling, and submits to the panic.

It beats against her, and beats against her.

Which is awful. But she deserves it.

So she'll take it.

And she does.

For a long time.

How long? Hard to say.

But eventually, she senses a change. Her heart stops racing. The awful sick falling sensation in her stomach recedes. Her hands relax their death grip on the duvet.

She comes back into herself, into the room.

She keeps her face buried in the soft linen but takes a few deep, steady breaths. She's never felt anything like that before. And now, does she . . . ?

Yes. She feels better.

Well, calmer, let's say. The fear battered her, wore her down to a smooth little nub, but that's okay. Being a smooth, quiet little nub is okay.

There's a distant crash. A muffled curse.

She lifts her head. The bed is empty.

She hears the toilet flush.

Should she check the news? It might disturb this fragile peace, and yet . . . she feels around in the duvet and finds her phone. Her heart kicks up as she searches but . . .

Oh. The news is definitely not awful.

@FDNY says the fire is close to being contained.

She double-checks, triple-checks, skims various sites. The internet is in rare agreement: the situation is under control. It's only a matter of time.

She allows herself a tiny bit of hope. They might be okay. This might be almost over.

The bathroom door slides open, and she turns away. The peaceful nub grows a few spikes. She's still furious. She hears him sigh, the soft thumping of pillows being plumped. He must pick up his phone, because here comes the tippy-tapping again. Christ, is he drafting his last will and testament?

No. He's certain that's not necessary.

The fool.

Well, he's not the only fool in this room, is he? This situation, this nightmare, is ninety-nine-point-nine-nine-nine percent his fault, for sure—the insistence on a whole night, the choice of this particular deathtrap-beg-pardon hotel, his withholding of information and of course his arguments why they should heed the intercom voice, not her gut or common sense, and stay.

But who allowed herself to be prevailed upon and persuaded? Who allowed their time to be frittered away with idle talk of brainwashing and phantom jizz?

She glances at him. He's sitting up against the headboard, shoes off, frowning at his phone. He's aging well. Six years older than she is, but doesn't look it. He's holding on to his hair. It's started going gray, which suits him. He keeps it cut too short, though.

She rarely gets to observe him from a distance like this. The sharp jaw, sharp chin, he's all edges and corners. Still slim. In better shape than when they started, in fact. Being a relentless tyrant must do wonders for the metabolism.

She refreshes Twitter. @nycfirewire says the FDNY is beginning smoke remediation efforts, aiming to clear the building's stairwells within the hour.

She considers his hands. They're long and slim, a little bony. Beautiful. She's always been a hand woman. A handmaiden, ha. His are rarely still. He never shuts up and his hands never stop moving, painting his words onto the air.

What is she doing? Why is she appreciating him, and getting all florid about it? *Painting his words onto the air?* She's so embarrassing. Meanwhile he's ignoring her, sheathed in his umbrage over there, his chagrin. He's the Chagrined King, scrutinizing his phone, lips pursed.

What's he studying with such concentration?

Porn. It's probably porn.

She turns away so he doesn't happen to look up and think she's smiling at him, because sorry, no, she still hates his guts and thinks he sucks.

She refreshes Twitter. @firechieftim, a retired battalion commander, applauds the FDNY's rapid and effective response, noting the department's unparalleled experience fighting high-rise fires. Couldn't agree more, Chief Tim!

Does she really hate Nick's guts? Should she? What's the point of staying angry? It's exhausting. It allows him to take up way too much space in her head. Even more than he's occupied lo these many years.

He remembered the room key. If he hadn't, they'd be roaming the halls right now, or hanging out in the little room with the vending machines and the icemaker. He's organized, he has forethought—points in his favor.

The little room with the icemaker? This isn't a HoJo, for God's sake.

Another point in his favor? She loved him once. It's been over for ages—lo these many years—but some tenderness lingers. Even back then she wasn't blind to his flaws, but he was alive. Most people are dead dead dead. He had a spark, in the way he spoke and looked. His intensity and outrageous opinions. The complete truthfulness of him when he was naked. He was vital. He dazzled her.

See? Even now she can't escape the absurdity of it, the spoony superlatives. We make so much fun of people when they carry on about falling in love, about getting swept away, because they sound so ridiculous. Love is ridiculous, from the outside. But when you're in it . . . oh God, when you're in it . . .

She thought it would be awful. Humiliating. And sometimes it was. But mostly, she was exalted. More absurdity, but she was. This outrageous, imprudent love, it was her thing, hers alone. She wanted without being wanted, and felt great power in it. Even in the ending of it. Not that that was easy, Jesus no, it was torture. But she did it.

It's reassuring, actually, to know that you can fall in love with someone, and fall back out, and survive. It's difficult, harrowing in fact, but you'll be okay.

Now? It's fine. Little things, like the wedding ring incident, occasionally tug at her, but mostly she's steady. Her love was a madness, but she's glad it happened. Once I loved someone, and he didn't love me back, but that didn't matter. I did it. It was mine.

And here they are now, here he is, the unwitting beneficiary of her buried tenderness. And her gratitude. She can't forget her secret gratitude to him, for turning her into a writer. A good one, college workshop instructors be damned. She might have become who she was supposed to be without him, but she didn't. She owes him that.

She hears a rustling. An aggrieved, slightly performative sigh. The click of his phone being placed on the nightstand. Is he . . .

Yes. He's getting out of bed.

He's coming over.

The cooling-off period has ended, apparently.

He walks across the room and pulls out the desk chair. He sits down on it, facing her across the coffee table.

He wants to talk. Good. If he apologizes, she'll grant him a little grace. In honor of her dead love and her very live gratitude. And the fact that he was so generous earlier. *Where are you, Jenny?* He fucked up after that, badly, but he has tried to be kind.

He gazes at her.

She gazes back.

Did you sleep with that director? he asks.

She blinks.

He crosses his legs. Folds his hands. Looks at her like, *Well?*

She erupts with laughter.

She can't help it!

Tears spring to her eyes.

Did she . . . did she . . .

Oh my God, *what?*

He's serious! Look at him, sitting there in his little interrogation chair. This—*this* is what he's been thinking about over there on the bed, while she's been melting down about the fire and her boys, Jewish mothers and him—how she loved him once. How she burned.

For this guy!

Wow. She wipes her tears away. Thanks. I needed that.

Happy to help. Will you answer the question?

Sorry, she says. I have no idea who you're talking about.

Jenny.

If you could give me a name, maybe I could help. Otherwise . . .

I don't want to say his name, he says. It's a stupid fucking name and I refuse to say it.

Oh! She slaps her forehead. Are you talking about *Juan Pablo?* Juan Pablo *Torrrrrrres?* The *muy guapo* director of my book *adaptación?*

Is there a reason why you're unwilling to answer a simple question?

Are you actually as anxious about the fire as I am? she asks him. Are you freaking out, and this is how you cope—by distracting yourself with random questions about my sex life?

It's not random, he says. I want to know if I'm safe.

You're not safe, Nick. You're trapped in a burning building.

I mean safe from disease, he says.

She takes that in. Safe from disease. You mean, a disease in my vagina.

There's no need to get upset, he says.

Hey. She holds up her hands. Who's upset?

I just want information. You said he hit on you. You didn't say whether he was successful.

Whether I fucked him, you mean. Whether I fucked another man, contracted an STI from him, then came here and passed it to you. That's what you want to talk about? Now?

Why not? I assume you've seen the news. The fire is under control.

I have seen that, she says. We'll be out of here soon. In the meantime, you want information? So do I. Let's lay it all out. Be completely honest with each other before our time here comes to an end. Sound good?

Before their time here comes to an end. He hears in those words an unmistakable note of finality. He has wondered, since they got back to the room, since she blamed and attacked him, whether this might be it for them. They had a good run. Six years. But they never built the kind of bond that could survive a challenge like this.

It's too bad. Still, given everything that's happened tonight, maybe it's for the best.

So they'll have it out. All their concealments and evasions. Not that he's concealed much, but sure. He'll tell her whatever she wants to know. Then they can part as friends.

Complete honesty, he says. Fine by me.

Good! We'll take turns. Why didn't you want to use the minibar?

What?

Earlier. I wanted water, and you were all like, she puffs out her chest, wags a finger, *We're not using the minibar, woman! It's extortionate!*

I don't sound like that. Also, this is what you want to ask me?

For starters, yes.

He stands and walks over to the television. They've cut away from the fire to a weather report. Looks like the snow will be stopping soon.

So it's over. Their *this*. Well, what did he think—it would last forever? They'd be hobbling into hotels into their seventies, eighties, rubbing their desiccated sex organs together in a desperate bid for one last watery orgasm? Jesus no. He didn't think about it at all. Jenny was always now, an intoxicating present, in both senses of the word. But that's over. She's to be relegated to the past, the place where all the good things are.

He's going to miss her.

He pokes around in the minibar and pulls out two small bottles. He returns to his seat. Bourbon or vodka?

Bourbon, please.

He cracks the cap of hers and hands it across the coffee table. He opens his own, and they each take a swig.

I feel sad after I come, he says. If I'm physically alone. It's . . . an emptiness. A loneliness. It passes quickly, but I need whoever—meaning, in this context, you—to stay beside me for a few minutes. So when you leaped out of bed, I wanted you back, and apparently I decided the best way to achieve that was to act like a controlling asshole. That's the answer.

You couldn't ask me to stay? Explain it to me?

Jesus, no! That's not what we do, Jenny. You're not my therapist, or confessor. I want to come in here and leave my issues, my weaknesses and neuroses, at the door.

It doesn't really work that way, she says.

It does, he insists. Most of the time it does. And it should. You're not missing anything. Trust me. You're getting the good parts.

He toasts her with his tiny bottle and finishes it off.

I didn't sleep with Juan Pablo, she says.

It's fine if you did. I have no right—

Oh my God, Nick, knock it off! I didn't. I know I lie sometimes. Because . . . well, it doesn't matter. I'm not lying about this.

He nods. He believes her.

She goes to the minibar and comes back with a package of peanut M&M's.

I did lie about Juan Pablo's come-ons, though. She smiles. They weren't ambiguous at all.

He laughs. Why did you say they were?

I don't know. He came up in conversation, you somehow guessed things had gotten weird . . . she sighs. I was embarrassed.

Most women would have bragged. Most women wouldn't make it through the door of this room without announcing that a hot young Spaniard was desperate to bang them.

Most women wouldn't come through the door of this room.

Jesus, Jenny, this again? Anyway, I'm not sure I agree.

She sips her bourbon. You think most people cheat?

I think many do, he says. And many more would, though they can't admit it. Most people can't even think about infidelity clearly. They're too terrified of it.

I take it you can think about it clearly.

I can. Enough to notice a contradiction, at least. Everybody agrees that cheating is wrong, it's vile, it's monstrous. And yet, he spreads his hands, it is also universal, persistent and indomitable. The most common crime there is, which all the social censure and moral opprobrium in the world haven't come close to rooting out. To the point that you have to wonder: maybe it's not the crime that's the problem, but the prohibition.

So that's how you do it, she says, fascinated. You reason yourself off the hook.

No way. I'm not off the hook. The prohibition may be ineffective and contrary to human nature, but for most people it's still very real, and to escape it I'm lying. Intentionally deceiving my wife. Maybe we should all reconsider whether it's so awful to want to sleep with people other than your spouse, but lying is unquestionably, categorically wrong, and the fact that I've chosen to do it is on me. What I won't do, though, is excuse it, or explain it away, or somehow delude myself about what I'm doing. I may be lying, but I won't lie to myself.

So you do feel bad? she says. Because the way you're acknowledging what you're doing, and just kind of accepting it . . . don't you *feel* guilty?

I do. But I limit it. By limiting this. There's my life, right? Ordinary life, which is one thing, you know, one big thing, then there's this. You and me. Completely separate.

Firm boundaries, she says. Even in your head?

Especially in my head. They have to be. It's like what they say about the Titanic. It wasn't the iceberg that sank it. It was the bad bulkheads.

The bad what?

Bulkheads, he says. They're the walls between compartments in the hull of a ship. On the Titanic, the bulkheads didn't reach the ceilings of the lower decks. So when the ship hit the iceberg, water spilled over from compartment to compartment, rather than being limited to the site of the breach. It couldn't contain the damage. That's why it sank.

She stares at him.

It's a good analogy, he says.

If you're the Titanic, what does that make me? she says. The iceberg?

Okay, forget the analogy. The point is—

Never mind. What was your great disappointment in life?

Pass, he says.

She throws an M&M at him. You can't pass!

Says who?

Fine. Why did you insist we spend a full night together?

He sighs. Jenny, can we not—

You kept bringing it up, she says, even though we've never done this before. You pushed me to add a day to my trip, you changed the date of your deposition so we'd overlap. Why?

He rises and moves to the window. Then the door. He returns

and grips the back of the chair with both hands, looking down at her. She's still wrapped in her duvet, cheeks rosy from the bourbon.

Let's be done with this, okay? This true-confessions bullshit? It's making my skin crawl. You want to know how I avoid feeling guilty? By not thinking—not talking—about shit like this. I'm a man, okay, a typical man, keeping it all locked up, and that's worked really well for me for forty-six years. So can we please stop with all the talk about feelings?

Sure, she says. Right after you tell me why you wanted a whole night.

Jesus Christ!

Fine. He sits down. When was the last time we saw each other?

She frowns, thinking. The Spencers' Christmas party?

The last time we *saw* each other saw each other, he says. Just the two of us. In a place like this.

Oh. Right. Was it . . . mid-November? I know it's been a long time.

It was early October, he says. October third.

That long? Wow. I guess we were both busy, there were the holidays—

No, Jenny. It was all you.

What? No.

I offered you half-a-dozen dates, but you were out of town, or had a reading, or the kids were sick. Every time.

They're always sick in the winter, Nick, I'm sorry—

I'm not blaming you. They were legitimate reasons, but their cumulative effect was such that . . .

Listen to him. Going all lawyerly. *Their cumulative effect was such that.* He needs to move. He stands and circles the room. He's going to break out in hives. But now that he's started, he might as well finish.

He stops in front of her.

It felt like you weren't trying as hard to see me as you used to. I wasn't important—*as* important, not that I was or ever could be important-important, I get that—but important in the very limited way in which I was once important, or thought myself to be . . . goddammit, I've completely lost the thread of what I was saying.

He's all worked up, running his hands through his hair, pacing again.

He stops, spreads his hands.

I thought I was losing you, okay?

Oh, Nick, no!

Let me finish, please, without the *oh Nick*s and the protestations and so forth—you wanted me to spill my guts, so I am. That's why I pushed for a whole night. To reassure myself. You could say I was testing my hypothesis, but I wasn't trying to trick you or trap you. I wanted to see you, it had been so long—

I wanted to see you, too!

He holds up a hand. Jenny, please. I wanted to see you, but part of me also needed some proof that the, whatever the hell we have here, the *connection,* is still in good working order. Your life has changed, you've become this—phenomenon. You're writing, you're watching movies be filmed of your work. You're a celebrity. Who am I? Some dickhead who came on to you in the weirdest possible way in a neighbor's kitchen one night! What we have, what we do? I know it's not supposed to be a big deal. But it is *a* deal. It's important to me. To you? I wasn't sure. Maybe you were ready to move on, and you decided to let me down easy, with a gradual fade-out. That's what I feared. And if I was misreading anything, well, a nice long night together might remind us why we do this.

She nods, not saying anything, just listening.

He sits beside her on the sofa and takes her hands.

And it worked, he says. You didn't cancel. And it was *so good,* as it always is. At least, I thought it was, until I found out you didn't come. You faked coming, in fact, which made me feel useless and confirmed—please, Jenny, let me finish—confirmed my worst fears about my value to you. Then we heard another alarm, and you were ready to fly out of here. Next, you mentioned this Juan Pablo clown, and I thought, well, that's it. I can't make her come, here's this hot young guy who probably can, maybe even has. Later, after we fought, I started fixating on him, and I . . . well, you should see what I've been googling the last little while. It's profoundly embarrassing.

The point is, I let myself get all worked up until I couldn't stand it anymore, at which point I marched over here and demanded you answer that utterly shitty question.

He's still holding her hands. He looks down at them.

I don't care if you slept with him, he says. You said you didn't and I believe you, but I truly don't care. As long as you don't stop sleeping with me.

He looks up now, into her eyes. That's it. My long-winded explanation for why I wanted a whole night, and why I didn't want to leave. The idea of losing time together, when we hadn't had time in so long? I couldn't bear it. I'm a greedy bastard. We should have left, we—

I came, she says.

What?

I came. Before. I said I hadn't, I faked it. But I didn't.

He releases her hands, sits back.

It was a mistake, she says. A momentary . . . I can explain if you want. Why I did it.

He stands. He walks away, then turns back.

You didn't fake it? he says. You had an orgasm?

She nods.

When I . . . we both came?

Yes.

He is still staring at her, like an idiot no doubt, because he feels like an idiot. He has been made into an idiot, by her. Reduced to repeating, once more, idiotically:

You came?

She nods again.

You . . . faked faking it?

Yes, she says.

At which point he completely loses his mind.

What the *fuck* is wrong with you?

Nick!

What is this, Jenny? You're playing games with me?

Of course not!

You are! he shouts. I just laid my heart bare for you, and you respond by informing me that you've been mocking me all night?

No, I . . . that's not why I told you, I told you because—

Who acts like this? He throws his hands in the air. I have no idea where I stand with you! You pretend not to be scared about the fire when you are. You knew a man was hitting on you but claimed you weren't sure. And you flat-out lie to me, *all the time.* Apparently you even lie about lying!

Oh, so I should be honest? she says, jumping up, chucking away her empty bottle. I should be honest, but you don't have to be?

What? I'm honest!

Come on, Nick! You made up some BS why I shouldn't get water from the minibar—

The minibar! he wails. Jesus Christ, can we *please* stop talking about the fucking minibar?

—you misled me about where the fire was, you insisted we spend a full night together without telling me it was some kind of test of my loyalty—

That is, oh, Jenny, that is *so* unfair, do not manipulate what I confided in you, do not—

Manipulate? she cries. You manipulate, you—you're the worst! You're always making fun of me, you make fun of my books, which you don't even bother to read—

Do *not* change the subject, he says. We are talking about your orgasm right now! Nothing else!

She stares at him. Will you listen to yourself?

He is listening. And he is hearing himself be ridiculous. He laid himself bare—only in part, true, and a relatively minor part, but does she know how hard even that is for him?—he handed her a small soft piece of himself. *I thought I was losing you.* He trusted her. And she responded by announcing that she'd lied, a lie whose only purpose could be to make him feel failed and weak.

She took his offering and threw it against the wall.

And now? They're fighting about a fake fake orgasm. An inane argument that only compounds his humiliation.

Afraid he was losing her? He never had her.

Have you always faked your orgasms?

Jesus, Nick, what a . . . of course not! Never.

Okay, he says. Okay. Then why did you say you faked one tonight?

She hesitates.

You know what? he says, hands up. Doesn't matter. I can't . . . I think we're done.

What?

This is not why we come here, Jenny. To bicker, and poke at each other, and play mind games.

You're breaking up with me? She's shaking her head, uncomprehending.

It's been great, he says. But tonight has revealed some things . . . maybe my instinct that something had changed these last few months . . . maybe this thing has run its course.

Should he be saying this? How can he not? She has hurt him. Seemingly on purpose. And hurting each other is definitely not what this is supposed to be about.

Fine, she says. Whatever you say. We're done.

You said our time here is coming to an end, he points out. Isn't that what you meant? That tonight has been too much for us, it's shown that we're not—

He is interrupted by a violent hammering.

She gasps.

He starts.

They both turn.

There it is again.

Sudden and explosive. Coming from the hallway.

Someone is at the door.

part three

hello, happiness

nine

He moves swiftly to the foyer, almost racing there because this is it, someone has come for them, thank Christ this nightmare is over.

Should he grab his shoes? No, let the guy in first, he'll give them time to get ready. He came to get them, after all, because it's over, this night is—

He flings the door open.

Nobody's there.

The hallway is, as it always has been, low-lit, immaculate and empty.

What the hell? What—

He hears the violent pounding again. It's so loud he jumps.

He leans out of the room.

Three doors down, a large man in a white bathrobe is beating frantically on a door.

While Nick watches, the man gives up and throws himself at the next door, pummeling it with his fists.

Not a firefighter.

Fucking hell, it's not a firefighter.

The disappointment is like a blow. It's like a—

Nick! What's happening?

She'd rushed to the door right behind him, but she can't see what he sees. The stranger must hear her voice, because he turns, sees Nick and with a hoarse cry comes barreling toward him.

And Christ, he isn't a large man, he's enormous, hurtling up the hall, growing bigger and bigger and babbling, what's he babbling? Bare feet, huge bare legs, flapping robe, terrified and honestly a little terrifying.

He feels the urge to duck back in and slam the door. The man is . . . he's just so massive, and Jesus he's fast, and he seems . . . but there's no time to think it through, no time to decide because the man is there, looming in the doorway, slowing down but not stopping, his size and agitation forcing Nick back into the room. Jenny retreats behind him.

The man slams the door and sags against it, quivering and sweating, looking none too steady on those tree-trunk legs. He gasps for breath, making sounds like little shrieks.

Luojan kiitos! Luojan kiitos! he says, between gulps of air. *Luojan kiitos!*

Jenny stares at him. Oh, no! I thought we were—

Tarvitsen puhelimen! the man gasps. *Missä puhelimesi on?*

Let's give him some space, Nick says. He guides Jenny back into the main part of the room, keeping himself between her and the colossus propped against the door, because he doesn't know, he's just not sure about this guy. He must be six-six, six-seven at least, three hundred pounds, maybe more. He's completely bald and dressed only in a hotel bathrobe. Also . . .

He smells like smoke, she whispers. Oh God, Nick, he reeks of it!

Hey. He takes her by the shoulders, looking into her eyes. Jenny? It's fine. We knew there was smoke out there. We ran into it ourselves. This guy has been through the same thing, that's all. There's no smoke in here, right? There wasn't any smoke in the hallway just now. When he calms down, we can ask him what he's seen, but right now we're perfectly—

The stranger launches himself off the door with a cry, practically knocking them down as he lumbers toward the window.

Jesus Christ, man! Take it easy!

But he can't—he's full-on panicking. He paces in front of the window, peering out at the snow, rubbing his bald head and muttering.

Nick takes a cautious step toward him. Hey. Hey there.

The man stops pacing and turns.

Do you speak English?

The man points out at the window. *Mikä suunta se on? Pohjoinen?*

So that's a no, Nick says.

Tarvitsen vitun matkapuhelimen! The man's voice is shrill. His eyes are bright and tiny in his wide pink face. He can't seem to control his breathing. His hands flutter helplessly at his sides. They don't belong to him right now.

It must be bad out there, she says. If he's acting like this? It must be so bad.

Jenny, please don't freak out on me, okay? I can't handle two—

The giant lurches away from the window, stopping in front of the television. He watches the news, his mouth hanging open. With his rosy baldness, his snowy robe and bare feet, he looks like a huge, confused baby.

Mitä helvettiä tapahtuu? he whimpers.

What the hell language is that? Nick says.

I don't know. It sounds like—wait! We can google it.

She moves to the sofa and shakes out the duvet. Her phone tumbles to the ground. The stranger turns from the television at the sound, and his wild little eyes widen.

Matkapuhelin! he says. *Joo!*

And as she bends to pick it up he's right there on top of her. Christ he moves fast. What's he going to do, snatch it away from her?

Hey, Nick says, again trying to insert himself between Jenny and the behemoth. Calm down, okay? If you need to make a call we can . . . no, don't take it from her, don't—can you chill, please?

It's okay, she's saying to the man, it's okay.

Nick is pushing the guy's hands away as gently as possible, but he keeps reaching for the phone. They're both talking at him and backing away, the man is babbling and following them, not angry, not forcing himself on them, and yet he's so very fucking large it's hard not to feel threatened.

Give us a minute, Jenny says to him, just *one minute*, okay? And we'll . . . look! I'm going to google it, I'm opening Google Translate—*translate*, yeah?—and we'll use it to talk.

She types swiftly. Here. Here it is!

Don't give him the phone, Jenny. We might not get it back.

I won't, I'm just showing him the . . . look! Look! She points at the screen, where there's a microphone symbol. Talk, okay? She taps the icon, then nods, touches her lips and makes a little exploding star with her fingers: *go ahead, say something.*

The man unleashes a torrent of sound.

Whoa, whoa! Okay. She taps the screen again. Waits.

It's Finnish, she says.

Joo! Joo! The man lets loose another flood of words as he reaches for the phone.

Easy there, pal. He's from Finland? How does he not speak English?

He probably does, he's just too upset to . . . okay, can you . . . she holds up a hand, which somehow shuts the guy up. She taps the microphone and speaks. Slow down, okay?

A text box pops up, reflecting what the microphone captured:

low down oak.

Oh no, she says, that's not—

Matala tammi, says a deep voice from her phone.

The huge Finn looks perplexed.

Jenny clears out the translation and tries again, enunciating carefully: Slow. Down.

Hidasta, the phone says.

Hidasta, she repeats, nodding at the man. *Hidasta!* Now. She taps the microphone. What's your name?

Mikä sinun nimesi on? the phone says.

The Finn blurts out a string of sounds. They wait while the app translates.

Give me the phone, the voice from the phone says. *I will find a way out.*

Jenny looks to Nick, baffled.

He taps the microphone. How will you do that?

The Finn fidgets as he waits for the translation. Then he speaks. Then they wait.

I am an engineer, the phone says. *I will locate the building plan.*

Nick and Jenny glance at each other.

Do you think he—

No time! the Finn cries. There is fire!

No shit, Nick says, but—

Give phone! the man insists. Give phone and I show!

He's looming over them, vibrating with impatience.

Give him the phone, Jenny.

But—

Just do it. Better that than he rips it out of your hands.

She offers the phone to the Finn, who grabs it eagerly. She shoots Nick a resentful look.

What? he says. I'm trying to protect you.

Yeah? You're doing a great job.

She moves away. The Finn paces by the window, typing and mumbling to himself. Nick watches him. What the hell is happening right now? How is there suddenly a gigantic stranger filling their room with his bulk and his anxiety?

Where did he come from? What did he see?

Is it really bad out there?

No. It can't be. The hallway was clear. Not a whiff of smoke.

Jenny comes back around the bed, holding his phone.

Unlock this, she says. I'll use it to talk to him.

I'm not sure he's in the mood.

We need to find out what he's seen, Nick.

He unlocks his phone. She starts typing, then frowns.

These keyboard sounds, she mutters. Jesus.

Are you okay? he asks her.

I'm peachy, thanks.

Look, he says. We both got upset just now, but let's be civil, okay? At least while we deal with whatever this is?

Go to hell, Nick. She walks away from him, typing.

Nice. No, really, that's sweet. But fuck this. He doesn't need a random European, or Google Translate—he'll call downstairs and get some information. An update, a timeline. It would also be nice to talk with someone who doesn't think he's an irredeemable asshole. He moves around the bed toward the room phone. She has no right to be angry with him. She's the one who lied, who toyed with him, who—

He picks up the receiver. It slips out of his grasp.

Because his hands are trembling.

He lowers himself to the side of the bed. He takes a deep breath. He's a little rattled.

No, not rattled. Disorganized. This is too much, all at once. They were shouting at each other, they were breaking up—were they really?—then came the banging, the rush to the door, now they're dealing with a plus-size Scandinavian who's shedding stress like a fucking virus. Who wouldn't be skittish in those circumstances?

What's your name? she says into his phone, then holds it up to the Finn.

He needs to get a grip. He's disappointed, sure. Bitterly. No rescue for them, no salvation, not yet. But there's nothing to be done about that, so he needs to let it go.

Edvin? she says. Hi, Edvin! I'm Jenny. She puts a hand on her chest. *Jenny.*

The Finn nods at her briefly, then returns to his study of her phone.

So did she have an orgasm or not? He thinks she did. Her confession had the ring of truth. And he'd been skeptical when she said she'd faked it. He knows her, how she feels when she . . .

Why the fuck is he thinking about orgasms right now? Jesus, he's all over the place. Outrage still twanging through him. Not to mention a cringing mortification. What was he thinking, exposing himself to her like that? Telling her he thought he was losing her? What did he expect?

Doesn't matter. It's over. They're parting ways. He suggested it, and she agreed.

The Finn—Edvin, apparently—is now chattering away as he scrolls and types. Jenny raises Nick's phone to capture what he's saying.

I tried to go down the stairs, the voice from the phone says, *but when I opened the door it flake force right moon.*

She sighs and taps the screen. Can you repeat that? she says into the microphone.

Calmer now, Nick picks up the receiver and dials the front desk. He proposed they be civil, and he will be, for the rest of this miserable night. That's two rings. He watches the Finn move away from the window and head for the television, trailing Jenny. Are they really done? Did he overreact? She'd lied to him, but she was trying to make it right. That's six rings. These useless clowns. Are they just not picking up now? Are they . . .

There must be someone downstairs.

Right?

He hangs up and redials. Of course there's someone downstairs. The hot NY1 reporter is still yakking away, though nothing is going on behind her. A few firemen strolling into the building, that's it. Look at that guy. Captain Sloth. Could he be more unhurried? He's not dashing toward an inferno—he's heading in for a colonoscopy.

Jenny is speaking into his phone slowly, eyes on the stranger's face. She's so generous with him, so patient. Must be nice. Word of advice, buddy. Don't expect straightforward answers about her sexual satisfaction, okay?

The mega-Finn is listening to her, scrolling on the phone and glancing at the television. He's like a carnival creature. In that scrap of a bathrobe that barely reaches his knees. You expect someone that size to be a little tougher. More self-possessed.

They're still not answering. He hangs up, considering whether he should do something that occurred to him a while ago, but that he decided was unnecessary, too dire, too . . .

Doesn't matter. It's time.

He dials 911.

The line is busy.

He and Jenny can't be done. He was bewildered, that's all, caught off guard. He still is. Why would she say she didn't come when she had? How can you know someone so well, physically, intimately, while inside they're a black fucking box? But then, why is he surprised? Her lies are always mystifying. Like the age thing. Why does she pretend to be two years younger than she is? Does she think he doesn't know how to google?

Ei, the Finn says. *Ei . . .*

His voice sounds different. A little hollow. He swallows hard.

Edvin. She touches his arm. Are you okay?

The Finn clutches his stomach and runs for the bathroom.

He yanks the door shut behind him, so hard it nearly comes off the track.

They hear the toilet seat slam down on the porcelain.

Then, a massive blast. A splash.

A fusillade of wet farts. A piteous groan.

They exchange a look.

Yikes, she whispers.

There's another sizable splash. Then another.

The poor bastard, he says. Did you learn anything?

A little. She's studying his phone. He's been here since last week, in a room on the forty-seventh floor. He heard a bunch of alarms over the weekend, which turned out to be malfunctions, so he wasn't worried when the announcement to stay in our rooms came over the intercom. But when he heard the shrieks, and the voices arguing, he realized this was different and rushed out of his room. The nearest stairwell was full of smoke, which spooked him even more, so he decided to go back and wait . . . which is when he realized he'd left his key in the room.

From the bathroom comes another groan. Then another substantial discharge.

He needs to think about flushing, Nick says. What then?

He started banging on doors. He eventually found another stairwell—the same one we tried, I think. He made it down a few flights when a big cloud of smoke came billowing up. So he escaped onto this floor and kept trying doors, until he got to ours.

They hear a flush. Then another.

Edvin emerges, holding up her phone.

I find plan, he says. Now we go.

He's pale, but perfectly calm. He moves toward them.

There is way. See?

There is in fact some kind of blueprint on Jenny's screen.

Where did you find that? Nick asks.

City, Edvin says. All cities has department.

His English has returned, along with his poise. He swipes the screen with steady fingers, expanding the image.

We are here, he points at the diagram. South side of structure. Television say fire on west side of structure.

Nick looks to Jenny. They did say that a minute ago, she says.

I try stairs B, here. Edvin points to one corner. No good. Then stairs A, to get here. You also try A, Jenny say, yes? All close to fire, see? Now we go stairs C, on north side of structure. Safe route.

The fire is almost out, Nick tells him. If we sit tight, we'll . . .

Edvin turns and disappears back into the bathroom.

Nick shakes his head. He's out of his mind.

He seems fine now, she says.

Because he's found something to feed his delusions. He was literally shitting himself with fear two minutes ago, now he's seen a single floor plan and he's Ferdinand Magellan?

He's an engineer. Maybe he knows what he's talking about.

She can't be serious. Jenny, he says. Please don't tell me you think this is a good idea.

We should at least consider it.

No time! Edvin says. He's back, his arms full of wet towels. No considering. We go.

He dumps the towels by the door and heads for the cabinets. Nick watches him open one and start rooting around. He turns to Jenny.

This is who you're going to listen to? The guy who didn't have the brains to bring his key with him when he galloped out of his room—in a bathrobe?

But I should listen to you? she says. The guy who persuaded me to stay when we could have gone? Who lied to me about where the fire is? Who—

Jesus Christ, I'm sorry, okay? I screwed up! Repeatedly, comprehensively. Trust me, I am very, very, *very* sorry we didn't leave. But that doesn't mean we should leave now, when the problem is almost solved. That's fucking insane!

He turns to find Edvin right on top of him, holding a laundry bag.

You should not swear at your wife, the big man says.

Nick sighs. Right. Thanks for the tip, chief.

Edvin moves to the fridge. He stuffs bottles of water into the laundry bag. He scrabbles around in the snack shelves.

You saw the news, Jenny. We'll be able to walk out of here soon. But not yet.

Edvin was so scared when he got here, she says. What if it's worse out there than what we've been told?

Then we definitely shouldn't go! It's . . . what the hell is he doing now?

Edvin has opened Nick's suitcase. He pulls out a pair of running shoes.

Okay, that's . . . Edvin? That's not cool, man, those are—

Edvin tosses the shoes aside and moves on to the desk. Nick

watches him ransack the drawers. She can't go with this guy. She can't . . . Christ, all night it's been like this. She tries to escape, he tries to stop her. He didn't want her to leave the bed, the room. Their *this*. He should have let her go when she wanted to go. They both should have gone.

But just because they should have gone then doesn't mean they should go now.

Edvin drops a ballpoint pen into his laundry bag. He picks up one of their robes from the floor, yanks the belt through its loops and shoves that in, too.

Nick reaches for her hands, but she draws back.

Jenny, please listen. I know you want to go. But—

Why do you care whether I go or not?

Why do I . . . because I care about you! Yes, I got massively pissed off a few minutes ago, but I don't want you to get hurt, and if you leave with Gigantor here, that's a real possibility. Look. We don't have to talk the rest of the night. We'll sit in opposite corners and ignore each other. But please please *please* don't go. Not now.

Edvin is messing around in the closet again. They watch him pull a hanger off the clothes bar and shove it into his bag. What the fuck does he need a hanger for?

Jenny turns back to Nick. Her eyes are full of tears.

I just want it to be over, she whispers.

Oh honey, I know. He cups her face with his hands. So do I, and I am so sorry it isn't. But leaving right now isn't the answer. People die doing dumb shit like what he's about to do.

I know, I know, I just . . . she steps back and covers her face, shaking her head.

But she's staying. He can tell.

Thank Christ, she's staying.

Is time, Edvin says. Is . . .

He picks up the wet towels and holds one out to each of them. They shake their heads.

We go now, Edvin insists.

We're staying, Jenny tells him. You should stay, too.

Edvin stares at her. He tries to speak, but he's lost his words again. He pulls her phone out of his pocket, types, then speaks. He turns the phone toward them.

Please come, the phone says. *My English isn't good. It's too risky to go alone.*

It's too risky, period, Nick says. Which is why we're not going.

Edvin throws his hands in the air. He taps the phone and speaks rapidly. He turns it to them, but nothing happens. Frustrated, he taps the screen hard and speaks louder.

Hey Edvin? Jenny steps toward him. Can I have my phone back?

No. He frowns at the screen. I keep.

But that's . . . you can't have my phone.

Edvin ignores her. She reaches for it. He holds it away from her.

Nick? Help me.

Edvin, give her the phone, man. It's not—

Edvin waves at them to hush as he speaks into the microphone. Then he holds it out to Nick, his round little eyes pleading.

Don't you want your wife to be safe? the phone says.

Okay, enough. Enough of this erratic presence filling their room with his stress and his demands, ransacking their belongings and beshitting their toilet. If he's leaving, he should leave.

My wife is perfectly safe at home, Nick says. But she'll be touched by your concern.

Jenny sighs. For God's sake, Nick.

Edvin needs a minute to puzzle it out. Then he draws back, looking scandalized.

Shame! His voice is low and righteous. Shame on you!

That's right, Nick says agreeably. Shame on us. Thanks for stopping by, Edvin. Safe travels.

He opens the door.

Is that what does it—the wide swing of the door, the view of the hall? Hard to say, but something breaks the big man. His panic comes roaring back. He drops his supplies, charges forward.

Then he turns, grabs Jenny's arm and yanks her through the door.

It's so unexpected, so sudden and fast that Nick doesn't react until she's halfway out. That's when he lunges, grabbing her other arm and hanging on, but the huge man is strong, so strong, they're a confused tangle, three bodies half in the room half out, more than half, but he doesn't have the key this time so he can't let the door fall closed, they'll be screwed.

He wedges a foot in the doorway, holding on to her, but she's slipping away, her blouse is so goddamn slippery, but she can't go, he'll hang on, he has to . . . he's shouting, thrashing, trying to beat the guy away with his free hand, trying to kick him, but he's too far away, he can't get at him properly. Her face is strained and white, they must be hurting her, she's trying to pull her arm away from Edvin's grip but she can't fight him off properly because Nick's got her other arm, but what can he do?

What is happening, what is happening, what the fuck can he do?

She's struggling, flailing wildly but making no noise. He is, he's shouting *Stop! Stop! Leave her let her go fucking get off her you fucking* hollering at the monster, he's not an idiot baby but a big bald menacing monster.

None of it's working, though, and his grip is slipping. He can't hold her. He's losing her. He's—

No!

She gasps it out at last, and yanking her arm away from Nick she grabs Edvin's hand and bites down. She must really tear the shit out of him because he screams and releases her, shoves her away in fact, into Nick, and as the two of them tumble back against the open door Edvin rushes down the hall, wailing and holding his injured hand.

He grows smaller.

He rounds a corner.

He's gone.

ten

Nick pulls Jenny inside the room, slams the door, locks it, bolts it.

Checks the lock. Checks the bolt.

Adrenaline is fizzing through him. He can't catch his breath, can't process what just—

Her face crumples, and she bursts into tears.

Oh honey! Come here.

She shakes her head, weeping, helpless, wordless.

You're bleeding, he says. Your mouth.

She wipes her lips, looks at her hand, confused. Looks at him.

Is it his blood? he says. Jesus, you took a chunk out of him, didn't you?

That makes her sob even harder. He reaches for her but she shies away, rubbing her mouth, spitting, trying to get the blood off.

Don't touch me!

Jenny, please. He reaches out again, coming to her rather than pulling her to him. Arms around her shuddering shoulders, her seized and wrangled body.

Poor girl. Poor girl.

This fucking night.

She gives in now, letting go, letting her legs do what they want, which is to turn to water, apparently. She has to cling to him so she doesn't slide to the floor. He holds her up, stroking her hair, murmuring into it. That feels nice.

Even though he's been such a dick to her.

And she's been so awful to him!

She starts sobbing all over again. He lets her blubber onto his shoulder for a while.

Then he sweeps her up. Just sweeps her right up into his arms.

He carries her to the bed and lays her down. She turns onto her side, away from him. She feels him hovering.

Do you want me to stay close, or should I give you some space?

Yes, she says.

He's so fricking brilliant, let him figure out what she wants.

He hesitates, then lies down behind her. He puts an arm around her waist.

Good. That's what she wanted.

And there's his breath in her hair again. That's good, too.

They're quiet for a while. Breathing in unison.

She squeezes out a few more tears.

We should never have people over, he says. They kill the vibe.

Oh my God, Nick, don't joke!

Sorry. His arm tightens around her. It's a reflex. I was—that was scary.

Were you scared? she says. Poor guy!

She's safe, after being manhandled and terrorized. She has earned the right to be truculent, to crab at him a little. Even though he saved her. Which is so frustrating! He's the worst, he ruins everything, but no sooner does he reach the apex of jackassery— accusing her of playing games, breaking up with her?—than he does something right. Noble, even.

It's infuriating, that contradiction, yet somehow, it's very him. Very Nick.

Noble, though? Let's not go crazy. Let's not start handing out good-conduct certificates. He did what any baseline decent human would do. Preventing her abduction by a Finnish headcase: pretty much the bare minimum. Especially since he's why she needed rescuing in the first place.

Edvin took my phone, didn't he?

I think so, yeah.

He wrenched my arm, too. And you weren't exactly gentle.

I'm sorry, he says. I was trying to—I'm sorry.

He was trying to save her. He grabbed her and he didn't let go.

I wasn't playing games, she says. Earlier. I felt awful that you thought you were losing me, so I—

Never mind. He strokes her hair. Just hush now.

Oh no! She sits up, twisting around to glare down at him. Don't tell me to hush!

Whoa, sorry, I just—

I just, I just! She mimics him in a high-pitched voice. I don't care what you just! And no more with the *whoas*. Don't tell me to *hush*, or *whoa*, ever again.

I won't, he says. I'm sorry. Please lie down. That's a request, obviously.

She lies down, relaxing into the pillows. Completely drained. He's close, but not too close. There's his good strong arm around her waist. His breath in her hair.

After a while, he gets up. She hears the bathroom door slide on its track.

Jesus, he mutters. The fan drowns out any further commentary on the state of the toilet.

How could Edvin turn on them like that? She can still feel his hand, his implacable grip. She was lost, she was basically gone, and like in a nightmare she couldn't make a sound.

Her shoulder aches. She must have bruises. She could check. But she doesn't want to see them right now.

She hears Nick come out of the bathroom. He enters her line of sight, peering out the window. He returns to the bed and takes a seat.

Can I do anything for you? he asks.

Yes. You can go check the stairwells.

What? No way!

She sits up. There was no smoke in the hallway just now. Maybe the stairs have cleared. What's the harm in checking?

He leans over, resting his elbows on his knees and pinching the bridge of his nose. It just seems incredibly foolish to me.

Then I'll go.

No chance. I'll go. He sighs. If you absolutely insist.

Circle the whole floor, to make sure you hit every stairwell.

So that's a yes, he says. That's a, yes Nick, I am absolutely insisting you go.

With a great show of resignation, he rises and finds his shoes.

Take one of the wet towels, she says. Do you want a bottle of water?

I'm not crossing the Serengeti, Jenny. I'll be right back.

He heads for the door, where he picks up a towel, then turns to give her one last martyred glance.

Well, he says, it's been real.

Thank you, Nick.

He gives her a little salute. Then he opens the door, and he's gone.

But he'll be back. She saw him pick up his keycard. Does he think she won't let him in? Does he mistrust her that much?

Retrieving his phone from the foyer, where she must have dropped it during the struggle with Edvin, she sits on the end of the bed, unmutes the television and scrolls for updates. The conditions downstairs look more or less unchanged. Juliana, the pretty NY1 reporter, keeps referring to the situation as a *significant blaze,* but it's unclear whether that's official terminology or infotainment hype. Juliana is currently explaining how smoke filtered to lower floors of the building via electrical conduits, creating initial confusion about where the fire was. Smoke also spread upward when fleeing guests opened stairwell doors.

The two anchors in the studio, whose names are Ron and Cheryl, listen and nod and look concerned.

The fire has made the *New York Times* home page: FDNY Battling Blaze in Midtown High-Rise.

Firefighters are now going room by room on the affected floor, making sure all flames have been extinguished and beginning smoke mitigation efforts.

Poor Juliana's nose is red. They'd be freezing too, if they'd left. No, they'd be in another room by now. In another bed. Asleep. Or fucking. Or watching the news, astonished, saying, that's insane. Can you believe it?

We were *just there.*

Shouldn't Nick be back by now? Chill, it's been like four minutes. She misses him. Has she ever been alone in a hotel room without him? *I get lonely after I come.* She understands now. The simple comfort of a body, near at hand.

She hadn't meant to upset him—she was trying to make him feel better! She'd listened to his explanation for why he'd insisted on a whole night, his heartfelt confession, and she'd felt awful. So she blurted out the one thing she had, her own confession, which she hoped would reassure him, but which, upon reflection, she can see might not be so reassuring. Of course he'd be confounded by what she'd done—what kind of psycho fakes faking an orgasm? Plus her reason, her ridiculous wedding ring misunderstanding . . . how can she explain that to him without sounding like a complete cuckoo?

She logs into Twitter on his phone. @firechieftim is describing the building's numerous safety features. It has advanced sensors, high-tech sprinklers and a buildingwide command-and-control system monitored by AI. Okay, but if the building is that spectacular, why was it so hard to find the fire in the first place? Answer me that, @firechieftim, you who seem to know so much.

I laid my heart bare for you. Okay, but . . . really? He shared a concern about their relationship, not some soul-crushing secret. Is he so fragile that a little vulnerability can knock him sideways—make him feel so bad that he needs to get rid of her, erase this awful stain on his sense of imperviousness? Is he really so defended, so . . . what? Allergic to consequences. No wonder he didn't take the fire seriously at first. How could something like a fire possibly affect him? He's invincible.

Or so he thought.

And persuaded her to think, too.

She hears two quick beeps, and the door opens. He takes two, three, four steps in, and by the time the door falls closed he's sitting beside her, taking her hands in his.

I have a proposal, he says. No more lies. We wipe the slate clean, and commit to total honesty from here on out. How does that sound?

Okay, but—

I'm saying this so that you believe what I'm about to tell you, which is that we are better off, significantly better off, staying put. I did a full circuit of the floor. The elevators are still shut down—the freight elevator, too. I checked all three stairwells. Our old favorite, A, is almost black with smoke. Impassable. The other two weren't as bad, but bad enough.

Black with smoke? she says, shrinking away a little.

But no fire, Jenny. Smoke rises, right? The stairs are probably clear farther down. Still, we won't make it through right now.

He presses her hands between his. Looks into her eyes.

I did as you asked. I'm reporting back. Do you believe me?

She nods. Did you see Edvin?

I didn't see anyone. He glances at the television. Any news?

Not much. The fire department is going room by room on the twenty-first floor.

Good. Nick looks around. He really did a number on this place, huh?

Together, they erase all traces of Edvin. He straightens up around the desk and returns the throw pillows to the sofa. She hangs the robes in the closet.

You expect Northern Europeans to be more orderly, don't you? he says. They've got such clean cities. All that minimalist architecture.

She folds the duvet and places it along the bottom of the bed.

He retrieves a bottle of wine that had rolled under the coffee table and checks it against the minibar menu.

Unbelievable! They're charging two hundred bucks for pinot noir. It's minibar robbery, she says.

Right? He reaches for the corkscrew. Obviously we're drinking it.

She returns to the end of the bed and bumps up the volume on the television.

> *Hotel management is working to determine how many guests remain in the building, but they believe the number could be more than a hundred.*

Over a hundred of them. It's unreal. There's no smell of smoke in the room. No flames visible out the window, or rippling black clouds. Just whirling snow. Juliana could be posing in front of a building in Moscow right now, or Minneapolis. Instead she's a few hundred feet below them, and they're a few hundred feet above a *significant blaze*, watching it unfold on television.

He brings two glasses of wine over and takes a seat beside her.

What if Edvin comes back?

We don't let him in.

But—

Jenny. We do not let him in.

Let's call him, she says.

Why the hell would we call him?

To find out if he made it. If there's a clear path down.

Yeah, but . . . he pauses. That's not a bad idea, actually.

Shocker, right? I'm not a total idiot.

He looks startled. Who said you were?

She wakes his phone. What's your passcode?

5455, he says. It spells Jill.

She unlocks the phone and dials her own number. She taps Speakerphone and sets it between them. It starts to ring.

Norman? she says.

What?

She points at the screen. Your phone says it's calling Norman.

That's how I stored your number in my contacts, he says. What's wrong with Norman?

The phone is still ringing.

I don't know, she says. I think of Norm from *Cheers*. A big, sweaty alcoholic.

You want me to use a sexier pseudonym? he says. Hot Mama? Killer Lay?

No, I—

Aphrodite of the Golden Distaff? Sexual Partner, Comma, Best I Ever Had? Kind of defeats the purpose of an alias, but—

Hi, you've reached Jenny. I'm not available to take your call, so—

She ends the call.

It hasn't been that long, he says. We'll try again later.

They shouldn't have called. Now she's going to worry about Edvin, of all people. She shouldn't. But she will.

> *The hotel opened less than a week ago. Its owners, a French hospitality conglomerate, claim that it's the most luxurious five-star hotel in Manhattan, offering a multifloor wellness spa, an aromatherapy lounge, three restaurants and a full-floor private club with panoramic views of the city.*

Aromatherapy! he says. Do I bring you to the high-class joints or what? Let's take a break from the news. They're just talking to keep people from changing channels at this point.

He mutes the television and heads back to the minibar. Strolls to it. He's not nervous. He returned from his expedition full of brisk energy. But is he telling her the truth about what it's like out there?

Are you telling me the truth about what it's like out there? she asks.

Yes. He's poking around among the snacks. Because no more lies, remember?

We'll see how long he can stick to that little edict. But he does seem as calm now as when he left. Still confident in their rescue.

But when? When?

Whenwhenwhenwhenwhenwhenwhen—

I guess it doesn't matter how you stored my number, she says. You'll be deleting it soon. Since we're done.

He doesn't respond.

Since this thing of ours has run its course, she adds. Quote-unquote.

She can tell he's watching her, but she doesn't look up from his phone.

Hey Jenny.

What?

Shut up.

She puts his phone down. We should talk about our fight.

He's studying the nutrition facts on a can of nuts. No we shouldn't.

You don't want me to explain the orgasm thing? You don't want me to apologize?

I'm good, he says. Clean slate, remember?

What if I want an apology from you?

I'm sorry, he says automatically.

Nick. We should clear the air. What else are we going to do?

He sets the nuts down and comes back to the bed.

He sits beside her. Puts a hand on her knee.

Smiles.

She stares at him. Are you kidding me?

What? It would relax us! Not to mention pass the time.

She laughs in disbelief. There's no way!

Why are you so outraged? This is what we do. It's what we're good at.

Right, she says. It's all I'm good for.

What? No, that's—what the hell, Jenny? That's not what I meant.

She reaches for the remote and unmutes the news.

*—and by the time backup units arrived, the wind was
blowing in a northerly direction.*

The camera is trained on the lobby doors. Still no Edvin, she
says.

They sip their wine and watch firefighters amble in and out of
the building.

*Reports further indicate that after firefighters collapsed
the hotel's revolving doors to facilitate the entry of
men and equipment, a gust pushed into the building,
which disrupted—*

How big do you think Edvin's dick is?

She tears her eyes away from the television to gape at him.

Gargantuan, right? As a matter of sheer proportion?

What is wrong with you? she demands.

So much, he says. Though at the moment I'm just trying to distract you.

By proposing we discuss a stranger's dick? A possibly dead
stranger's dick?

You're right, he says. That's totally inappropriate. Let's discuss
mine instead.

At which point she bends over, setting her wineglass on the
floor.

She stays like that, covering her face with her hands.

She's trying desperately not to laugh.

She shouldn't be laughing right now! But she doesn't just want
to laugh—she also wants to weep and scream and run out the door
and beat him to death with the remote. She needs him, she wants
him, she hates his fucking face. Because here she is, marinating in
a slew of awful feelings, a witch's brew, she was just *physically assaulted*, they're in a predicament terrible enough to be the focus of
the evening news, not to mention earning one of those dire red

Breaking subheads from the *New York* fricking *Times*... and he wants to talk about dicks!

Witch's brew. That's what Ben calls a soup Tom makes, with tomatoes and beans. The first time he tasted it he hid under the kitchen table and cried. Natey joined him in solidarity.

Oh, Ben. Oh, Natey. Her little weirdos, her menaces. She sits up and opens her photos on her phone, so she can see their sweet faces.

But all she finds are pictures of Jill and a bunch of documents.

Right. Not her phone.

Her phone is gone.

This is all bad, so very bad. She doesn't want to think about it. So she reaches for her glass and drains it.

Not that big, she says.

Beg pardon?

Edvin's dick. I saw it. His robe fell open while we were standing up at the television.

And you looked! he says. You hussy!

I couldn't help it! It was right there.

She has shocked him, which pleases her. He gets the wine and refreshes their glasses.

I need every detail, he says. Start at the root, proceed to the tip. Or go the other direction. Up to you.

She shrugs. Eh.

Eh? he repeats. You're a novelist, woman! Use your formidable powers of description.

I don't know what to tell you. It was a basic pinkish schlong. The hair around it was copper-colored. There was a lot of it.

Insulation for those Arctic winters, no doubt. But sizewise, you weren't impressed?

It was normal. Small, even.

Fascinating. Still, imagine when he gets hard. It must smack the ceiling. He must need a special hoist to position it, like in a shipyard.

I can't believe we're talking about this, she says. We're awful.

Ve're the vorst, he agrees.

—and the force of that wind pushed through the elevator shafts and stairwells of the building, causing smoke to mass on the upper floors.

See? he says. The smoke is rising. The fire is still far below us.

She picks up his phone and checks her go-to sites. The fire, once nowhere, is now everywhere. People are posting photos and videos on social media, the news sites are buzzing.

I wish he hadn't left, she says.

He mutes the television. Edvin? He couldn't help it.

Why, because there's no such thing as free will?

I was thinking it was because he'd completely lost his mind, he says, but sure. Also because there's no such thing as free will.

You just muted the television, she says. You went to law school, years ago. You got married, had a child. Put on a blue shirt this morning. You're saying all those decisions were completely out of your control?

Yes, because they were each the result of earlier decisions, which were themselves the result of even earlier decisions—as well as the product of my upbringing, my genetics, prior experiences, environment. There's a chain of prior causes, stretching way, way back, through our lives, through time, through the history of the world, and they form the sum total of the conditions we find ourselves in at any moment. Everything we do is the direct result of things that already happened—things we had absolutely no control over.

Fine, earlier decisions and circumstances led me here, she says, but why does that mean the next decision I make isn't free? It feels like it is. It feels like I spend half my life agonizing over my choices, wondering whether I'm doing the right thing.

That's an illusion, he says. You were always going to do the thing you end up doing. You just didn't know it.

There's something wrong with his logic. She just doesn't know how to articulate it.

She glances at the television. Still no Edvin.

So when I thought I was deciding whether to go with Edvin, I wasn't? That choice had already been made?

Well, it wasn't even a choice, he says. It was an outcome, already determined, based on who you are, how you think and behave—everything that's ever happened to you led you both to vacillate about staying, and ultimately to stay.

Why did you persuade me so hard to stay, if you knew the outcome was already whatever—fixed in place?

Because I had no choice either, he says. That was my predetermined course of action.

Okay, there's definitely something wrong with his logic.

It's like your argument about women being brainwashed, he adds. In fact, if we circle back to that discussion—

You're actually bringing this back to blow jobs, she says. Incredible.

As we say in the courtroom, you opened the door, sweethcart. So. Imagine we have a woman. And this woman happens to find herself in the presence of a tasty-looking dick.

Ha! she says. Now we're truly in the land of illusion.

Be that as it may. We have a woman, we have a dick. Said woman perceives said dick. Thinks, hey, that looks good! So she wraps her lips around it, and proceeds to—

Thank you, she says. I get the idea.

Great. Now if—as you yourself insisted—she made that choice because she's been trained to do it, persuaded by forces beyond her control, then how is her choice in any way free?

Because, she says, well, because . . . she still chooses. Sure, she's influenced by her environment, but that doesn't mean she's completely . . . I mean, it doesn't strip her of all . . . shoot, what's the word?

Agency, he says. And I think it does. There's no such thing as partial freedom.

Dammit! She doesn't know how to circumvent his reasonableness, how to articulate what she feels in the deepest pit of herself to be true—that her choices are hers. *She* elects, *she's* responsible, all blessings and faults her own. His big words and irritating logic don't matter.

Oh, but they do. They do matter, because she's a frozen duck!

She glances at the television. The anchors are discussing construction delays at LaGuardia. The fire is getting boring—that's a positive development. Though it also means she can't see whether a big man in a tiny robe has emerged through the lobby doors.

She tries calling her number again.

It rings and rings.

Norman's not picking up, she says.

Isn't that a good sign? I mean, it's awful for him, but it shows we were right not to go.

She feels Edvin's hand on her again, pulling her. Just thinking about it . . . she stands and moves to the window. She's getting worked up again. Riled by these four walls, this unbelievable situation. She wants to fling herself around the room and shriek. Tear the stuffing out of the pillows, throw herself on the floor and pound on it with her fists.

Instead, she looks out at the snow and takes deep calming breaths. Inhale, one, two . . .

Why, though? Why hide her rage, her fear, her burbles of hysteria? She hides them and hides them, all night she's been hiding them. Or trying to, and failing miserably.

Why hide anything? It never really works. Maybe it shouldn't.

She turns from the window.

A man, Nick. A man who was just here with us is almost certainly dead. Maybe a lot of other people are, too. That's not a *good sign*, of anything.

We don't know if he actually tried to leave, he points out. He could have found a room down the hall where a nice, non-adulterous couple is roosting. Maybe they're all holed up in there right now, drinking overpriced wine and discussing the blessings of compulsory monogamy.

Goddammit! she cries. Stop fucking joking!

Sorry. He rises and comes to her. I'm sorry. It's a bad habit. When things get stressful, I tend to make jokes, rather than—

What, have feelings? Be genuine?

Hey. He takes her hands. Let's not attack each other again, okay? It's important to stay united. We've never faced a situation like this before.

A crisis, she says.

Okay, a crisis. And I think that's why it's been rocky. We needed some time to adjust to how we each deal with this sort of thing. Now, we need to be a team.

A team? We barely know each other.

What? We've known each other for years.

Really, Nick? What's my middle name?

She watches him struggle. He can't admit that he doesn't know.

It's Grace, she says. Where was I born? What's my favorite movie?

Those are random facts, Jenny, they're not important, or—

Racine, Wisconsin, she says. And *Moonstruck*. But we've never talked about the important stuff, either. Not much. Which is fine, we spend our time doing other things. But it means we don't really know each other. Do you even know why I started sleeping with you?

Because of my ferocious cock and my magnetic sorry sorry sorry! He grabs at her hands as she pulls away. I told you, it's a reflex. But what is it you want? Opening up, sharing our secrets—that hasn't gone so well for us tonight.

Why are you so against talking about real things? she demands. Why are you so typically, tiredly male about not sharing your feelings?

Jesus, Jenny, I—

It's so boring, she says. Aren't you bored?

The room phone rings.

eleven

It rings again. He moves swiftly toward it.

Hello?

Please. Please please please let this be good news.

Okay, sir? he says. Let me stop you right there. Should we be evacuating?

He listens. Their eyes meet.

He shakes his head.

Understood, he says. No, we won't . . . we did, but we won't try again.

She watches him listening. Is someone coming to get them? Is there a plan?

Please let there be a plan.

How about you tell me something first? he says. Why has there been zero communication since the deranged announcement we heard a few hours ago?

Oh no. He shouldn't get angry. Lawyerman needs to shut up and listen.

Why hasn't anyone been answering the phone downstairs? You call me when you want information, but when I call—no no, let me finish. This is outrageous. What little we know about what's happening we're getting from New York fucking One!

He pauses, listening.

Okay, he says. Okay. And how long . . . uh-huh. That's good news.

Good news? She likes good news! She unclenches a little at good news.

Hang on, he says, opening a drawer, pulling out a notepad and pen. Go ahead. He scribbles something. Smoke? No, not in the room or the hallway. The stairwells, yes, quite a bit, though it varies from . . . what's that? There are two of us. No, no injuries, or . . . yes, that's me.

He listens. Then he glances at her.

What is it, Nick?

I'm not comfortable giving you that information, he says.

What are they asking?

He motions to her with his free hand, like *Relax. I've got this.*

I understand that gathering these details is part of your standard protocol, he says. Part of my standard protocol is checking into a hotel and not being trapped for hours by monumental incompetence.

Jesus, Nick. Tell them my name!

Fine, he says. Fine. Her name is . . .

He glances at her again.

Grace Gryzb, he says.

She drops down onto the sofa.

Sure, he says. G as in George . . .

She lets her head fall back. She gazes up at the ceiling.

I know, he says. It's Polish.

No more lies! Wow. And he's not just lying. He's erasing her. He gets to be named, and counted. But Jenny Parrish? Sorry, there's nobody by that name here. There never was.

The lies are inescapable. Even though lying is categorically wrong, he said. The true problem of infidelity. Once you've started, you can't stop. You lie to spouses, to each other. To people trying to rescue you from disasters.

You just can't lie to yourself. That, to him, is key.

Lie if you must, but know yourself.

Though, why *must* you lie? Because of who you are, and what you've done? Genetics, environment? Because you literally have no choice?

Yes, he says. Understood. Thank you.

She's still staring up at the ceiling. He comes to the sofa and sits beside her.

That was a fire chief of some kind, downstairs at their command center. He said we should absolutely not leave the room right now.

Then it's bad out there, she says. It's really bad.

Only the smoke, Jenny. He said the operation is going well, despite initial holdups caused by some mechanical problems and what sounds like criminally inexperienced hotel staff. But the FDNY is in control of the situation, and they foresee no additional problems in extinguishing the fire. Though the process is going to take a while. What the news said they were doing—going room by room—is taking a long time because all the doors are locked, and the software that allows them to open them all at once in an emergency is—surprise, surprise—not working. Bottom line, the fire department is being meticulous, and they think it will take most of the night. They said 911 is overloaded right now, and gave me a separate number to call if we want updates. When it's time, someone will come up to get us. Probably closer to morning.

She says nothing. She's thinking about meticulous processes. Firefighters following a plan. That's all she wanted—to know there was a plan.

This is good news. Really good news.

I'm sorry about the name thing, he says. But this is an exorbitant hotel. People are probably hoping that celebrities and evil billionaires are stuck in here, to raise the drama quotient. If the guest list leaks, and surely it will . . . it's bad enough they've got my name, but you're a big deal. You'd be noticed.

Excuses, excuses. She should give him a hard time—first she's Norman, now she's Grace?—but her irritation is already dissipating. She's so relieved about the plan, the meticulousness. She wants to enjoy that feeling, not keep sniping away.

I'm not that big of a deal, she says. But whatever. They know there are two of us in here. That's what matters.

He nods and squeezes her hand. Then he goes to the foyer and looks through the peephole. He opens the door and pokes his head out.

Still no smoke, he announces.

He shuts the door and walks to the window. He looks down at the city, rubbing the back of his neck. Then he takes a seat on the side of the bed, facing her.

We're going to get caught, he says. I don't know how public it's going to be, I hope not very, but I don't see how we get out of here without Caroline and Tom finding out.

This is still your concern, she says, marveling at him. Your sole concern.

The FDNY just called, Jenny. They know we're here, they're in charge, and as the whole world knows, they're good at this sort of thing. So while this is messy as hell, we're not in physical danger. What happens after tonight, though, in our real lives? I know you hate when I bring it up, but I feel compelled to point out that we are well and truly fucked.

He looks defeated. For the first time! Not in the stairwell, not when they opened the door expecting a firefighter and finding a babbling maniac. He was tense then, but composed. Man in Charge. Well, not in charge, because he has no free will, duh. Still. He's extraordinary. Master of the universe, undone by the fear of losing the wife he's been deceiving for years.

Fearing Caroline more than the fire.

That's interesting. Very interesting.

He's bent over, elbows on his knees, studying the floor. She moves from the sofa to the desk chair, turning it to face him.

Interrogation time!

Why are you so scared of getting caught?

He gives her a weary look. Because I don't want my wife to leave me, Jenny.

I didn't leave Tom when he cheated on me.

Tom's a lucky man. But if I recall, he didn't cheat on you for over half a decade with a woman you both know.

Caroline never remembers my name, she says. I've introduced myself to her about twenty times.

I don't think that's going to make her feel any better about this. Also, don't take it personally. She's awful with names.

She glances at his phone. The battery is low. She goes to the bathroom, gets her adapter out of her bag, plugs it in and sets it on the nightstand.

Tom slept with someone from work, she says. Twice. I was pregnant. I didn't leave.

She's told him this before. They do talk. It's not as if they meet up, undress silently, hump frantically and part without a word. They chat about work, neighborhood gossip, their kids. And they trade some limited confidences. More so in the early days. He spoke of midlife depression, what he called his malaise. She spoke of restlessness. But that was back when they had to explain how they'd ended up sneaking into rooms like this together, had to tell themselves a story about why they were breaking promises that made the breaking, not okay, but explicable. They had to identify their prior causes.

So yes, they know a few things. But not much.

I couldn't leave, she says. Then I got over it, and I didn't want to.

He reaches for his wine. His pointed silence means drop it, Mrs. Gryzb. Move on.

What's Caroline like? she asks.

Are you serious right now, Jenny?

So, you want us to be united, she says. A team. But it's your team. You're the captain, and you decide how the game is played. That's the idea?

He's about to respond, but instead, he gives in. Throws his hands up with a look like, *Fine, have at it.*

She persuaded him. She won! With an argument about fairness. That's what's effective.

She needs to remember that.

We'll take turns, she says. We'll each say one thing we love about our spouse and one thing we can't stand.

This taking turns thing, he says. It's big with you.

I have two boys. If taking turns didn't exist, we'd all be dead. You go first. What's something you love about Caroline?

He thinks it over. Well, obviously . . .

And she can tell by the look on his face exactly what he's going to say.

Jesus, Nick!

I'm sorry, but she's beautiful! It's not a knock against you, you know I think you're—

Stop! She covers her ears. I'm not fishing for compliments!

I'm just saying you shouldn't be jealous. You're—

Stop! And of course I'm jealous. Who wouldn't want to look like her? But the fact that it's the first nice thing you have to say? That's a little messed up.

Kind of you to be defending my wife right now, he remarks. She'd be so grateful.

If she remembered my name, she says.

He raises his glass to her. Touché.

She glances at the television. The two anchors appear to be discussing corruption in Albany. She sighs. Caroline really is beautiful.

I know, he says. Not that it does me much good anymore. We don't, he clears his throat, I mean, we do, have sex, occasionally, but—

Uh-huh, she says. So she can check that question off the old list. They still sleep together. That's good. It would be awful if he only got some once or twice a month, with her. Though the way he has at her sometimes you'd think he just escaped from a monastery.

So yes. Good for him. For them. Why should she care? She doesn't. But she always assumed . . . that is, she didn't expect . . .

Oh, hell. What does it matter?

Tell me something real about her, she says. Why is she so great that you hate the thought of losing her?

While he mulls that over, she goes to the nightstand and checks his phone. The fire is on the CNN homepage now. @firechieftim is in the middle of a thread about how smoke spreads through zoned mechanical exhaust systems. The fire nerds are on high alert tonight, man. This is pyro Christmas.

But it's fine, because of the meticulous processes. Because the FDNY has a plan.

She refreshes the *Times* website. No updates. She googles: arguments in favor of free will. The first result is a page titled: Why You Probably Don't Have Free Will.

Awesome. Thanks.

She sets his phone down. She's not going to look at it for a while. The television is on, the fire department knows Nick and his vowelless Slavic princess are here. If something important happens, they'll hear about it.

She returns to the chair. He empties the last of the wine into their glasses.

Caroline is a great partner, he says. She's conscientious and smart and thoughtful. We're in sync about the big things—how we raise Jill, how we spend money, dealing with in-law bullshit. She's fully committed to the life we have, which is smooth-running and comfortable, thanks almost entirely to her. We communicate well and look at the world the same way. We have similar tastes, similar opinions. The same things interest us and bug the shit out of us.

So what you love about her is that she's a lot like you, she says.

He laughs, shaking his head. You're really breaking my balls tonight.

I pitied them earlier, she says. I'm trying something new.

Lucky me. Can I say what I don't like about her now?

Go crazy.

She's overly preoccupied with the opinions of other people. Family, friends, the neighbors—she's deeply concerned with what they think about her, about us, about the state of our landscaping. Way too many of her decisions are dictated by how other people will react to them. I'm not only talking people we know—I'm talking total strangers. Given the chance, she'll always take sides against me with a waitress, or a salesperson. Even when I'm not being a dick. Go ahead, look shocked, but I am, occasionally, not a dick. I'll be asking a question, or maybe *mildly* objecting to something, and Caroline starts making these little consoling faces. Like she has to soften me, in order to protect them.

You want her to be on your side.

Or to stay neutral. Whatever, he says, it's not a big deal, and it's far from the only thing she cares about. But it's frustrating.

Has she always been like that, or has she changed? Wait, I forgot, she says. People don't change.

No, they don't. And she hasn't. It just took a while for me to see it. But you know how it is, he says. Insufficient information never stopped anyone from falling in love. In fact, it's pretty much a prerequisite.

True, she says. Very true.

Can I say something else I don't like about her?

No, she says. Or, you can, but you have to say another nice thing first.

Fine. She's a generous and patient caretaker to her aging parents. Also, she's totally lost interest in sex.

But you just said—

I know. We do have sex. She even initiates sometimes, which totally stumps me. Because she doesn't want it. She doesn't delight in it anymore.

Has she said that?

She doesn't have to. Her mind is clearly elsewhere, every time. I'll have just finished—making sure she came first, of course—

Such a gentleman.

I do try. Anyway, I've just finished, I'm lying there trying to catch my breath, gather my wits. I'm feeling replete, it's very quiet.

Then out of nowhere, she'll say something like, Did you remember to call the guy about the tuckpointing?

Jenny laughs, choking on her wine.

How long she's been thinking about the tuckpointing guy I don't know. But she's moved on from our mutual pleasure. I haven't. I need a minute.

Because of the loneliness, she says.

Because of the loneliness, exactly. I want to rest inside her, me and my poor, detumescing cock. I don't want to discuss home renovations. But if I dawdle, pretty soon I feel this two-pat, quick, on my ass. *Pat-pat.* Like, that's it, bud. Pack it in.

She laughs again. She can't help it.

And so I do, of course. I pack it in. I get the message: she's not into it. Or me.

Is that what you meant when you said her beauty doesn't do you much good?

Did I say that?

Yes, just now. You don't get to enjoy it, linger with it?

There's definitely no lingering, he says. What did I mean? I appreciate her beauty. I see it. But I suppose . . . it doesn't move me anymore. Not the way it used to.

Maybe that's why she's thinking about the tuckpointing. She knows you're not really thinking about her.

But I am.

Not in the same way, she says. Not if she doesn't move you.

He stares at her, irritated by her presumption. Until something changes.

His shoulders slump. He looks dejected.

You nailed it, Jenny. We've lost something, Caroline and I. Obviously, or I wouldn't be here. I can't seem to articulate it— I don't know why I'm even trying. It's not that her beauty, her body doesn't do me any good. It's that I don't do her any good. She doesn't touch me anymore. She hasn't for ages, since long before you and I . . .

He's on his feet now, heading for the minibar. But he changes his mind and swerves back to the bed.

It's very difficult to be *moved*, to be attracted to someone who has no interest in you, someone who . . . you know, sometimes I touch her, and she flinches? Actually flinches. We don't embrace, or hold hands. But the worst thing about it—the very worst? It's only when we're alone. When we're around other people, she touches me plenty. Flirts with me, even. Not because she wants to, or even to please me. She's putting on a show. The Nick and Caroline Show—look at the happy couple! Which we are, that's the killer of it all, we're generally content. But in this one way, this one very vital, necessary way . . .

He sighs. Scratches his cheek. Frowns at the television without really seeing it.

It sucks, he says. To live with someone every day, she's right there, and she doesn't want to touch me. It really sucks.

She nods, taking that in for a moment.

Then she stands and comes over to him.

She takes his hand. She brings it to her lips and kisses it.

Well, I think she's missing out, she says.

twelve

She kissed his hand! And now she's smiling at him. He doesn't deserve her kindness, he's been a thousand varieties of bastard to her tonight, but he'll take it.

He watches her move away, moseying to the window. Caroline would lose her mind if she knew Nick was telling tales about their sex life, especially to the woman who—okay, but Jenny hounded him into it. He feels a roil of unease, the sour aftertaste of having shared too much—oh, the horror!—and he's tempted to flee to his mock-heroic mode, to kiss her hand in turn and say *why thank you, kind lady, how gracious, how bounteous is your rue* or some equivalent horseshit.

But he resists.

He didn't hate laying it all out like that. He felt some queasiness, mild skin-crawling. Provoking her sympathy didn't feel pleasant, in other words, he hasn't seen the light and begun some transformation into a different person, a Good Guy, one of those sincere characters who go around being emotionally available and practicing gratitude and whatever the fuck else they do, he doesn't know because he's not one of them.

Still. He's feeling okay right now.

Tell me something, she says.

And now she's going to ruin it!

Why not make a change? she says. Find someone who can be all that for you—the worldview, and the compatibility, and the touch. Not me, obviously, but . . . marriages end all the time. If you're dissatisfied, why stay?

I might not have a choice after tonight, he says. Jenny has no idea how comprehensively, how expertly Caroline is going to rake his ass over the coals if—when, come on, you know it's when—the truth comes out. Yes, it's going to be a big old Holloway barbecue, far toastier than anything he might encounter down on twenty-one.

Speaking of which. He glances at the television. The anchors are checking in with the hot reporter, but seem disappointed she has no juicy new details to convey. Should he call the number they gave him? No, it's too soon. He doesn't want to unsettle Jenny. Though he does wish that firefighter, or command coordinator or whatever the hell title the caller used, he does wish the guy had expressed a little more confidence about the situation. Been a bit heartier. He had the perfect New Yawk accent for bluff assurance. While he listened Nick could practically see his salt-and-pepper mustache bobbing up and down. But his words had been flat. Careful. Just the facts, sir.

Overall, the conversation hadn't been quite as reassuring as he'd implied to Jenny. Not that he'd misrepresented anything—no more lies!—but there had been a hesitation. A hedginess.

Or he's reading too much into it. Professional reserve, that's what it was. A reluctance to be pinned down to specifics. He can relate.

It doesn't matter. They're going to be fine.

Unlike his marriage. Yes, he's in for it. As he should be. He is the villain, after all. Though he did try to be discreet. He never wanted to humiliate her. Now it seems inevitable, and he's sorry. Caroline will never show it, she'll never crack—they're alike in that way, too. But he has failed her. And behind the cold scorn and lashing indifference she will be hurt, terribly.

Especially by his choice of partner.

Did you know one of our neighbors published a book? she said one Saturday morning, two or three years ago.

He felt every muscle, every cell in his body, tense up. He took a long sip of coffee, playing for time.

You mean Roger's tax manual? he said.

God no. A novel. Becca Dodge's friend wrote it. Jenny something. The woman with the two demon children?

I have no idea who you're talking about, he said, hating himself.

Caroline persisted. She was at the Keanes' Labor Day thing. Dark hair, a laugh that's a little too loud—

Not ringing a bell, he said. Do you want me to take Jill to tennis?

She's already at tennis. I'm going to pick up a copy—Becca says it's fabulous. Do you need anything from the bookstore?

She stood at the kitchen island, waiting for his answer, looking so innocent. Did she not remember berating him just a few months earlier for buying Jill the very book they were now discussing? Had she, instead, found his copy in the back of the filing cabinet in his office upstairs, done a little digging, made a few elementary deductions? Did she, in fact, know everything, but rather than confront him was engaging in some elaborate psyops for her own amusement, before very justifiably kicking his ass to the curb?

I'm good, he said. She nodded. The conversation moved on.

Until she came charging into his office the next weekend, startling the hell out of him as he stood at the window, lost in thought, looking down at the Parks' back porch.

This is amazing! She was holding up Jenny's book.

Oh, that book? he said. I bought it for Jill, remember? You said it was too mature, so I—

Well it is, for her. Maybe in a few years. She thrust it at him. Look at the photo—don't you recognize her?

He flipped to the back, feeling his heart kick up. Though he was pretty sure he was in the clear. Caroline's enthusiasm was too genuine for this to be some twisted game.

She does look familiar, he said, handing the book back.

She thumbed through it, stopping to read a paragraph, smiling. She's so talented.

Good for her. Hey, did you pay the water bill?

We should have them over, Caroline said.

Jesus Christ!

Fortunately, that never came to pass. Jenny soon got busy with her massive success, becoming scarcer at social gatherings. When they did meet, Caroline was struck with uncharacteristic shyness, which manifested as hauteur. But she continued to think the world of Jenny.

It's been translated into thirty languages, she said. She's about to come out with a second one. She's pretty, too. Don't you think she's pretty? Nick?

So yes, that disclosure is going to sting. And his marriage is going to end. He'll have to start over. That sounds fun. Find someone new. *Not me, obviously,* Jenny just said. Thanks, he's well aware. She made clear the limited boundaries of their arrangement long ago, the time he suggested they meet more often. The look on her face . . . he'd quickly backtracked. Which was fine. But the point is, no. Not her, obviously.

Plus, it would never work—the two of them, as a legitimate couple. Nobody trusts a relationship founded on cheating, especially the people in it. And they have nothing in common. Only the body thing. The sex. Which never lasts. He had it with Caroline, too, long ago. And not just the sex—she was everything. She made him believe for a while that he hadn't screwed up his life, coming home from England. That he'd made the right decision, because he'd found her.

And now he's going to lose her. He will be scourged, shunned by friends and family, a mongrel skulking away from the community of the righteous, the decent—aka the cowardly and the not-yet-caught. He'll have to move back to the city, the suburbs being too depressing for a single man, a Sad Dad. Jill will hate him. Hate him, reject therapy, start vaping, acquire an eating disorder, be groomed by a youth sports coach and hop onto a carousel of addictions.

What? Calm down. Jill is great. She's a good person. He's not sure how that happened, but he'll take it. And she loves her dad. She'll despise him for a while, sure, but she's a teenager. She despises him every other day as it is. He'll win her back. Though some other man will be arriving promptly to help raise her, because Caroline will replace him right fucking quick.

He feels a pang, thinking of his girl. His Jilly. He only has three more years of her in his daily life, then she's off to college. He can't miss that time. Why is he assuming he will? Yes, Caroline might find out, but that doesn't mean they're through. People get over this sort of thing. He'll repent, he'll plead and persuade. He's a persuasive bastard, it's how he got her to go out with him in the first place. He will atone. Whatever it takes.

He'll have to give up Jenny. But he's given her up several times tonight already. He can do it for real. It's fitting punishment.

What about her? Will she suffer if Tom leaves her? She doesn't seem concerned by the prospect. Which makes sense. Tom's such a zero.

Your turn, he says. Tell me something you love about Tommy boy.

She's sitting cross-legged on the sofa. He's an amazing cook, she says.

Good man. What's something you hate?

He lost half of our money in crypto.

Beg pardon?

She nods.

He is motionless. Staring at her. You're joking, he says.

I wish I were.

He gets up and walks to the window. Walks back.

Please tell me you're joking.

I can't, she says. I'm not.

Okay. He's frowning, raking his fingers through his hair, trying to work this out. Okay. But when you say half of *our* money, you mean your joint savings, right, not your money, what you earned from your—

Everything, she says. Including the royalties from my first book.

What the *fuck*? he cries. What the fuck was he thinking?

He thought he was setting us up for life, she says.

He's pacing the room, beside himself. He stops, struck by a horrible thought.

This is why you took all the toiletries! You're broke!

No! She laughs. Honestly, it's not that bad.

She's laughing! Sitting there so placidly.

Why am I the one freaking out here? he demands. How can you be so calm?

I wasn't at the time, trust me. But it was a while ago, after the first big crypto crash. Or maybe the second. It's hard to keep track. Anyway, I got over it.

You were supposed to be buying that house on Mountainview, he says, remembering. The historic place. Everybody was talking about it. Then you didn't.

We're staying on Tuxedo for now. I don't mind—I love our house. And we have plenty of money, especially with the final book coming out, and the movie stuff. Plus we have a financial adviser now, so . . . we're fine.

You never told me, he says. You never said a word.

Why would I?

That stops him. He stands before her, head cocked.

Why would you, he repeats. Interesting. So, fair to say I'm not the only one of us who leaves my shit at the door?

She rolls her eyes and goes over to the nightstand. She reaches for his phone, then changes her mind and veers to the window.

Did he do it on purpose? he asks.

Tom? No way!

Are you sure? Maybe he was threatened by your success.

He's not like that. He's delighted for me. For us. He encouraged me to write for years. When I finally buckled down and did it, he was thrilled.

Does he read your books?

He does. Teen romance doesn't exactly thrill him to the marrow—you guys have that in common—but he's very helpful.

Tom must have read the third book already. He pissed away the money she earned, yet he gets to know how the cliffhanger at the end of the second book resolves. And how the whole story ends. Bastard!

She drifts back to the nightstand. He watches her pick up his phone and swipe it awake. A lock of dark hair falls against her face.

Tom's not a bastard. He's an overgrown boy, with boyish enthusiasms like motorcycles, and fantasy football. Mystifying. But Jenny is fond of him. She shows none of that smug superiority some women have for their husbands, whom they seem to tolerate only so they have someone around to gently deride, and ask to open jars. Even when she was describing Tom's masterful financial moves, it was obvious she cares about him.

Do they still have sex? Does she flinch when he touches her? She writes about romance so beautifully. She nails the experience of falling in love. He knows novelists have imaginations, they're not all memoirists. But when she writes about love, is she writing about Tom?

Surely not. Because why would she be here?

What are you looking at? he asks, because she's glued to his phone again.

News sites, she says. Social media. A retired fireman on Twitter is providing a blow-by-blow of what the fire department is doing. Other people are posting videos from downstairs.

He glances at the nightstand clock. It's almost one. These people don't have anything better to do?

Apparently not. You were right, by the way. Everyone's trying to figure out whether there are celebrities in peril. Apparently Helen Mirren stayed here over the weekend.

Helen Mirren! Why couldn't she come to our door in a bathrobe?

She smiles and keeps scrolling. He returns once again to the minibar. Not hungry or thirsty. Just bored. He hadn't described it well. How he and Caroline had changed. The poverty of their sex life, the loss of touch—those are easy gripes. Sticking to the surface allowed him to avoid the bleaker truths.

They are still excellent partners. They feel strong affection for each other, regard and respect, love of a kind. But, love *of a kind*? What bullshit is that? He doesn't want love *of a kind*. He wants what they used to have. Love, flat-out, impetuous and overwhelming. Love that makes you feel like you're going to die, that makes you feel like a god, not that you'd ever admit that out loud because it's so embarrassing, so cringe as the kids say nowadays, but it doesn't matter what the kids say, what anyone says.

Because you're in fucking *love*!

Or, you were. It's gone now, that love—when had that happened, how, surely he was to blame, was he to blame? Passion had been watered down to affection.

Affection. Jesus Christ.

Love is the most powerful thing in the world when you're young. It's tidal, it capsizes you. You've found the One, the necessary, inevitable other, good God it's a miracle! You cling, you coalesce, you build a life. Then somewhere along the way, somehow, love dies. The deathless thing, the best fucking thing, just slips out the back one day.

What a scam.

Does Caroline feel scammed? Does she miss what they had? She must, if she loves Jenny's books so much. He came upon her not so long ago, reading the second one. She looked up at him, eyes shining.

She gets it, Caroline said. She really captures it. How it feels, to . . .

She trailed off, looking down at the page.

He didn't ask what she meant.

He knew.

A pleading voice is coming out of his phone.

What is that? he asks.

A TikTok posted by a woman looking for her daughter, Jenny says. She lost track of her as they came downstairs. She thought she'd find her when she got outside, but . . .

Enough, Jenny. Give me the phone.

She snorts. Fuck off, Dad.

Fuck off, he says. Go to hell, Nick. You've never sworn at me like this.

Sure I have, she says. Inside my head I have.

Is that right?

She taps her forehead. It's a raging river of obscenity in here.

She looks up from the phone, and they smile at each other. But the pleading voice calls her back. She sighs and taps the screen.

Love slips out the back, huh? Love's a scam? How convenient: endowing love with volition, blaming it for disappearing, when surely he was the problem. Him and his struggle, what he would come to call his malaise. He was thirty-six, thirty-seven when it started. Jill had just started first grade. They showed up for Parents' Night, and when he entered her classroom a hundred sense memories of his own elementary school reared up and knocked him sideways. The squeak of shoes on the floor, the colorful corrugated borders on the bulletin boards. And the smell—the smell was *exactly* the same.

He took it all in and was overwhelmed—swamped—with regret.

Because it was over for him. The hopefulness of youth. Possibility. He'd lost his chance when he came home from England fifteen years earlier, scurried home, running headlong into this life. *My prime of youth is but a frost of cares.* Because of course he would find the perfect poem to reflect his mood, a knack that only reminded him of what he'd really wanted, what he'd lost and could never get back.

So he was one, swamped, and two, infuriated at himself. Because as tormenting as the malaise that had descended was his awareness that it was *all so fucking ordinary.* He was an unremarkable man, wallowing in the most banal self-pity. He had everything. This was when life was supposed to be roses. Instead, it was fucking . . . carnations, it was dull autumn mums, and he was a miserable cliché. Cultivating a midlife crisis, bang on schedule. Good job, golden boy.

And though he tried to hide it—the sense of loss, the self-loathing provoked by the sense of loss, a meta-malaise, how sophisticated—it must have showed. The disappointment and self-disgust must have emanated off him, like a stink. Surely that's why Caroline lost interest. Pulled away. Started flinching.

Unless their growing distance was part of what prompted his struggle in the first place.

Which came first, the bullshit or the asshole?

Impossible to say.

He hadn't even begun to describe to Jenny how awful it was. No physical closeness with Caroline, no warmth. He still had Jill, his girl who wrapped her arms around his neck and kissed his cheek and told him he needed to shave, which was heaven, but not the same. Not the same.

To want without being wanted. It's the worst.

And so he muddled on for a while, several years in fact, an ungrateful cretin trapped in an enviable life. Another New Year's Eve came around. Their next-door neighbors threw a party. Everybody got dressed up and left the kids at home. People let loose. Dancing, drinking like they were back in college, smoking pot—naughty parents!

Loud talk, loud laughter.

Good, good times.

He wanted to kill himself.

Not that it showed. Caroline wasn't the only one who knew a thing or two about appearances. He was, as always, clever Nick Holloway, full of funny rants and stories and entertaining conversation.

Reliably amusing.

Quietly annihilated.

Because he looked around the party, at his friends and neighbors, and he knew nothing was ever going to change. These were his people, this was his life. Despair descended, choking and bleak. Then fury at himself for being so goddamn tiresome. He tumbled once more down the spiral, all by himself, because in this crowd of revelers he was alone, alone, he would always be alone.

He tried to rally the troops. Come on men! Look alive! He had a drink, then another, then three more in quick succession. Maybe they'd help lift the malaise from the cluttered seabed where it had lodged, raise it up so it could float away.

What has greater density—despair or Johnnie Walker? Let's find out, boys!

And so he got drunk. Drunk enough, around two in the morning, to go looking for the mildly (okay, intensely) alluring stranger he'd been trying so hard not to notice for the previous year and a half.

He'd never gotten to know her, the woman who'd snagged in his mind, with her smile, her hapless charm. He'd kept his distance, not wanting to go *there*, didn't he have troubles enough? Yes, but just now he needed a kind face. She had one. And she was funny, wasn't she? He thought she might be. Hot, too, but that was irrelevant. Was she even at the party? He thought he'd spotted her husband earlier. He'd track her down, they'd have a friendly chat. That's all he wanted.

He found her at last in the kitchen, getting a glass of water at the sink. It was the year women wore their necklaces close at their throats and hanging down their backs. She was in black, a long loop of pearls falling between her shoulder blades. Her hair was up.

He stood right behind her and inhaled deeply. He couldn't smell a thing—maybe because he was soaked in booze. As she reached for the tap her dress shifted, exposing a bra strap.

Good God! *An erring lace! A sweet disorder in the dress. A something something wild civility.* Who wrote that?

Who fucking cares?

She turned the tap off, and her necklace shifted. He wanted to pluck it up, wrap it around his hand, hold it like reins and bend her over.

He couldn't. He wouldn't!

But if he could. That would be life.

'Twould be life.

Christ he was hammered.

Which is why, rather than clear his throat, or tap her on the shoulder, or back quietly away from her and from a potentially reputation-destroying error—instead of choosing any of those sane and respectable courses of action, he picked up the end of her long strand of pearls and put it in his mouth.

She must have felt the necklace move. He saw a hand go up and touch her throat.

Then she turned, to find him standing right on top of her.

With her necklace in his mouth.

Her eyes went round and baffled. Of course they did!

He spit out the pearls.

He stood before her, hands at his sides, helpless.

Instantly, horribly sober. And fucked.

So fucked!

But she didn't scream, or kick him in the nuts. She took his hand and led him out the back door, onto the deck. It was freezing. She pulled him into the shadow of the roof overhang. He stumbled, bumped into her, he didn't know what to do.

She leaned against the side of the house and guided his hand to her hip. Oh, that's, yes, that's a woman's hip, warm under the slippery black fabric. Her hand on top of his, holding it there. He put his other hand on her neck, his fingers skimming up the nape, into her hair. It was so dark he could barely see her. Their breath clouded between them whitely.

He leaned in. Pressed his lips to hers. They were dry. Then their mouths opened, and . . .

Well, it was bad, frankly.

It was fucking awful.

Teeth knocking, noses bumping. He made some critical mistakes with his tongue.

But they didn't give up. They were old enough to know you have to be patient sometimes, you have to adjust. So they adjusted.

Then something clicked, and good God.

It was tremendous.

They made out for ten minutes. He put his hand up her dress. She pushed it back down, which, fair. She did let him have a go at a boob, though. Thank you, gentle lady, oh thank you, his first encounter with her perfect, her exquisite . . . he was a teenager again, feeling up a girl for the first time. She pressed herself against his erection. Who was this woman? Why was she giving him this gift? He felt her hand on the back of his neck. Her fingers in his hair.

I will do this forever, he thought. For the rest of my life, I will be here, on Tim Park's back porch, kissing this delicious, this beautiful and generous stranger.

Then a door slammed, somewhere in the house.

They broke apart.

Wait, she said.

She slipped inside.

He waited.

She didn't come back.

Well, he thought blearily, stumbling home across his lawn later that night, that's that. She came to her senses, a delayed but perfectly reasonable reaction to having some pathetic slob's desperation foisted on her. He hoped she didn't feel assaulted, or regret it too much.

He hoped she wouldn't talk.

He was exalted and more depressed than ever. He would never do anything like that again. It was too risky. It was wrong.

Three days later, she texted him. He still doesn't know how she got his number.

And six years later, here they are. She's improved his life so much. *Changed me fundamentally?* No, but she's been such a balm for the lack of touch, of warmth. For the fewer tomorrows than yesterdays. She vanquished the malaise, helping him to be a better human. A better version of who he's supposed to be when she's not around.

Life works now. His marriage works. He'll have to find a way to keep them both working. But she should leave Tom. She can do so much better.

He'll find her a good divorce lawyer. The best.

thirteen

Jenny, please put the damn phone away.

He's back on the bed, legs outstretched. She's hovering by the window, watching another video. She looks troubled.

He wishes the fire department guy had been more reassuring.

I'm sorry, she says, I—

Look at these fools. He points at the television, where the two studio anchors are yapping about the Oscars. They haven't cut back to the fire for twenty minutes. Because nothing's happening. It's a waiting game at this point.

He hopes he's right. He plumps a pillow for her. She takes a seat beside him, setting the phone on the nightstand.

Let's talk about something else, he says. Do you and the Crypto King still sleep together?

Nick.

Let me rephrase. How's your marital sex life?

Good, she says. It's very . . . solid.

Solid. So, you enjoy it? You don't ask him about the tuck-pointing?

Oh, I ask him about the tuckpointing all the time, she says. It's our dirty talk.

Is that right?

All those crumbling bricks, and tight crevices? She wiggles a little. Ooh, baby.

Nice, he says, heading for the minibar, not to get a drink but so that he can covertly adjust himself, because fucking hell if she hasn't made him hard by talking about tuckpointing.

Tight crevices!

You do all right then, he says, stooping to peer into the fridge. You never need to fake orgasms with him, or fake faking orgasms, for utterly obscure reasons?

Is there something you'd like to talk about, Nick?

Nope! He pulls out a can of ginger ale, looks for a fresh glass. He meant what he said about wiping the slate clean. Though . . . it's slightly infuriating that she'll jerk him around to no evident purpose, but when it comes to her husband and their apparently quite satisfactory love life, she doesn't play games, or—

Let it go.

He sits in the desk chair, propping his feet on the bed and crossing his ankles.

A solid sex life, he says. That's great. So, no problems. No complaints.

I didn't say that, she says.

Ha! He knew it!

It's nothing major, she adds. But Tom can be a little . . .

Inept? he suggests. Impotent? Microphallic?

Nick, she says.

What?

I know you don't like him, but you don't have to be mean.

Tom's fine, he says. I like Tom.

She laughs. Sure you do.

Go ahead. I won't interrupt.

But she waves him off. We shouldn't be talking about this. We're breaking the rules.

What rules?

What rules? she scoffs. You know what rules. We don't talk about our spouses.

We just did! he protested. We took turns.

That was a one-off.

Fine, he says. We'll stop. Right after you describe Tom's massive failings in bed.

She only laughs at that. She reaches for his phone again, notices him watching her, gives him the finger. Flipping him the bird—what's that about? There's a fizzy energy between them. Is it the fraught situation, or all the things they've been telling each other? He shouldn't have asked about her sex life. He's still hard from the tuckpointing thing. He'll probably never be able to look at brickwork again without getting aroused. Will the torment ever end? His penis doesn't care about her lies and evasions, their shouting match, her great anxiety, even his own concern about the fire.

His penis *does not care.*

They're still dressed from their attempted flight. He could take off her clothes again. All those little buttons. He loves to strip her naked. He doesn't usually get to do it twice in one night. Actually, this would be the third time, thanks to her first, Herve-driven effort to flee.

A third disrobing. Glorious!

Would she let him? Is she game?

You asked why I don't make a change, he says. Why did you stick with Tom when he cheated on you? Was it the kids? A religious scruple?

She gives him a wry look. You mean obedience to my international crime syndicate?

What? I never called it that.

Nick, she says. You've called the Catholic Church that literally dozens of times.

Sorry. But is that the issue?

He shifts in the chair, uncrosses his legs to ease the pressure. Why is he bringing up religion? Jenny's Catholicism, the faith that's so wonderfully, voluptuously specific concerning its carnal proscriptions. Concerning lust.

Such a great word, *lust*. It sounds rich and dirty, feels exactly as it should in the mouth.

Lust. Lust. He mouths the word.

Lust.

No, she says. It was more personal than the church.

The church. Jenny in a church, confessing her sins in a whisper. Her erotic crimes. Getting aroused, starting to touch herself, right there in the shadowy confessional—

I made a promise, she says. To Tom. And to the family we planned on having. It was a commitment, you know? It was—is—very important to me. To stick to it. No matter how much either of us screws up.

He nods, trying to listen, but he's distracted because in his head he's taking her from behind in front of a baroque altar, the scent of candles is overpowering, chanting echoes through the cathedral from some nearby monks.

Monks? He needs to stop. He needs to pull out of Sister Jenny right now and—

So it's more about the social contract, he says. You agreed to a set of terms and conditions, mutual rights, and you feel honor bound to abide by them.

Well, except I haven't been abiding by them for years, she says.

Maybe not all the terms, but that doesn't mean you're in breach of the entire agreement. Or that you're willing to terminate.

This is becoming very legalistic, she says.

It is, because he thought using dry, analytical terms like *terminate* and *mutual rights* might quell his now-raging horniness. Instead he finds himself in a courtroom, fucking her on a file-strewn counsel's table in view of the jury, she's wearing a skirt suit, and her legs are—

To recap, he says. You won't leave him, but you'll cheat on him. Why?

Well well, she says, smiling at him. Look who's attacking the bulwarks.

Bulkheads, he says, smiling back at her. And look who's deflecting.

Me? Never! She stands. But I do have to pee.

Back to the old throne room. In and out this time, though, no loitering. Because she's really not deflecting—she has a small bladder! She'll tell him whatever he wants to know.

Does he really want to know anything, though, or is he tit-for-tatting, maintaining the balance between them? As if there's ever been a balance.

Okay, maybe she'll loiter a little. She brought his phone with her—she scrolls through the latest videos taken outside the building. So many fire trucks. But the crowd seems thinner. Gawkers getting cold, and bored—that's a good sign. She's certainly not bored, though she's felt surprisingly calm this last little while. Flares of panic few and far between. The call from the fire department helped.

She should check on Edvin. She dials her number. Sorry, Norman's number. What was Nick's suggestion for a new phone pseudonym? Aphrodite of the what?

Also, Best Sex Partner Ever? Is that true?

The phone rings and rings.

Then it goes to voicemail.

That's unfortunate. That's unsettling. She rises and flushes and goes to the sink.

Caroline doesn't enjoy sleeping with him. Does she find him too demanding? Maybe it's gotten stale, too familiar. But she and Tom are familiar, and she still enjoys sex with him. Though it's different. She's different. Tom would probably love to meet Best-Sex-Partner-Ever Jenny, Aphrodite of the Whatever. But he never has.

How could he? She can't be that Jenny with him. They have a completely different relationship—longer, deeper, encompassing almost every aspect of their shared lives. If she was better in bed, she'd be worse in other ways, the ways that make them work. And she wouldn't even know how to be different. There's

Jenny-with-Tom, and Jenny-with-Nick—women who don't just fuck differently, but talk differently, or at least about different things. Who move differently, probably even think differently.

Which one is real? Or are they both just roles she's playing, and once again there's some baseline Jenny lurking inside, unified and coherent? A just-Jenny, no male modifier required. No lies necessary.

Who knows? Even if there is some primal Jenny, the Jenny out here will never find her. She'll remain a mystery. Like Caroline. So poised and cool. Does that explain her lack of interest in Nick? She could be cold, one of those women who doesn't enjoy okay now you're being sexist. It could be some fundamental physical mismatch, a pheromonal thing. Or maybe Nick is kind of a doofus in Caroline's eyes, the way Tom is a doofus in hers.

There must be a reason. Caroline has a side of the story, after all, her own narrative of their relationship. Full of small grievances, battles not picked. Hills not died on, which nevertheless dot the landscape, reminders of all the accommodations necessary to a functioning marriage. What did he call theirs? A good partnership. One that, if they are found out, will be wrecked.

She doesn't want to touch me. She'd never seen him so undefended. He didn't seem to mind it at the time, but is it bothering him now? Is he this moment being racked by a vulnerability hangover, she's going to go back out and be grilled about whether she made out with an Amtrak conductor on her way into the city and caught herpes?

She scrolls through a few more videos, but they're a waste of time. Like everything on the internet. And like worrying about what Nick is thinking, whether he's uneasy, whether he's this, he's that. His reactions, what's really going on in that big brain of his, have often been her preoccupation. But they're not actually her problem.

She washes her hands and leaves, barely glancing in the mirror.

When she comes back into the main room, he's rifling through the minibar again.

Am I the best sexual partner you've ever had? she asks.

Absolutely, he says. He holds up a bag of chips. Can you believe they want twenty-two dollars for this? It's five ounces of potatoes!

She's about to inquire further—absolutely?—but the television distracts her. The reporter is speaking intently into her microphone.

Juliana looks worried, she says.

He tears open the chips. She's probably just constipated. Unlike you, she hasn't taken a bathroom break for hours.

She unmutes the television.

> *—and after a significant amount of time with no*
> *apparent progress, the hotel is demanding more*
> *information from the FDNY, who, they say, have not*
> *been forthcoming regarding their initial difficulties in*
> *locating the fire.*

That's not good, she says.

It's fine. Our ace reporter is manufacturing a controversy to keep people from changing channels. He holds the bag out. Truffle chip?

When are you going to admit you don't know what you're talking about?

Jenny, come on. I just think—

I know what you just think. It's what you keep just thinking, and saying. It's fine, it's fine! But you have no idea. We're stuck in here, and there are fire trucks *surrounding* the building, which doesn't seem, to me, to be the definition of *fine*.

He sighs. She has vexed him. You know what? Too bad. No— it's good. Let him be vexed. Let him be wearied by her legitimate concerns.

She's done letting him rest easy in his delusions of safety.

> *Employees of the hotel have told us that the slow*
> *preliminary response to the fire stemmed from the*
> *FDNY's decision to send only one unit to investigate the*

initial alarm, after multiple incidents over the weekend
were determined to be false alarms. A source at the
FDNY strongly denied this claim, insisting instead that
unaccountable delays on the part of the hotel's third-
party alarm monitoring service led to—

Let's not fight, he says. We've been doing so well. And much as I'd love it, we can't expect Dame Helen to barge in and separate us if we start going at it again. So let's be friends, okay?

As suddenly as it came, the irritation leaves her. The urge to bicker. Friends. Sure. Whatever.

She scooches up the bed to lean against the headboard. He takes the chair.

Where were we? Right. You were about to tell me why you cheat on your husband.

You don't really care, do you? You're only asking because—

You *are* deflecting, he says. Fascinating.

I'm not! But it's not like I'm used to talking about this, either. I opened up to one friend, years ago, thinking she wouldn't judge me, and, wow. Was I wrong. Don't look so terrified. I didn't tell her your name.

She needs a minute to gather her thoughts. She has many. She's been thinking about this for six years. But talking about it? No. Not since Diane.

You described not being touched, she says. The loneliness of it. Which I get—and it sounds awful. I have—had, really—a different problem. We're talking six, seven years ago, when you and I . . . when this started. You weren't touched? All I was, was touched.

By the boys, he says.

By the boys, yes. Two wonderful, amazing, also exhausting and clingy little boys. They were always *on* me. I was this mother ship. Hugged and pawed and hung off of. Loved, too, of course, but it was like . . . I belonged to them. My body did. To be clear, it was wonderful sometimes, and above all it was the deal, you know? But I didn't expect it. And I couldn't help but think back—no, really *feel* back—to being alone. A single person, living in the city, my time, my body, everything my own. I could walk down the street and I wasn't weighed down by strollers and bags and small articles of clothing. I wasn't this docking station.

You'd lost your autonomy, he says.

I'd given it away! And I was happy to. Mostly. But I did start feeling this occasional, intense irritation. At the end of a long day, after I was mauled and used up. I'm not the only mother who feels this way. It's a big thing online, women who feel overtouched. But for a long time I wasn't even aware it was bothering me. Until one day. Night, actually. I'd put the boys to bed, and I was on the sofa, just zapped, you know, wiped out. After a while, Tom came home—

Cue ominous music, he says.

She laughs. Right. He'd been out somewhere, or working late, I don't remember, but he came home, plopped down beside me, and . . .

She gives her thigh a good, hard slap.

It was a greeting, a friendly thing. But it made this resounding . . . I don't know if the jeans I was wearing were too tight or what, but it made this loud *whack!* And I saw his hand spread there on my leg, pressing down on it a little, and it was like he'd smacked a mare's flank. The sound, the ease with which he did it, so familiar, like, ah, here's my trusty nag! Jenny the Pony.

And I was *stunned*. Remember, I was exhausted, my brain was goo at that point, and so this was probably a complete overreaction, but I felt like I didn't matter. I didn't exist, aside from the parts that could be patted and handled.

So you needed to reclaim your body, he says. Infidelity became an act of feminist rebellion.

Yeah, she says. That's . . . yeah. Basically.

She picks up a half-empty glass of champagne on the night-stand and takes a sip. He's not getting it. She wasn't making some grand statement. She was . . . God, it's impossible to explain. Maybe she doesn't get it either.

She reaches for his phone and calls her number.

It rings and rings.

I don't like that Edvin's not answering, she says.

Try again, he suggests.

She does. Still no answer. They turn to the television, where indefatigable Juliana is doing her damnedest to make compelling news out of the fact that nothing is happening.

He goes into the bathroom and returns with two tumblers. He finds a small ceramic jug of tequila on the liquor shelf and comes to sit beside her on the bed.

You think we should get drunk right now?

Not at all, he says. But I do think we should each have a shot. To relax us. It can't hurt. We probably have hours to go.

Her heart sinks. Hours?

Better they take their time than rush, right?

He cracks the cap and pours. They drink.

Oh, that's nice. It spreads right through her, warming her.

I can't believe that fucker stole my phone, she says. Just took it. Like he was entitled to it.

Men, he says. Am I right?

She holds out her glass. Give me just a splash more.

He does. Tell me, Norm. How is my number saved in your phone?

Under the name Farthead Buttinski, she says.

He laughs. You really are the mother of boys, aren't you?

I really am. But saving you under a name like that would be a terrible idea. They'd find it and start calling you constantly.

They already do, he says. I was talking to Ben the other day, telling him what an astonishing lay his mom is.

Nick! You're disgusting!

That's what Ben said. Should we have more tequila?

Yes, she says. No. Just a little.

He pours. She sips it, savoring it. Mulling over her inadequate explanation. Describing the Tom thing, the thigh slap—that implies the fault was Tom's, when it wasn't.

Poor Tom. Deceived. Disparaged. She'd said he was a good

cook. That was her bit of praise. How is that any more meaningful than Nick loving Caroline because she's beautiful? It's worse, in fact, because it was a setup. She knew she was going to drop the crypto bomb, and that Nick would lose his mind over it. She thought *amazing cook* made a nice contrast.

That's classy. Mocking your husband for the amusement of your . . . of a man who makes no secret of his disdain for him. But Nick's wrong. So wrong. Tom is a gentle, sincere, generous soul. And an *awesome* cook. He's sweet and playful. Not so much lately. Lately he's been a bit down. A bit dark. The crypto thing devastated him. She'd had no idea it was happening, not until he came to her one night with a white, strained face. *Jen? We need to talk.* And her stomach flipped. He knows. Oh God oh God he knows. Then he started talking about money, and her relief was immense. Until he started sobbing.

She lied to Nick when she said she'd been upset about it. She'd never truly cared, not even at the time. Tom lost some of the money she'd earned from books inspired by her love for another man? That's not a screwup. It's justice.

But it happened ages ago. He can't still be down about it. Has he done something else? Should she log in to their accounts?

No way. He's just in a funk. Frustrated with her. You're never home, he'd complained, as she was leaving to go upstate. Even when you're here, you're not here. It wasn't true—she works so hard to be present, to be there for him. He was being shitty and unfair. Still. She should reach out to him. Say hi, tell him she loves him. She'll send him a quick text. She picks up the phone and opens her messages.

But they're not her messages.

Because this is still not her phone.

Panic surges up, quick and hot. She stands, feeling helpless. She can't reach out to the ones she loves. For how much longer? She plugs the phone in to charge, then swings by the door and takes a good long sniff. Still no smoke. She returns to the end of the bed and stares at the television. She finds the remote and starts flipping. No other news channel is covering the fire. That's a good sign, right? That's promising.

Promising, promises . . . she'd made a promise to Tom. What did Nick call it? A social contract. Whatever, Vocab Man. It was a vow. *I do.* Or maybe *I will*, she can't remember which terminology they ultimately settled on for the ceremony, she had a sinus infection that day and was completely zonked out on antihistamines. I do, I will—I promise. And it matters to her that she did that. It means that unless something truly dire happens, she will not call it quits. Because if you buy into the whole marriage thing—which she does, obviously—it's for life, and you have to try. You don't have to be flawless. Marriage is . . . well, it's a challenge. It's an AP course. The most you can hope for is a B. Maybe a B-minus. And that's fine! The semester could last fifty years or more, so you can bomb one test. Or an entire unit! And still pass. Still succeed.

But no dropping. No switching majors. Unless you absolutely must.

Plus, people improve with age. Sometimes. They flower. She flowered. Herve said so. He said she was like a fine wine. What a goof. Maybe Tom hasn't hit his prime yet. *(You must always recognize the years of your prime, girls.)* She has to wait for that. Because she promised. Promised to be there. Even though she's not really there much anymore. With him. For him.

Is she just like Caroline? God no. She touches Tom, she doesn't flinch, she . . . she's trying.

He'll be so hurt, if Nick's right and they're about to be busted. But they'll get through it. Not as easily as they got through Tom's lapse, but they'll survive. Will he leave her? Surely not.

Probably not.

How did you get my number? Nick asks now.

What?

Way back. After the party. Who gave you my phone number?

Caroline, she says. I introduced myself for the fortieth time at

Pilates and said I wanted to make out with you some more. She handed it right over.

Their infamous New Year's Eve. What a shock that had been. This guy? The one she always noticed, who she glanced around for when they showed up at a party? He'd barely said ten words to her in two years. There he was, right up in her business. And so drunk! She worried later that she'd taken advantage, dragging him out onto the porch. At the time, though, she didn't care. She was so pissed. Because it had happened again.

A few hours earlier, she and Tom had walked through the door and were set upon by a sky-high Marla Park, who started raving about how great Jenny looked. *Cocktail attire!* the evite had said, and for the first time in a long time, she'd made an effort. It was New Year's, she'd lost the last of the Natey weight, so she put her hair up and crammed herself into an LBD from the old days. Tom stood beside her, listening to Marla's compliments. He grinned, put a hand on the back of Jenny's neck, and squeezed. Gave her a little shake.

And she dropped dead.

Right there in the Parks' foyer.

Not because what he'd done was controlling, or possessive. No, she died because she'd seen him do the same thing to their golden retriever. Grab her around the collar and give her a shake, like, *you scamp!* It was friendly. *Love ya, cutie!* Trixie didn't mind, Trixie fricking loved the attention. But Jenny minded. She didn't want to be a dog, or a horse. She wanted to be a woman. Clichéd as it sounded it was what she wanted and what she hadn't been for years. She longed to be Jenny again. Walking down a city street, arms swinging. Free and full of possibility.

So a few hours later, when she turned and found Nick standing behind her with her necklace in his mouth, well, it wasn't exactly a gesture of grand romance, but it would do.

It would have to do.

Was it revenge? On Tom, and his pats and shakes? No. But it

was a reaction. Tom put his hands on her. Nick had only touched her pearls. She's the one who pulled him outside. Kissed him. A few days later, texted him. And a week after that, took a train into the city to meet him.

She walked from Penn to a hotel near Gramercy, a place that's closed now. I am on my way to an assignation, she thought, and laughed at herself. Idiot! But she felt different. The world looked different, too, tinted by her secret knowledge. I am on my way to meet a man. A man who has no right to me, nor I to him.

It was a terrible idea. She barely knew the guy! But it would be just the one time. One adventure, one slip. Hardly a slip—Tom always said it would be okay. *If you ever feel like you want to get even, I'll understand.* Like betrayal was a game, with a score to be balanced. She brushed it off. She never wanted to get even. But she did want this.

So Tomwise, she was in the clear. As for Nick's beautiful, forbidding wife, well, Jenny felt awful, but again—it would be just the one time! And Nick said he would be discreet.

Thus did she push her qualms aside and do, for the first time in a long time, something purely for herself. The fact that it was wrong, well, that was unfortunate. Or maybe it was exactly why this was the thing she had to do. What better way to assert her freedom, her right to her own body, than by using it in a way she was absolutely not supposed to?

To be an individual again. That's what she wanted. Not part of a family unit, not mother or wife, but her own, owned self. That's why she did it.

Feminist rebellion? Please.

She just needed a little fricking privacy.

The hotel bar was crowded when she slipped in. He was ordering a drink, his back to the door. When he turned, she was looking right at him. And she saw it.

The terror.

He was terrified!

Then they were upstairs, kissing and undressing each other. She had forgotten what it was like to unbutton a man's shirt. To pluck up the crisp cotton, feel it in her fingers, push the thick, translucent buttons through their holes one by one, exposing the chest underneath. A new body. And she was new, too. To him and to herself.

He was far unsteadier than her, that first time. But it didn't take him long to pull himself together. As they kept meeting (just the one time? oh you sweet innocent!), they became themselves. He grew bossy and secure. She retreated a little, lost that heady feeling of control.

Still, she never forgot what a boy he was, that first time. How uncertain. And out on the porch, too, the way she'd had to practically show him what to do.

Does he remember? He's probably told himself a different story.

She says none of this to him now—it's too much, too complicated—but he's obviously still thinking about what little she did tell him as he flips through the channels.

So you were slapped, and pawed, you missed being the person you used to be, he says. Why didn't you let Tom know? Wouldn't he have understood?

He might have, she says. I don't know why I didn't tell him. Maybe because that would have been one more thing I had to do. Not only experience the problem, but have to communicate it, then manage his feelings about it. Why should that be my obligation, too?

If he didn't know something was wrong, he couldn't help you.

Kind of you to be defending my husband right now, she says. Why didn't you tell Caroline you needed to be touched, and not just when other people were watching?

Fair point. Seems like a little honest communication might fix all our problems.

Maybe we should try it, she says.

Right now?

Sure. Let's call them.

He smiles, taking up the challenge. Now there's an idea. Who goes first?

We'll tell them at the same time, she says. Have a little group therapy.

I'm in. Where's the phone?

They both turn to the nightstand, see it and lunge for it. She gets there first, grabbing the phone and swiping it awake.

Let's see . . . favorites . . . oh, look! Caroline is listed under her real name. How nice for her. Here. She holds the phone out. You dial.

He takes it. When she answers, we'll loop Tom in.

And tell them the whole truth, she says.

Every bit of it, he agrees.

Their eyes meet.

fourteen

They're smiling.

Daring each other.

His finger hovers over the screen. Moving closer and closer to Caroline's name. Waiting for Jenny to stop him.

He's almost touching it . . .

He breaks first, laughing as he tosses the phone on the bed. She watches it land.

Why can't we do it? she wonders. Show them our true, whole selves. Just put it all out there.

It's too risky, he says. If they knew the truth about us—not just this, but everything we hide, every unkind thought, every untoward impulse—they'd stop loving us. Plus, it's impossible to show ourselves in full. Words are inadequate. Another person will never truly understand what's going on in your mind. He taps his forehead. We're alone in here. Inescapably partitioned.

She looks out the window, depressed suddenly. They're alone. Not just the two of them, but everyone. A collection of separate souls, little self-pods, careening around the universe. Banging off one another, or missing one another completely. Never uniting. Always lying.

Why must they lie?

Because the truth is impossible.

Is it, though?

Let's try, she says. Tell me something monstrous. Something you've never told anyone.

He leans back in the chair, yawning, thinking it over. He doesn't resist, or imply by his expression that she's a nosy pest. Has she worn him down, vanquished his balustrades? Not balustrades—she keeps forgetting his nerdy boat word. Is he starting to feel more comfortable opening up, confiding the secrets of his innermost heart?

I love jerking off to your author photo, he says.

She is speechless.

I do it a lot, he adds. And by a lot, I mean, a lot.

She bursts out laughing.

It's such a great photo, Jenny. Do you even realize?

Did you buy a copy of my book?

Multiple copies, he says. One for every bathroom in the house. One for my car, my office, the backyard shed . . .

Nick!

I'm probably why you're still on the bestseller list, he says.

You perv! They're YA novels. I'm supposed to look kind, and friendly. Not sexy.

That's what's so fantastic about it. You're so demure, but with this hint of sluttiness—

What?

The way your head is tilted, he says, that lacy collar on your blouse, good God, and how your hands are crossed in your lap—

You've really studied it.

Two to three times a week, he says. Sometimes oftener.

She falls back on the bed and howls.

He comes over, stretching along the bottom of the bed at her feet. I can't be alone in finding that picture irresistible, he says. Trust me—in bunk beds and bathrooms across the land, in camp cabins, school libraries, juvenile detention facilities, Young Adults are rubbing themselves raw to that toothy smile of yours.

She lifts her head. Is my smile toothy?

That's your takeaway here?

She props herself on her elbows. Do people in real life know what a depraved horndog you are?

Alas, he sighs. Passing few.

Because God forbid you reveal your true self to someone, right?

Hey. He flicks the bottom of her foot. Be nice.

You wouldn't know it to look at you, she says. You look so normal.

Tone it down with the compliments, okay? You're making me blush.

It's true, though. It always throws her when they run into each other out in the world. When he's clothed, ironed and spectacled, dropping Jill at the town pool, holding a drink at a party. Seeing him that way, who would believe he's such a filthy-minded, dirty-mouthed sex fiend? Ardent, endlessly inventive, so wholly, utterly intent on . . .

She shouldn't be thinking about his sex fiendishness.

Or sex, period.

She's stopping. Right now.

Stopping thinking about it.

Your turn, he says.

What's that?

He's inspecting her toes. Tell me your deepest, darkest secret.

Well, the choice is obvious. And impossible.

Though what if she did? What if she unloaded the biggie on him?

A few months after we started sleeping together, I fell seriously, ridiculously in love with you.

Preferably sexual, he adds.

I was completely infatuated. Then I started writing, to try to channel it.

She won't tell him, of course. But imagine his reaction.

It would Blow. His. Mind.

Even more than the crypto thing.

Don't worry, I forced myself to fall back out again.

But for about six months?

I loved the shit out of you.

You're smiling. He holds her ankle lightly, gives it a shake. It must be good.

Well . . .

But of course she won't. She'll never tell him. That secret belongs to her alone.

He hasn't let go of her ankle. Speak, woman!

Instead she glances at the television. Firemen are hurrying into the building. Is something happening? She sits up and reaches for his phone.

He sighs. You and that fucking phone.

She feels a flash of irritation. Right, I forgot, she says. You want me to be bothered by what bothers you, our chances of getting busted, but not what bothers me, our chances of dying.

Dying? Jesus, Jenny, we're not dying.

She checks her go-to sites. No updates. She glances at the television. Was it nothing?

Hey, he says.

She's scrolling through her social media feeds, looking for updates from a guy who's been posting videos from outside the hotel. Maybe he saw something.

Jenny.

Hmm?

What say we screw?

She looks up from the phone. He's lounging along the end of the bed, that unmistakable look in his eye. Behind him on the wall, Juliana speaks earnestly into her microphone.

How can you even suggest that?

Why the hell not? he says. You act like there are right and wrong things for us to be doing in this situation. Let's do what we're good at. You can have an orgasm, or fake having one, or fake not having one—ladies' choice, okay?

Her irritation flares. Because he's being a jerk.

And because she does want to sleep with him again.

Maddening!

Okay, but what if they did? A quickie. To distract, get the jitters out and what? No!

What's wrong with you?

I'm trying Edvin again, she says.

Because that's a much better use of your time, he says. Give him my regards.

She dials. It rings.

Once. Twice.

Then the ringing stops. The screen reads:

0:00

0:01

Edvin? she cries. Edvin!

0:02

call ended.

Nick! She jumps up, holding the phone in both hands. He answered! Then the call dropped. Is the reception bad in here?

She moves to the window. He's off the bed, right beside her. She dials again.

It rings. Then:

0:00

0:01

Edvin! she yells. Edvin, are you there?

Silence. No, some kind of rushing sound. Breathing?

Nick leans close. Edvin! Can you hear us?

Auta, says a voice from the phone.

Edvin! she cries. Where are you?

No answer.

Where are you, Edvin? Are you okay?

Auta. The voice is weak and flat.

Tell us where you are! Nick shouts. We can call the fire department. They'll send someone to help you!

They hear nothing in response. Just that rushing, windy sound. Edvin? Edvin!

call ended.

Try him again, Nick says.

But before she can, it happens.

It. What is *it*?

She can't tell, not at first.

The room goes silent.

As if all sound has been sucked out of it. The air feels strange, almost charged, like—

Then comes sound.

A massive boom. Rolling up from below.

So loud, so horribly loud! Like a monster trapped in the center of the earth has broken free and is roaring, mouth wide open, sound pouring out.

It's a blast of sound, an intolerable wall of it.

She drops the phone and presses her hands to her ears. Nick is doing the same.

But the roar continues.

Then the room begins to move.

It doesn't shake, or sway.

It shudders.

A single, slow and queasy shiver. The floor seems to rise, the ceiling to bear down.

Reeling, terror-struck, she turns to the television. People are running. The camera jerks and tilts to the side. Nick is watching, too, hands covering his ears.

Juliana is turning, looking up. Something is falling.

The picture freezes, then turns to snow.

The room is quiet. It's stopped moving.

Is it over? Are they over?

Is everything about to fall down?

No. The ground holds. The noise is gone.

The lights, which had flickered, snap back full force, as does the television. The anchors in the studio look terrified.

> *Our live feed just cut out. We're not sure what . . .*
> *Juliana?*
> *Juliana can you hear us?*
> *Juliana, are you there?*

Jenny takes one stumbling step toward the door.

Then another.

Then she falls to her knees and wraps her arms around her head. Making a noise between a whimper and a howl.

Her fears come back, they come roaring back, like the roar that just filled her ears.

She is doomed.

They are dying. Here.

They are dying here tonight.

fifteen

She becomes aware of him, of his hands, his arms around her, pulling her—where? Up? She doesn't want up, she wants to stay on the floor, grounded, as grounded as she can be so high in the air. Forty-two flights! They are dead. Dead people. She resists his pulling hands, jerks away. More hands, men's hands, won't they leave her alone?

She feels him relent, crouch beside her, holding her huddled, quaking self. He's talking but the stream of words makes no sense, it might as well be Finnish because a blanket has descended, a choking blanket of dread, letting noise in, his voice and the yammering television, but no meaning, no thought.

She is meaningless, thoughtless, and alone, all alone.

She doesn't want to come up on the bed, fine, they'll stay down here. He holds her as close as he can, hunched awkwardly, smoothing her hair.

Jenny, he says. Jennyjennyjennyjenny. Hey. It's over. Try to breathe, okay? Take a deep breath. Can you do that? Can you . . . it's okay. I've got you. We're okay. We're alive.

This is how you calm a panicking person. He remembers it from Jill's birth, that literal bloodbath, how the doctor instructed him to stay close, hold Caroline's hand, talk to her. Low voice. Short sentences. *Model calm*, the ob-gyn had ordered him, as she and the nurses worked to pry the goddamned baby out of his wife's body. It had been twenty hours. Caroline was weak and desperate, certain the baby was dead, it must be dead, why couldn't they find the heartbeat? He couldn't answer that but he could follow the doctor's instructions and hold her, speak simply and quietly to her. It worked then, so he's going to do it again now, hold this woman, soothe her, not hush her—Jesus, no hushing or whoa'ing, ever again—and bring her back to herself.

Jennyjennyjennyjenny. It's okay. We're here. We're here.

But he also needs to find out what the fuck just happened, and whether it's going to happen again. Because that was . . . that was . . . Jesus. Holding on to her is what's keeping him from falling to pieces himself. That's what the doctor explained to him later, when they were sewing up Caroline and he was holding his screaming daughter. *I was trying to stop you from losing it as much as her.*

Right. Well, he didn't lose it then, and he won't now.

He will make a plan.

First, he'll call the number they gave him. Hi there, yeah, just checking in, wondering if you have an ETA on our evacuation, or maybe a best guess as to whether *the building is fucking collapsing?*

Sure, I'll hold.

But he can't get to the phone and comfort Jenny at the same time. He's going to have to coax her into a state of minimal composure before he can move.

Let me go, she says. I have to leave. We have to leave. Nick, let me go. Letmego. Letmegoletmegoletmego.

We can't, honey. Not now. We have to—

She wails, so piteously. Like a lonely animal. He wraps his arms around her and whispers close to her ear.

Jennyjennyjennyjenny. I know, honey. I know. Breathe.

What if she tries to make a break for it? He'll have to hold her down. She can't go, so he'll have to force her to stay. He's never forced a woman to do anything, never dreamed he'd have to. He's held her down plenty of times, plenty of wonderful times, pretended to force himself on her as she pretended to struggle, and she loves it, when he holds her wrists over her head and . . .

But this is different. This is so horribly different.

Still. He can't let her out that door.

So. Step one: calming Jenny.

Step two: calling those fire department fuckers.

Should he also call Jill? Caroline?

What? No. That's hysterical thinking. Premature. The building stopped moving. Though what the fuck? He glances at the television. The studio anchors, the ones to whom intrepid Juliana has been reporting all night, look completely out of their depth.

> *We're trying to get more information about what*
> *occurred at the scene . . .*
> *Witnesses on the ground are posting videos that, that*
> *seem to show . . .*
> *Juliana?*
> *Juliana, can you hear us?*

How is this happening? How has the fire, which was under control, escalated into some kind of epic cataclysm? And how are they in the middle of it?

Pressing questions. But humped over on the floor like this, he's not going to get answers.

Jenny honey, I should find out what's going on. I'm going to get up. I'm—okay, I won't. I won't leave you. I'm here.

You know what? Let's go together. Come on. We'll scoot over to the phone. It's not far. Come with me.

Like a weird pair of conjoined snails, they crawl across the floor to the nightstand. At least she's not making those awful noises anymore. Clutch away, my dear. Whatever helps.

He manages to reach up and find the notepad. He picks up the receiver, starts to dial . . .

The line is dead.

Fucking hell, the fucking line . . .

He taps the little button. Yes, it's dead.

Okay, but they still have lights. The television is working. They just don't have a landline. So what? Landlines are obsolete. Fuck it, they don't need it.

Jenny, I need to get my phone. I'll pull the duvet over you, it's nice and heavy, it'll . . . let me go, honey. I can see my phone on the floor over there. I'll just go and grab it. You can watch me the whole time, okay? Watch me go and come right back. Here I go. I'm standing up. I'm walking . . .

He thought Jill was dead when they pulled her out, putty-colored and still, the cord twisted around her neck. His face was right next to Caroline's, he was narrating to her, until he saw what the blue sheet protected her from seeing, a dead gray baby, and he faltered, and his life fell to pieces for three or four sickening seconds, until the doctor plucked the cord away and gave the dead baby a tremendous whack on the ass, and it started screaming, because it was fine, the baby was alive, like he is, like Jenny is, too.

Everybody's alive. Nobody's dying tonight.

He comes right back with his phone. The room feels steady. Not swaying or . . . what does a building feel like when it's about to fall down? Not this solid, surely. Buildings sway in bad weather all the time. He was in Chicago once for a deposition, high up in a skyscraper. He glanced away from the witness at one point and noticed the window blinds were moving from side to side. Happens all the time, opposing counsel told him.

Modern architecture is a miracle. High-rises are engineered to withstand astonishing amounts of stress. Built by brilliant humans, performing endless calculations to assure structural integrity under all sorts of conditions.

He dials the fire department number.

He gets a busy signal.

He tries 911. Same thing.

At least the storm seems to be passing, Jennywise. She's sitting up, wedged against the nightstand. She's not shaking anymore. Poor girl. He gathers her and eases her onto the bed—always trying to drag the poor woman into bed—where she flattens herself against the headboard.

Her charging cord is dangling across the nightstand. He connects his phone to it. Just in case.

Now then. They need information. NY1 has become useless. He finds the remote on the floor at the foot of the bed and starts flipping.

He stops at CNN.

WATCH LIVE: Catastrophic Fire Rages at Manhattan High-Rise.

So they're national news.

She said it was becoming a big story, but she'd been checking the internet. Celebrity hangnails are a big story on the internet. He didn't think . . . that is, he didn't fully grasp . . .

CNN. Christ.

He glances at her. Maybe he can change the channel before she—

Leave it on. Her voice is low and ragged.

> . . . on what we believe is the twenty-fifth floor,
> the twenty-fifth floor of the building, a significant
> escalation of a fire that was thought to be nearly
> contained. Glass from the windows rained down on the
> street—we're getting reports of multiple casualties . . .

He dials the fire department number.

Still busy.

> We're receiving word—and I would caution viewers
> that this is speculation at this point, we do not have
> confirmation—we're getting word that the twenty-fifth
> floor is an open space of some kind, possibly an event
> space.

CNN is showing a different view of the building than the one they've gotten used to, its crew having opted, wisely as it turns out, to position themselves farther down the block.

The camera pans toward the sky.

Midway up the building, an entire floor is spewing orange flames.

Oh God, she whispers. Oh God oh God.

He puts an arm around her and holds her close. The reporter, a young guy with red cheeks and too-short CNN hair, looks stressed out. In the background, sirens are blaring.

> *. . . trying to make sense of what's happening, it's a scene of chaos as first responders attempt to reach the wounded on the street. It's still not clear what precipitated what appears to have been a, a massive detonation several stories above the known location of the fire. Here's footage from a few minutes ago, capturing the event.*

The screen cuts to a view of the building from the street. Unremarkable. Then a stripe of orange appears, running left to right across it, flaring behind the windows, blooming and bursting through, sending glass showering down. The crowd starts screaming. Jesus Christ.

CNN plays the explosion again. And again.

He redials again. And again.

Busy.

He was in New Haven in September 2001. Starting his second year of law school, holed up in the offices of the Law Journal one morning, editing an article, when another student burst in—it was Justine Dillon, he remembers that specifically—babbling about a plane crash in New York City. She turned on the TV in time for them to see the second plane hit the South Tower.

It's going to fall, Jenny says. We're going to fall.

Honey, no. It's okay.

We are, she says. We're falling. We're dying.

She's leaning forward, her duvet cocoon pushed away. Staring at the television.

Jenny, we're here, okay? We're right here. I'm trying to get some information about—

You're so calm, she says. Aren't you scared?

He smooths her hair back, looks into her eyes.

Of course I'm scared. This is . . . this is not good. It looks like it was worse for the people who were outside the building, but yeah. I'm scared shitless.

He laughs. See? I'm laughing. A classic hysterical reaction. But I'm also trying to—

Edvin's dead, she says. He must be dead. Is Juliana dead?

I don't know.

She is, she says. Juliana's dead. We're dead.

Jenny, honey, that's not true, we're—

Jenny honey, she says. Jenny honey, Jenny baby, baby baby baby sweetheart what say we screw? Still wanna screw, Nick? Wanna screw me?

Okay, he says, so you're not . . . are you with me here, or are you—

This is my fault, she says. All of it.

The CNN reporter is chattering away. Nick mutes the television and puts his arms around her. Back to the holding, the nearness, the low voice. He leans toward the nightstand for his plugged-in phone.

It's okay, Jenny. I'm going to keep trying this number. I'm going to dial until I get through and find out what's going on. We're going to sit here together, and we're going to breathe. It's still busy. The fucking . . . I'm trying again. You know what, though? That's a good sign. It means lots of people are calling. Lots of people are alive in this building, like us—

Dead, she says. Like us.

No, that's . . . hey. Would you maybe like to pray? You could take a minute, collect your thoughts—

She turns her huge, dark eyes on him.

Who am I going to pray to, Nick? Not my mafia God. Not my Catholic crime boss God.

Jenny, I am so sorry I ever insulted your—

That's not who you mean, right? Because he won't help me. He put me here. He made this happen. These flames, this fire? God did it.

Honey, no, that's not—

Yes it is! she cries. It is true! Don't tell me it's not true! I've never lost. Never lost anything. It's time for me to lose.

How the hell is he supposed to respond to that? What does she mean?

Is she going to bolt for the door?

He takes her hands. How can I help you?

Kill me, she says. No. Fuck me.

How about another drink? That might steady both of us—

Is that why you wanted me to pray? she says. So I'd kneel, and you could take me from behind? Fuck me in the ass, like you've always wanted to?

Absolutely not, he says.

Why not? Why *absolutely* not, Nick? Let's do it. Let's screw. You wanted to before the building blew up. You always want to. I always want to, even tonight, even if I can't admit it. I want you. It could have been anyone but you. But no. I had to pick you.

She pushes the duvet away, rising up onto her knees on the bed, unbuttoning her blouse.

Jenny, there's no way we're going to—

Yes there is! she cries. We're fucking, Nick! Right now. It's why we're here. It's all we're good for, right? So let's do it.

He watches, helpless, as she tears her blouse off, shoves her skirt down and wiggles out of it, naked quickly because she didn't bother with her underwear the last time they dressed, neither of them did, when they left and fled down the stairwell.

They should have kept going. Held their breath and rushed down the stairs as fast as they could, past the firefighter with his bullhorn, past the fire, down down down.

Take off your clothes, she says.

Jenny, I don't think I can—

You will! she shouts. You will do this, or I will run out that goddamned door, and I will rip your dick off if you try to stop me!

Oh hell.

Fucking hell.

That's what this is. Literally.

It's fucking hell.

He stands. He unbuttons his pants.

Shirt too, she says. I want it all off.

He removes his pants. His shirt. The look in her eye as she
watches him. Unhinged is such an overused word. Jill is always
telling him to calm down, he's acting unhinged. But the way
Jenny is staring at him right now? It's truly unhinged.

How do you want me? she says. Should I turn? On my knees,
and you can stand and—

No, Jenny. Let's . . . let's lie down, okay?

She stretches out on her back, legs spread, clearly expecting
him to leap on top of her and start pumping away. Instead, he lies
down beside her. This is awful. There's no way he can . . . the flesh
is decidedly not willing. Maybe if he touches her gently, she'll calm
down. He places a hand on her stomach. Kisses her shoulder.

She grabs his cock and begins to yank on it.

Jenny, that's—ow!

She kisses him hard, a hand on the back of his neck pulling
him down on her. She bites his lip. He feels her tongue deep in his
mouth.

And there it is, folks!

The tingling, the warmth.

Jesus, the thing really is indomitable.

She's kissing him, digging her nails into his back. She's never
like this. Peremptory, almost cruel. But by God is it working! He
feels the growing heaviness in his cock, the sense of something
uncoiling, so pleasurable in itself. She pulls him onto her and
reaches down to guide him inside her.

But surely he's not . . . okay, he is, he is ready, and this is, this feels . . .

Oh, he's missed this.

He has. He's been missing it for hours, for the whole night, missing it for years, for his whole life. She wraps her legs around him, grabs his ass, forcing him deep inside her. So demanding! And he's happy to oblige, he's hers completely. This was *such* a good idea, it's exactly what they should be doing. Fucking as the walls collapse around them. He'll do anything she wants, she owns him utterly, so what if they're burning, they're done for, it's all worth it, if she wants him she can have him, she can have this.

Though, does she really want it?

Is she in her right mind?

Definitely not.

So, this isn't . . .

No. This isn't right.

And with that, he feels himself soften.

He keeps moving inside her, trying to hold on, but as abruptly as his erection sprang to life, it departs again. He slips out of her.

Please, she whispers. Please.

Jenny, I can't, I'm sorry. And I'm not sure—

Go down on me, she says.

But—

Do it, Nick.

What if he refuses? Will she really try to leave? She can't. She just can't. So he moves down her body, between her long parted lovely legs. This is all they're good for—she said that as if he'd said it first, but he hadn't, had he? It's not all they're good for, but they are in fact good at it, so he will go down on her now and maybe she'll snap out of it. He spreads her apart and puts his mouth on her. He'll make her come this way. He always can, sometimes several times in a row, until she's breathless and laugh-begging him to stop. She seems satisfied now, the way she's moving, and sighing. He feels her hands in his hair. And he doesn't mind this at all, lapping at her, she's so delicious and warm, he could do this all night, he's still soft but that's okay. She's responding, pushing up to meet his mouth and murmuring.

Is Tom all about the penis? Is that why her sex life with him is solid, rather than spectacular, as theirs is and always has been, spectacular if infrequent? Never enough. *Tom can be a little . . .* not him. He's not a little anything when it comes to her. He's all about the everything, including her bewitching, peerless cunt, a rude word some think, but he doesn't, no, it's a holy word for her sublime and matchless apparatus. Okay, golden boy, don't get fruity, focus on the task at hand, calming this traumatized woman lingually, as per her request.

Not a problem. Happy to help.

And they're fine. This is a strong building. Brand-new. They just need a shitload of water aimed at the fire. He reaches up to stroke her breasts as he bites her gently, a finger deep in her now, two fingers, fucking her slowly with them, which she seems to be enjoying. It probably takes a lot of time to get that much water where it needs to be. Or do they use foam? Sand?

Whatever. Point is, the logistics must be daunting. But manageable. And being managed.

Maybe he can get hard again. Is he . . . yes, he's definitely getting hard again. He presses his mouth onto her forcefully now, plunging his fingers deeper, he'll wait until she's at the very edge, then he'll turn her over, pull her up onto her knees like she suggested and . . .

He stops.

Raises his head.

Is that . . .

Yes.

He smells smoke.

sixteen

There's smoke in the room.

He pushes back onto his knees. She sits up. She smells it, too.

The door, she says.

He jumps up. She follows him to the foyer, where he looks through the peephole. Is it smoky out there? Hard to say. She picks up the wet towels left in a heap by Edvin. He helps her wedge them along the bottom of the door. Then they turn and survey the rest of the room.

The vents, they say at the same time.

There are three, high up on the walls. He ransacks his laptop bag and finds a paper clip, then climbs onto the chair and unscrews the cover of the one above the desk. She hands him a pillow, then another, then a third. He stuffs them in tight and screws the cover back on.

He tackles the vent above the bed while she gathers more pillows and blankets from the closet. The sofa cushions. A cashmere throw.

She moves quickly around the room, fixed in her purpose. She passes the thermostat near the bathroom, stops and switches it off.

The air looks clear. There's no haze. Just the smell of it. The very faint smell of it.

As he finishes screwing the cover onto the vent above the sofa, she disappears. He hears water running.

He goes to the bathroom door. She's bending over the tub, filling it. Still naked. So is he. He hadn't noticed in the rush of activity.

Are we supposed to save water?

I read it in a novel once. It can't hurt.

He plugs the sink and turns on the taps.

Is the phone charging? she asks. We might lose power.

He goes back into the room and checks. It's charging. He sits on the edge of the bed and googles: how to shelter in place during a fire.

Millions of results. Excellent.

The first one appears to be an emergency management pamphlet issued by Tufts University. He taps on the link. Scrolls.

Close all windows and doors. Done.

Turn off the A/C and air-handling systems. Jenny did that when she switched off the thermostat. Smart.

Move away from outside windows.

And that's it.

What the hell? Surely there's more they can do. But what did he expect? Tufts is such a mediocre school. He returns to his search results. What else . . . ah. Here we go. A FEMA site: Shelter-in-Place Guidelines for Ten Different Hazards. He taps on it and scrolls.

Hazard number one: Active Shooter.

Jesus Christ. FEMA makes a list of potential disasters, and Crazed Gunman is number one?

This fucking country.

Moving on. Chemical Hazard. No. Earthquake. Flood. Hurricane. Nope.

Fifth on the list? Nuclear detonation. Wow, that's a little . . . whatever. He scrolls on. Pandemic. Thunderstorm. Tornado. Blizzard.

That's it. Those are the ten hazards.

What the fuck, FEMA? You offer tips on dealing with nuclear war, but not a goddamned fire? The priorities here are just . . .

She comes out of the bathroom. Try the fire department again.

He does. It's busy.

He ends the call. Dials again.

Busy.

He lowers his head, rubbing his eyes and pinching the bridge of his nose.

I feel, he says, gathering about him all his patience, his great forbearance, drawing it around him like a kingly robe, that the management of this disaster leaves a great deal to be desired.

She takes the phone out of his hand and sets it down.

She pulls him to his feet and embraces him.

They hold each other for a long time.

What should we do now? she says, remembering when that question provoked the jaunty answer, *maybe a little light fellatio?* She'd been profoundly uneasy back then, no matter how she'd tried to hide it. But those were golden times, compared to the present.

Let's get dressed, have a drink and catch up on the news, he says.

Get dressed. Because they're still naked. Which doesn't feel remarkable because they're usually naked when they're together.

I don't want to get dressed, she says. I'm sick of clothes.

An attitude that would normally gladden my heart, he says. But with the heat off, and that big window, it's going to get chilly in here.

He brings the robes out of the closet. She doesn't want to put on one of those, either—they remind her of Edvin. But better a robe than her tired, tiresome skirt and blouse. Picked out so carefully last week, when she was packing for her trip, anticipating this night. Silky, clinging things, intended to arouse him, very briefly, before he tore them off her.

So robes it is. He pours them each a glass of champagne—they've barely touched the second bottle, given the events of the evening—and they sit at the end of the bed.

He unmutes the television.

Though the hotel isn't commenting, and the FDNY is a little too busy to entertain media inquiries at the moment, journalists, fire experts and internet sleuths have been hard at work piecing together what happened on the twenty-fifth floor. The leading theory, relayed to them by Brian, the self-serious CNN reporter, is that while firefighters were busy dealing with the fire on twenty-one, flames were sneaking upward via the building's electrical conduits, as smoke had traveled to different floors earlier. Trapped inside metal tubes, the fire triggered no alarms or sprinklers as it snaked past the twenty-second, the twenty-third, the twenty-fourth floor.

At last it hit twenty-five, a vast open space, intended to be an exclusive lounge with views of the city. The space was still under construction when the hotel opened last week.

> *Sources tell us that the floor was serving as a staging area for building materials that construction workers, racing to meet the opening deadline, didn't have time to remove. Those materials are believed to include large amounts of oils and solvents used in the hotel's decorative paintwork, as well as dozens of lithium-ion batteries used in cordless hand tools.*

Fucking hell, he says.

> *When the fire reached the unfinished floor, it escaped the exposed conduits, hit the highly flammable materials, and exploded.*

Jenny takes the remote and changes the channel. Fox is reporting on the fire, too. She keeps flipping. ABC, NBC, even BBC America is covering it. The chyrons blare phrases like:

Deadly Blaze
Historic Calamity
Urban Conflagration

She flips past channel after channel. If it's on Al Jazeera, they're truly fucked.

Look at that. A little humor. A touch of irony. Even now.
She cycles back to CNN.

> *. . . has not officially disclosed whether any first*
> *responders have been killed, but a source tells us that a*
> *crew of firefighters, dispatched to evacuate guests on the*
> *upper floors, is believed to have been near the twenty-*
> *fifth floor at the time of the explosion, approximately*
> *one forty-five a.m.*

Dead firemen. Possibly dead firemen. That's . . . hoo, that's not great. She takes a swig of champagne. Does another self-check-in. She's nervous, but not freaking out. Calm? Ha, no. More like, spent. Scoured out. It's as if she has a tank of feelings, and once it empties she has to idle, waiting for a refill. She knows she's petrified—she must be, she was only recently losing her shit—but she can't access it right now.

She observes her own numbness with a kind of wonder.

Nick is intent on the television. Leaning forward, gnawing on a thumbnail. It took a skyscraper-shaking explosion, but he's finally worried. He was so good to her. It's a blur now, but she knows he held her and spoke to her. He took care of her. When he must have been so scared himself. He said he was. That, she remembers.

She nudges him with her shoulder. Thank you. For before.

He notices how he's going at his thumbnail and stops. Which part?

Soothing me, after the . . . after whatever happened. Wrangling the wild beast.

He nudges her back, holding his shoulder against hers. You're welcome.

> *Questions are mounting regarding the fate of what's*
> *believed to be scores of guests still trapped in the upper*
> *stories of the building.*

She goes to his phone. The internet is now consumed by the fire. It's an onslaught of speculation, analysis, utter nonsense. They have a hashtag. No, several.

She checks in with @firechieftim, who has been a sane, steadying voice throughout. He's got a long stream of new posts. The latest:

> remember the old firefighter's saying, folks: a
> building on fire is a building under demolition.

Jesus Christ.

Not helpful, Chief Tim.

Really not helpful!

> *Though hotel management is remaining tight-lipped,*
> *social media is alight with rumors and evidence of*
> *celebrity sightings at the luxury hotel in recent days.*

Called it! Nick says. The jackals.

He called it, huh? He was right about something? She was right about something, too. A big fricking something. She should be angry—she should be enraged at having been right, and having been ignored by him, having ignored herself. She should be kicking herself, kicking him, kicking the door down.

But she can't find her anger. It must be hiding out with her fear. Waiting to be topped up.

She moves to the door. Still no smell of smoke. If she pulls the towels away . . .

She's not going to do that. Why would she do that?

The towels are fine where they are.

She wanders back into the room. No, she's not angry. Certainly not at Nick. Look at him, peering at the television. One of his knees is juddering up and down.

CNN is playing footage of the explosion filmed from different angles, including at what looks like the same height. People must be watching from other buildings. Filming with their phones.

> *Guests are frantically calling loved ones and posting on social media, looking for any information they can find. We're about to show you a video filmed by—have we confirmed this is genuine? Okay, we're about to play you a video posted by a man on the thirty-seventh floor, who identifies himself as Howard Beale.*

Is CNN really going to . . . yes, they're airing a TikTok from inside the hotel. A man holding his phone way too close to his face starts explaining what the explosion felt like. His voice is strained. The image is shaky. He's five floors below them.

Look at all the likes at the bottom of his screen, Nick says. He's going viral.

He's going infernal, she says.

He turns to her, surprised. I thought we aren't allowed to joke.

You can't joke, she says. I can do whatever the hell I want.

That earns her a smile. She sits and leans into his shoulder. He leans into hers.

> *The FDNY has issued a statement, which they've asked us to read for the benefit of hotel guests who may be unable to get through on the dedicated line.*
>
> *Continue to shelter in place. Do not leave your rooms unless accompanied by fire department personnel. The FDNY is aware of the location of every guest and is making plans for your evacuation. We urge you to remain calm. Make sure your doors are shut completely, and block your ventilation ducts with any available materials, such as blankets or pillows.*

Gold stars for us, he says. Get you anything from the bar, my lady?

She watches him root around in the fridge. Gold stars. They're well-fortified, tucked in to wait for rescue. All guests are accounted for. Even the pseudonymous ones.

Are there others in the building right now, people like them, who shouldn't be here, but are? Maybe they passed some of them on the stairs, everyone averting their eyes as they slipped back to their rooms. Other Graces, other Normans, who aren't here as their real selves, but as slightly skewed versions. Who talk and think and fuck differently, in service to their personal deceptions.

Why is she so hung up on what he named her? Compared to the lies they've both told to keep coming to rooms like this one, the hundreds, thousands of lies, to spouses, friends and families, to themselves—a name is nothing! Hell, she changes her identity every time she walks through one of these doors.

She has lied, and lied, and lied. Categorically, provisionally and by omission. She has lied to the whole world. And now she's lost.

She rises and heads to the window. Is this an existential crisis? Now, when she might be about to stop existing? She presses her forehead against the glass. You exist. You're here. The room is here. Nick is here. Breathe. He came to her the instant the building began to sway. He held her tight. It must have been an instinct, like his jokey bravado. Instinct, too, when he dragged her away from Edvin—kept her from being hauled off, anyway, until she could pull herself together.

He returns to the bed with a bottle of green juice. She checks his phone. On news site after news site—*The New York Times, The Washington Post, USA Today, The Wall Street Journal, The Guardian, The Financial Times*—the fire is the top story.

Breaking

Developing

Leading

9+ updates

It's frustrating, how he's constantly having to rescue her. Is it an instinct, or something learned? Maybe men are conditioned to protect women. To attack and destroy them, too, of course. Are the impulses connected—to save and to ruin? Stemming from the same attitude toward women's bodies. Not ownership, exactly. Some kind of managerial urge.

Has she been trained to collapse, then, to need male managing? Can't she keep her shit together on her own? She wouldn't have expected it before tonight, all the tenderness he's shown, the care. Or the far-from-heroic shit he's been up to, either. Not to mention his surprising confessions: about his marriage, how he was afraid he was losing her.

How did she fall in love with him when she didn't really know him? What did he say—insufficient information never stops it from happening. You gather scraps and fragments, and project the rest. Your creation holds together, or it doesn't.

Maybe if she'd known him in all his fullness, she never would have loved him.

Or maybe she never would have stopped.

Well, but she did.

She did.

She goes to a site that tracks trending topics across social media. The fire is number three.

The whole world is fixated, she says.

It's a Tuesday night in February, he says. Nothing else is happening. And this is hot stuff—pun intended. A burning building, loaded with rich people? What's not to love?

People don't love this, Nick. They're horrified. It's a compelling story, sure, but they want a happy ending.

What they want, Jenny, is a high body count.

God you're cynical! Remember the Thai kids stuck in the cave? People around the world were praying for them. And those Chilean miners from way back? Nobody was watching that ordeal thinking, gee, I can't wait to see them haul a bunch of dead bodies out of that pit.

There's a big difference between us and the Chilean miners, he says. They were hardworking bastards who got stuck in a hole in the ground. We're wealthy assholes trapped in a three-thousand-dollar-a-night hotel room. Trust me, the world wants to see us suffer. We . . . why are you looking at me like that?

You paid three thousand dollars for this room?

I did.

Three thousand? she says. For one night?

I was trying to impress you, remember?

That's insane! she cries.

You aren't flattered? I picked the finest room, for the finest piece of—

Oh my God, stop!

He sips his juice. I thought you'd be pleased. It's a junior suite. And the price was even higher because . . .

Because why?

He doesn't answer. He's suddenly absorbed in whatever Brian is saying.

Why was the price higher?

He sighs and rubs his face.

Nick?

The price was higher, he says at last, because I chose a room on a high floor.

She sits down heavily and covers her face with her hands.

He rubs her back.

The good news is, the FDNY believes that the steel-frame structure is fundamentally stable, despite the severity of the explosion. A team of engineers and architects is working to assess the situation, but structural damage may be minimal.

He flips through the channels. She walks in a circle, twirling a lock of her hair.

*The fire department has also confirmed that the original
fire on the twenty-first floor has been contained. All
efforts are now being directed to the situation on the
floors above.*

What did you mean when you said you'd never lost? he asks.

What?

Earlier. When you were, you know . . .

Out of my mind?

Basically. You said this was all your fault, and God was going
to make you lose. You were so distressed. What's got God all
worked up?

She roams over to the sofa. Then the desk. Circling again.
There's nowhere to go. She comes back and sits beside him.

It's this superstition I have, she says. It's nagged at me for a
while now. The feeling that something horrible is going to happen
to me because I haven't suffered enough in life.

Jesus, Jenny.

I know. It's totally irrational, but it preys on me. Because I've
never ever experienced anything really bad. I've got great health, I
love my work, I have money, wonderful parents who are still alive,
happy kids, a loving partner. I've never been traumatized, never
truly grieved. And sometimes I think, well, it's coming for me.
And the longer it takes to get here, the worse it's going to be, you
know? Like an overdue earthquake.

Tom cheated on you, he points out. A lot of people would consider that traumatic.

She shrugs. It was temporary. I got over it.

Well, I don't think your overdue earthquake is happening tonight.

No? She laughs. How reassuring. Because your predictions have
been spot-on so far.

Hey, he says. Don't forget what they say. A clock that's wrong
twice a day isn't necessarily stopped.

What? That's . . . how much have you had to drink?

I'm thober, mother, I thwear. Look. He holds up the juice. I'm antioxidizing. Actually, fuck this vegetal filth. And the champagne's gone flat. Let's have more wine.

Nick . . .

It's fine, he says. He's already back at the minibar, hunting among the bottles. We'll nurse this one. Look, it's a screw top. Classy. Now, as to our situation, I don't deny it's bad. But it's not hopeless. Did you see the statistic CNN just had up on screen? Five hundred firefighters have been deployed downstairs. And these aren't a bunch of schmoes, Jenny. It's the FDNY. The greatest fire department in the world.

You find it comforting that we're in a situation that requires five hundred firefighters?

He hands her a glass of wine. I'm saying we have resources. And this is a brand-new, high-tech building. It's not like we're in some rickety piece of shit thrown together with Popsicle sticks and Scotch tape. This is America. Things don't burn down here.

Things don't burn down here? She laughs in disbelief. Things burn here *all the time*, Nick. They burn and collapse and rot and wash away. Guys like you, who can drop three grand on a hotel room? You don't burn. That's why you can't believe this is happening.

Of course. He whacks his forehead with the heel of his hand. This is all about my privilege. I'm a rich, white, heterosexual American male, whose many and varied crimes have brought him to this room. How did that slip my mind? He toasts her with his glass. Thanks for the reminder, rich American white lady.

She toasts him right back. Here to help, sweetheart.

Speaking of total assholes, you said something else odd. That it shouldn't be me. It could have been anyone, but not me.

What? I never said that.

Yes you did.

Weird, she says. Can I have more wine?

When you stop bullshitting me. No more lies, remember?

She sighs. Nick, can we not—

Can we not! he cries. Can we not, begs the woman who's been hounding me all night, demanding confidences, details, secrets! No, Jenny, we cannot *not*. We can, and we must, and we—

Tom gave me a pass to sleep with someone else, as long as it wasn't you, she says.

His mouth falls open.

He felt terrible about cheating on me. After we got through it, he started mentioning from time to time that if I ever wanted to do the same, he'd understand.

Sorry. He's still stunned. This—you—this is *allowed*?

Not at all, she says. He was clearly imagining a one-off thing, not a . . . not something like this. Plus, like I said, he set an important condition.

Anybody but me, he says. Why?

He doesn't like you, she says.

Tom doesn't like me?

She shakes her head.

Fuck that guy! What's his problem?

Let's talk about something else.

No chance. Please. Enlighten me as to my grievous shortcomings, according to your high-quality husband.

Nick . . .

I'm a big boy, Jenny, I can handle criticism.

She takes a swig of wine. Courage!

He says you're way too impressed with yourself and not nearly as funny as you think you are. He also hates how you always interrupt him when he talks.

I see. Is that it? He reaches for the hotel notepad. Or should I start making a list? We could divide his complaints into categories, and—

Why do you care, Nick? You don't like him, either.

Yes, but I have good reasons. Tom is a complete—

Nope! she says.

Fine. But for the record? I only interrupt him because he talks too slowly. Not to mention that his conversation is about as stimulating as watching algae bloom on a retention pond.

So this is how big boys handle criticism? she says. Good to know.

He stares at her. Then he laughs.

What the fuck, Jenny? I can't believe you never told me!

Crazy, right? It's almost like I had a premonition about how well you'd take it.

Hold on. I didn't know you when he cheated. Weren't you still in the city?

She nods. The condition got added after we moved to town, and he got to know you.

Only one condition, he muses. Yet you violated it. You couldn't help but taste the forbidden fruit.

Oh God. She covers her face. I should have known you'd twist this into some huge compliment.

I am a massive egotist, after all. But it sounds like I should be even more impressed with myself than I am. I'm irresistible.

Only to me, she says. I always go weak at the knees when some drunk asshole starts eating my jewelry.

He bursts out laughing. You're really something tonight.

What kind of something? she says.

Honestly? Kind of a bitch.

She laughs. Mortal peril will do that to a person.

You called me sweetheart a minute ago, he says. You never call me any sort of endearment.

He's right about that. She trained herself to be careful, early on. Not to give herself away.

He takes their glasses to the minibar and pours them both more wine. What do you call Tom? In your tender moments, I mean. After some of that solid sex.

She thinks about it. Babe. Tommy. Sometimes we call each

other babyloves, but that's only because we're making fun of another couple.

The Goldmans, right? They're disgusting! And totally sincere about it, too. Oh, hey. Brian's looking excited about something.

She reaches for the remote and bumps up the volume.

> *. . . planning is in the preliminary stages, but we're told the FDNY is exploring the possibility of evacuating via the rooftop, using helicopters and—*

We can't get to the roof, she says. The stairwells are full of smoke.

> *—which would involve firefighters transporting additional sets of breathing equipment as they descend through the building, locating each occupied room and leading guests out individually or in pairs, up to the roof, where—*

Jesus, that'll take forever, he says.

> *—a painstaking process, as guests' rooms would essentially be cleared one by one.*

Old Brian's reading our minds, he says.

> *—also depend on weather conditions, particularly wind gusts at the roof level. Our source cautions that this is only a contingency plan, and despite the seriousness of the fire the FDNY is still optimistic about evacuating all occupants of the building by traditional means.*

She turns to him, smiling innocently. Do you think guests who paid extra for their rooms will get priority?

You better hope not, he says. There are penthouse suites above us, babyloves.

She gives him the finger—again! Two birds, one night! He heads once more to the minibar and tops up his wine. He is not drunk, as it happens, and he fully recognizes the hazards of getting sloshed. But he is booze-mellow, pleasantly hazed. They shouldn't be having this much fun. Because this situation is not good. Still, better to stay positive. He doesn't want her falling apart again. She seems all right now, but that could change.

Jesus, it's been a night. So very different from what he'd planned. And Jenny so very different, too. Mortal peril bringing out something new. She's being hard on him. Driving him crazy from time to time. Being so insistent, and contrary. It's a whole new side of her.

He likes it.

As he busies himself among the bottles and glasses, he glances over at her. Her face is tilted up, catching the light of the television. She's never lost? Impossible. She's got an upbeat disposition, that's all. An essential happiness. It must be hard for her to be trapped here, with so much to lose. Her family, her soaring career. Things that could be damaged even if they get out of here.

If? Where did if come from? This is not an if situation. They're getting out. He's concerned, sure, there was a goddamn explosion after all. It might be dangerous, difficult, but they're a long way from last rites.

She's never suffered, she said. Never grieved. Well, she shouldn't. She deserves only good things. Does she know he thinks that? She's said things tonight that suggest she doesn't. *Shocked I'm not a total idiot?* she'd said. *It's all I'm good for*—meaning sex. But that's not true.

Though she is good for that, of course. His compliments do tend to center around her body. And he has said some things tonight that . . . some less than generous things. Accusing her of lying, manipulating, et cetera.

He also broke up with her. And he just called her a bitch.

But that was in fun!

She knows, doesn't she? What he really thinks?

He tops up her wine, sits beside her and is about to put a hand on her leg but stops himself. He doesn't want to be accused of walloping her like a mule.

Jenny?

She's flipping channels. Hmm?

You're extraordinary.

She looks startled. Then she laughs. Okay.

I mean it. You're an extraordinary person.

Are you making fun of me?

What? No! Am I so awful you can't believe me when I say nice things about you?

Pretty much, she says. Oh, don't look like that! I'm joking. She pauses. Sort of.

This is not going as planned. Not that he'd planned it. Which may be the problem.

It's not you, she explains. I have a hard time believing people when they say nice things about me. I have to deflect them, or downplay them, or joke them away. Anything but, you know, accept them.

This confounds him. Why?

She shrugs. It's a midwestern thing, I think. And a woman thing. Praise is a trap, you know? If I take the bait, I might be found out. Exposed as a fraud.

Look, he says. I expose frauds for a living. I also conceal and deny them as the occasion demands. The point is, I know frauds. You aren't one. You're amazing.

So are you! she says instantly.

He shakes his head, mystified.

You are, though. I've read about your cases in the *Times*. That big antitrust one last year?

Sure, he says. Asshole Gets Asshole Corporation off the Hook. I'm a credit to the species. But we're not talking about me.

He takes her hands. You, Jenny Parrish? Are great.

She tries to pull away, but he holds her tight.

Stop it! In the time I've known you, look at what you've done. You were a, what, a stay-at-home mom with two kids, frazzled, exhausted, being mauled and manhandled all the time. And the work you'd done before that hadn't been anything special, right? What was it?

I was a digital marketing manager.

I have no idea what that is.

It involves using the internet to . . . you know what? she says. Doesn't matter.

Right. Anyway, you had this full life, crammed with people and their wants and needs. Always grabbing at you and making demands. Even more when I came along. But one day, you had an idea. You started to write, fitting it in—before the kids woke up and after they went to bed, you told me once—and you did it!

She's looking away. She's blushing! Too bad. He's not finished.

You wrote, with no experience, no outside encouragement, not knowing if it would come to anything or if anyone would ever read it, and now you're famous! Your books are everywhere. I saw them in the Dubai airport last month.

It's not like I took any risks, she says.

Just like you can't take any goddamn compliments, Jenny, Jesus!

I mean it, she insists. We had money, I didn't sacrifice, or—

Why is that the metric? What astounds me is that you did it. You reinvented yourself. Two huge bestsellers, a third on the way—and who knows what's coming after that?

You're awfully impressed by my books all of a sudden, she says.

I've always been impressed.

By the author photo, sure. She smiles. You might not be so thrilled by what's inside.

Right, he says, nodding. I . . . right.

He rises and walks to the window.

The snow is scanty now. Just the occasional flake whipping by.

He looks out at the night. Feeling a little killed.

She has no idea what he thinks of her, and she doubts his sincere compliments, because he has consistently diminished and mocked her. Pretended he's too good for her books, made crude jokes about them. Showed no consideration for how she might feel about her accomplishments.

He leans forward and rests his forehead against the glass. It's pleasantly cold.

Who wouldn't feel undeserving of praise if they were belittled, teased, all in the guise of good fun?

He nearly confessed, earlier. When she asked for his deepest secret. He almost said:

I've read both your books. I think they're phenomenal.

But did he? No. In fact, he went the opposite direction, implying that her work was valuable only as a tool for his sexual gratification.

He bangs his forehead lightly against the glass. Once. Twice.

You. Are.

An. Asshole.

He turns from the window.

Jenny?

She's flipping through the channels again. Hmm?

I've read them.

seventeen

She stops flipping. What?

I've read your books. Don't—please don't smile like that. I'm serious.

She watches him closely, still not comprehending.

I bought the first one the day it came out, he says. I pretended it was for Jill, but it was really for me. I read it a week later. The second book I preordered and read as soon as it arrived.

Does he have to tell her he's read them both twice?

Hell no. Let's not go overboard here.

I don't believe you, she says.

Okay, well, how can I prove—

What's Sophie's father's name?

Sophie's father? he says. His name is James.

What does her mother do for a living?

Sophie's mother, he says, getting the hang of this little game, restores historic buildings.

How did Julian die?

How did he . . . ? Shit. He has no idea. What could it be? Smallpox? Consumption?

Wait. She's trying to trick him!

We don't know how he died, he says. He doesn't remember.

Holy shit, she whispers. You read my books.

Do we find out how Julian died? Is that in the third book?

Yes, she says. So you didn't buy them just to jerk off to my photo?

No. I mean, I do that, too. But I have read what's inside.

Is she furious? He can't tell. She should be. He's been such a dick about this.

You must hate them, she says.

What?

You never told me you read them. You must not have liked them.

Oh God. This is torture.

I do like them, he says. Very much.

You like my books, but you never told me?

Well . . .

No, it's not that you never told me you had, she says, it's that you told me you hadn't.

Technically I implied it, he says. I never explicitly said—

Shut up, she says. Why didn't you tell me?

He sits beside her. I don't know. I meant to tell you after I read the first one, but by the time I saw you next, I felt like . . . you were already getting all this praise. What did you need to hear it from me for? And I was embarrassed about how much I liked them. They're for teenagers! I'm a snob, an elitist. I have my dead Austrians and so forth. It was uncomfortable to find myself so taken by something I wasn't supposed to like.

You were having feelings, she says. We know how much you hate that.

I would have gushed, he says. You know me. I don't gush. About anything. I joke. I play. So that's what I did. It was a way of talking about them without sharing what I thought. To praise them would have required a level of sincerity that's difficult for me.

You praise my tits sincerely all the time.

True, he says, but that's . . . actually, that's a good point.

Gush.

What?

Gush about my books, she says. Now.

But you hate compliments.

I'll cope.

Okay. Well, you created great characters, and a totally believable world—even the supernatural stuff. You have a natural ear for dialogue. Julian in particular is so witty, so alive on the page. The story is propulsive—I was never waiting for you to get a move on. And that's only the first book. The second is even better.

Most people prefer the first book, she says.

Fuck most people. They're useless. The second book is richer, and fuller. And sexier. But the best part of both of them? How you write about love. Jesus your books are romantic, Jenny! The way you describe how Julian and Sophie look at each other, how they react to each other, their conversations. How they touch. You capture what it really feels like to fall madly in love.

That's enough gushing, she says. I can't—

It's epic, it's ridiculously over-the-top, but so is love! he says. No wonder people go apeshit over your books. I don't know how you did that, it's—

Stop! She hides her face in her hands. I can't take it!

Are you pissed I didn't tell you?

Maybe, she says. I should be. You've given me so much shit about them.

I know. I'm sorry. But the good news is, I'm really looking forward to reading the third book. When does it come out?

For you? Never.

I can't read it?

Nope. You're banned for life.

That's bullshit, he says. Also, good luck. I'll be able to buy it anywhere.

Not if I cancel publication.

You'll deprive the whole world, just to thwart me?

Absolutely. She reaches for his phone. I'm calling my editor right now.

She's joking about it! She can't be too upset. That's a relief.

They turn their attention once again to the news. CNN is showing more clips of the explosion. It's a near-constant loop, interrupted only by occasional shots of grave-faced Brian. Where are they getting all this footage? Are they just harvesting videos off the internet now?

He watches her go to the plugged-in phone to check for updates. Is she really not bothered by his yearslong deception? She lies to him about something trivial, and he blows up. He lies to her about her life's work, and she shrugs?

He'd always assumed some part of her was disappointed that he hadn't read her books. But maybe she truly doesn't care. About his opinion. About him.

It's always been obvious what he does for her. He satisfies her, consistently and extravagantly. He amuses her. Is that it? Does she agree with Tom that he's an egotistical prick? *Has this changed you?* She wanted to know, and he'd answered truthfully, more or less. He never asked if he changed her.

Is he one of the good things about her life that she treasures, one of the things she's afraid to lose?

Hey Jenny, he says.

She looks up from the phone.

He holds up the bottle. More wine?

Additional firefighting units are arriving at the scene as the FDNY continues to assess the strength of the fire and the extent of its casualties.

I'd better not, she says. I'm already a little . . . she waggles a hand in the air. I'll take a pop, though, if there is one.

He roots around in the fridge. Pop. Another of her midwesternisms. Along with, apparently, an inability to accept praise. He finds a bottle of twee-looking artisanal cola and takes her wineglass into the bathroom to rinse it out.

She can't see herself clearly. But then, nobody can. And most of the people around us can't offer much assistance. Their views of us are distorted, too, by past and circumstance, their own hangups. So when we turn to them to know ourselves—have I done right, have I done wrong, does this make me look fat, am I any good at all?—they can't help us.

Though they can try. They should. She says Tom is a good partner, but can he be all that great if she thinks so little of herself?

Also, what's his failing in bed? *Tom can be a little . . .* what? A little what?

He's dying to know.

What he's not dying to do is have sex with her right now. An absence of lust. Unprecedented. Wanting her—craving her—has been a prevailing condition of his life for more than half a decade.

It's fine. It'll return. It always does.

He leaves the bathroom. There she is, perched at the end of the bed. The woman who doesn't know herself. Still, she must be happy, right? Even if she feels insecure and imposterous, even if she can't appreciate herself the way she should. Even if Tom can be a little . . .

What, goddammit?

A little what?

He holds out the soda, but she doesn't take it. Her eyes are fixed on the television.

Look, she says.

CNN is showing an aerial view of the scene. There's the building. No flames are visible from overhead, but plenty of smoke, streaming up two sides.

That's plenty distressing. But what stuns him is the scene on the ground.

The blocks surrounding the building are jammed to a standstill with vehicles and equipment. Three, four, five blocks in each direction clogged, this late at night, with what must be hundreds of cars, trucks, ambulances. And people—so many tiny figures clustered, or running. Hundreds? No, thousands.

Thousands of people.

It's Times Square on New Year's Eve. It's a shot from an old disaster movie.

Midtown is shut down.

New York City is shut down.

This is not okay.

His mouth is dry. He sips his wine. Brian is describing and assessing, for the edification of viewers at home. Safe viewers, gloating, warming their hands over this toasty little—

You love what you do, he says. Right?

She turns to him, surprised by the question. I do.

You do. He nods. You enjoy writing. That's good.

Yes, she says. I mean—it's hard.

I don't doubt it.

I'm on my own in this fake world I've created. Trying to make it plausible. And I have no idea if I'm succeeding.

He nods, eyes on the screen. There's the aerial shot again. It must be from a helicopter or a drone. More tiny vehicles are approaching, crawling along the perimeter.

You do what you love, he says. That's great.

His glass is empty. When did that happen? The camera cuts to a shot of the mayor, standing a few blocks from the hotel, nodding and listening to a fire chief of some kind. That intersection was mayor-free when he'd hurried through it earlier. When was that, ten hours ago, eleven? He'd left work early, telling his associates he was headed to the airport. It was freezing out. The streets were filled with that gray-purple light that saturates Manhattan around four o'clock in winter. But he was humming. He was light of heart. Because Jenny was coming.

He strode toward the building. She hadn't canceled. In fact, she'd texted: train on time. see you soon.

He passed through the doors of the hotel. Checked in.

Jenny was coming. It had been so long.

He came upstairs. Let himself into the room. Brushed his teeth. Chilled the champagne.

Every step, leading him to this moment.

He hasn't tried the fire department in a while. The damn phone is charged enough—he unplugs it and brings it with him to the end of the bed. He dials.

Busy.

I take it you don't? she says.

What's that?

You don't love what you do.

Oh, he says. No. It's fine, but . . . it's a job.

> *Guests inside the hotel are cautioned that social media sites are being swamped with misinformation concerning the severity of the fire and the availability of escape routes. In fact, we've learned that a video we aired earlier, purporting to be a man trapped on the thirty- seventh floor, appears to be a hoax. We apologize for any confusion.*

He wishes they would stop cutting back to the aerial shot. He's sure the technology is expensive, CNN wants to get its money's worth, but it's excessive. Voyeuristic.

He takes a couple of deep breaths. Surreptitiously. He doesn't want to worry her. He sits up, trying to release the pressure in his chest. When did that start? Hey, how about a heart attack right now, wouldn't that be fun? He has occasionally worried about keel- ing over while in bed with her. Sometimes it's felt like he might. On the one hand, no better way to go, on the other . . .

He doesn't want to go. He doesn't want to die.

Ever, ideally, but especially not tonight.

He sets the phone on the bed. His hand is unsteady. He picks it up again. He'll hold on to it. Give his hands something to do.

> *And while the fire department has provided a dedicated number for trapped guests, we're told that the line is overloaded, and people aren't able to get through.*

He opens his mouth to make a crack about that, but he can't think of anything. The urge to joke has deserted him.

First the lust, now the wit. Gone.

His stomach is jumping. He's never nervous. In fact he's famous for his composure. Unflappable even in the big moments—during opening statements, or when the jury is filing back in with the verdict. No butterflies, no sweaty palms. People are so impressed.

They don't know it's because he doesn't care. Doesn't give a shit about any of it.

He hasn't cared for years.

We're attempting to verify online posts that appear to be from guests on the thirtieth and thirty-first floors, reporting heavy smoke conditions. If these accounts are genuine, they suggest the fire is spreading upward at an alarming rate.

The fire looks like it's receded from the twenty-fifth floor—it's not visible from the outside anymore. Why not mention that, Brian? Why always focus on the next worst thing that could be happening?

You did it, he says, a touch too loudly. You went for it.

She turns to him, confused. Of course she's confused—what the hell is he talking about? If only he could pour out all his apprehension to her. Lay his head on her lap and tell her his troubles. He used to do that with Caroline. He would list his problems, and she would stroke his hair and listen, not saying a word until he was finished. Then she would ask questions, sort and rank his fears, accepting some as valid and dismissing others. He always felt better afterward.

They haven't talked like that in years. When did they change, why, how did they let it die? Should he have tried harder? Taken that messy New Year's Eve as a warning, a signal to back the fuck up and figure out what went wrong with the woman who had once been everything to him?

But Caroline had pulled away, too. It wasn't just him. They'd both lost each other.

And now everything is ruined.

If only he could tell Jenny his troubles now. She's a balm, she would be sympathetic. But he can't. He can't go back, can't keep starting over, repeating the same goddamn pattern. He's a grown-up, for Christ's sake. He's been the strong one—he is the strong one. If he wusses out now it might upset her, and that won't fly.

He needs distance from the news, and that gruesome image. He walks over to the sofa.

I went for it? she says.

I just mean, what we were talking about before. Your work. You do what you love. Being a lawyer was never something I wanted. It was a backup plan. I wanted . . .

His eyes stray to the television.

No. Focus on her. Look at her. Waiting for him to speak.

And say what?

I went to Oxford, he says. Like your buddy Juan Pablo.

Did she sleep with him?

Oh for fuck's sake!

I thought you went to Brown, she says.

I did, for undergrad. Oxford came afterward. I was a Rhodes scholar.

Wow, Nick! That's amazing!

He shrugs.

I can't believe you never told me. Don't make that face! Who's downplaying their accomplishments now?

Okay, sure, he says. It's a big deal. And it was a big deal to me, back then. It was something I'd wanted since I was twelve.

What did you study? Law?

Jesus, no. I . . .

Why is this so hard to talk about, like it's a crime? Well, maybe it is. A crime and a shame. Everybody's ashamed, she said. Looks like she was right.

I studied poetry, he says.

Poetry. She's trying very hard not to look surprised.

Indeed, he says. Indeed, madam, I sought to scale the heights of—

For Christ's sake. No distancing ironies now. None of your mock heroics.

I studied literature at Brown, he says. The Elizabethans. The Metaphysical poets. All the grand old English men. And some women. I fell in love with them, with how they wrote. The sounds, the images, the emotions they evoked. How it felt to speak them out loud. So I decided to go to England. Worship at the altar. My plan was to get a doctorate in literature and spend my life researching them, teaching them. Surrounded by ivy, ideally, and old books.

Why is he telling her this? Why flee to this, of all places, as a salve for his anxiety?

We're told the governor is en route from Albany.

It sounds wonderful, Nick.

Doesn't it? It was a very pretty dream. It lasted about eight months.

Oh no!

Oh yes, he says. I had to get there to find out that my guys were out of fashion. People were interested in the obscure, the undiscovered. And—though none of my professors were blunt enough to say so, being very English and very polite—I wasn't cut out to be a scholar. I didn't have original thoughts—not enough to build an academic career on.

Hold on, she says. A person doesn't get to Oxford, on a Rhodes scholarship, when they're not good enough.

I had a lot of passion, he concedes. I was smart. But I didn't want to develop a new theory or critical approach. I wanted to study the very greatest of them, to know them deeply, inside and out. That wasn't enough. I wasn't rejected outright—it was my decision to withdraw. I didn't see a way forward. Not a . . . true way.

They're quiet for a moment. She doesn't say anything, doesn't try to console him, which he appreciates, more than he could possibly say.

Anyway, he says. You asked, earlier, if I'd ever been disappointed. That's it.

She nods. I'm so—

Hello? Hello, are you there?

Brian is speaking loudly into his microphone.
Nick rejoins her at the foot of the bed.

Ma'am? Can you hear me? Barbara? It's Barbara, right?

A woman speaks, only to be interrupted by a burst of squawking static.

*Barbara? Can you turn down your television? It's
causing feedback on the line.*

Brian appears to be talking to a woman inside the hotel.

That's better. Thank you. How are you doing, Barbara?

Well, uh . . . I'm not great.

A nervous laugh. Barbara sounds shaky, maybe elderly. How did they find her? Did she call into CNN? Who would do that?

Tell us what's going on.

I'm sorry, Nick, she says. It must have been hard, giving up your dream.

Oh, it's fine, he says, already regretting his confession. His sad spewing. It was a long time ago. I have a good life. I can't complain.

It's not too bad here in my room, but when I look out the peephole, all I see is smoke.

And you still have the poetry, right? she says. You can enjoy it, even if it's not your whole life.

The chyron reads: Woman Trapped on 33rd Floor Describes Deteriorating Conditions.

Oh no, he says. I don't do that.

What do you mean?

I don't read it anymore. Random lines come to me sometimes, when I . . . but no. I haven't opened one of my old books in years.

You gave it up?

He doesn't care for her tone. Or the way she's looking at him with such disbelief. He goes to the minibar.

I was crushed, Jenny. My whole idea of what my life would be, who I was going to be, had changed. You say you've never lost, never experienced true grief? I have. When I went back and tried to read it, I was only reminded of what I'd lost.

What you gave up, she says. The idea of you quitting in the first place is surprising—

I know when to cut my losses.

But it was your dream, she says. You just let it go?

I would have left, but they told us not to. They said there was no problem.

Who said that, Barbara? Was it the hotel, or the fire department?

Could you stop looking at me like that? he says.

I'm sorry, I just don't get it. You had something you loved, enough to devote your life to it, but when it couldn't be everything, you threw it away? That's crazy.

What's crazy, he says, controlling his temper with effort, is what you're doing to me right now.

*I keep trying the number they gave us, but I can't get
through. I'm in touch with my family, and they're calling
too. Nobody knows anything.*

Once again, he says, I've offered some part of myself to you,
I've exposed a vulnerability, and once again? You're using it to attack me.

I'm not attacking you, I'm—

Oh, fuck off, Jenny! You are! I guess this is what you do, huh?
Coax confidences out of people, so you can weaponize them?

I'm all alone up here, I . . .

Barbara breaks off. There's a sound of quivery breathing. A
whimper.

I'm just so scared.

What the fuck were they thinking, putting this poor woman
on television? he says. I'm turning it off.

We need to know what's going on, Nick.

Not from Barbara we don't. He changes the channel, then turns
to face her. So what is this? Are you punishing me about the book
thing? You're upset I pretended I hadn't read them, but instead of
admitting it, you're trying to make me feel shitty about myself?

No, I'm curious, she says. Could you really have loved your
poetry all that much if you abandoned it when—

He throws his hands in the air and walks into the bathroom.
The door bangs shut behind him.

She picks up the remote and flips back to CNN.

The chyron reads: Prospects of Rescue Grow Dim as FDNY Struggles
to Contain Historic High-Rise Fire.

eighteen

Empty your mind.

She scooches back on the bed, pulling her feet up and sitting cross-legged. With her elbows she presses down on her knees until she feels the stretch in her inner thighs. That's good. She presses harder. Focusing on her body. Fingertips propping up her temples. Eyes closed.

Inhale. One, two, three.

Allow thoughts to enter, acknowledge them, then usher them out. Kindly, firmly show them the door.

Thanks for stopping by, thoughts.

Thank you, but you can . . .

Thank you . . .

She's terrible at this.

She uncrosses her legs and lies flat on her back. Meditation won't work now, when it's never worked before. Not even when she subscribed to the app everybody said was foolproof. Sorry, guys—it's no proof against this fool!

Her thoughts don't leave. They loiter. The FDNY struggles, it struggles, why is it struggling, please don't struggle. And now Nick is scared. But it's no triumph, having a partner in dread. It's a little sickening, in fact.

She stares up at the blinking smoke detector. She went after him too hard about his so-called disappointment. See, there, she still doesn't take it seriously—*so-called*—even though it's obviously a big deal to him. He's right: she's upset about the book thing. She wasn't at first, but the more she thinks about it . . . all his little jokes, his superiority, for *years*. And now he thinks he can praise her, show a little interest, and it's fine?

But she also genuinely wants to understand. Why didn't he persevere, instead of renouncing what he wanted in a huff? He doesn't read his beloved poetry anymore. What a man. He couldn't just love it, he had to win it, conquer it. Possess it on his terms. And when he didn't get his way? It reminds her of nothing so much as when she offers the boys a cookie, and they demand two, and she holds firm at one, and they storm off, insisting that if they can't have two they'll have none. Nick did that. Rejected one cookie because he couldn't have two. Hurting only himself, because guys? Nobody gives a shit if you don't have any cookies.

It's sad. But also interesting. The kind of thing he'd have examined endlessly, had it been someone else under the microscope. Her, for example. Oh, he'd have had a field day, delving and probing! But she asks a few questions and she's attacking him?

He needs to get his story straight. Either she's an extraordinary person or a scheming emotional terrorist. She can't be both.

> *Seventeen people are confirmed dead, including three members of a New York One news crew stationed where the majority of the debris hit the ground.*

Oh, Juliana! Here she is thinking about her books, and cookies, while people are dead. She needs to move. She jumps off the bed and nearly loses her balance. Easy now. She begins to walk toward the window. Heel, toe, heel. Small, careful steps, the length of her feet. When she gets to the window, she'll turn and come back the same way.

She watches her feet. She used to have to move like this in dance class when she was a girl. Her mother had signed her up, hoping to cure her clumsiness. She loved it. The feel of the wood barre, polished by decades of eager little hands. Watching the older girls slip on their candy-pink toe shoes, crisscrossing the satin ribbons up their calves.

She didn't last long enough to get those shoes. She was a terrible dancer. But she did stop falling on her face so much.

Now she steps. Steps again.

This is her.

She is here.

Nick storms back into the room.

This is a disgrace, he says. I'm calling again.

He finds the phone on the bed. She's made it to the window. She turns and begins heel-toeing back.

Busy, he says. Of course!

He hurls the phone down, but instantly picks it up again.

—hearing rumors from numerous sources concerning a lax permitting process and numerous violations of the city's building code during construction—

How do I search Twitter? he asks.

She looks up from her feet. Tap the magnifying glass at the bottom of the screen—

What are you talking about? he snaps. What magnifying glass?

Go to the browser. Tap the button at the bottom right of the screen. You'll see all the pages I have open.

He taps. Taps again. Jesus, Jenny. What is all this?

Choose Twitter, she says, refusing to be riled by him, as he so obviously wants her to be. You'll see a magnifying glass icon at the bottom. Tap it, and a search bar will pop—

Fine fine fine. What do I type in?

There are a couple of different hashtags. Do manhattanhotelfire. All one word.

He types. She continues her slow walk toward the bed. She curls her toes, feeling the carpet. Barely lifts her feet, so her soles brush along the plush surface as she steps.

Jesus, have you read some of this shit?

She inhales. Steps. Exhales.

You didn't tell me people were making jokes.

> *Questions are also being raised about what appear to be*
> *a series of systemic failures, particularly concerning the*
> *building's sprinklers, which, if they have been*
> *functioning at all, have completely failed to extinguish—*

Nick? Do you think maybe we should make some calls?

They're not answering, he mutters. The line is completely tied up.

I mean, should we call Tom and Caroline?

He looks up, outraged. Why the hell would we do that?

I think it might be time to—

No. That's—that's just dumb, Jenny. It's a dumb idea. Why are you walking like that?

I'm sorry I upset you, she says. But there's no need to be—

Upset me? Please. Nothing you could say would ever . . . oh, for fuck's sake.

He's looking at the television now. She follows his gaze.

CNN is showing another TikTok. This one is of a girl dancing to a pop song. The screen splits, showing footage of the fire beside her. The explosion on the twenty-fifth floor repeats in a loop as she dances, her moves synchronized to the song and the blooming fire.

> *. . . provoked outrage, prompting calls to improve their*
> *content moderation regarding—*

Unbelievable, he says. We're fucking entertainment.

She resumes her walk toward the bed. Deep breaths. In and

out. Avoiding looking at him, though she can feel the agitation vibrating off him as he gets up. Sits down. Rakes his fingers through his hair. He jumps up again, grabs the phone.

CNN is condemning it, but they're still showing it, he says. This is . . . people are *amused*. They're cheering.

He predicted that himself, not so long ago. *The world wants to see us suffer.* She doesn't remind him. It wouldn't help.

And the conspiracy theories, he says, shaking his head at the phone. Migrants set the fire, China did it. George Soros is behind it.

Did you see the one accusing PETA? she asks. They don't get blamed for much anymore. It was a nice throwback.

Jesus, Jenny! How can you be joking right now?

She's trying to be patient with him. She's been scared for longer, she's more used to the feeling. But come on.

I guess it's a reflex, she says.

He scowls and returns to the phone. You've got me pegged, don't you? I'm a failed clown. You and your husband can agree on that.

Nick, I don't agree with him—

Whatever, he says. I don't care. He can think what he wants. So can you.

Put the phone down, she says. Let's lie on the bed a minute.

I'm fine.

Come on. I'll rub your back.

Fuck off, Jenny! You think you can comfort me? Because you're calm now? How do you think you got that way?

Because of you, she says gently. You helped me, Nick.

You're goddamn right I did. So you can't be all serene now, okay, and hold that over my head, all that power, and—

Power? she says. How is this about—

He drops the phone—almost throws it onto the bed. He puts his hands up.

Why am I getting worked up? He waves his hands at the phone, the television. Humanity, sinking to a new low—it shouldn't shock me. I'm wasting my energy. Being angry won't change a goddamn thing.

He walks past her, not even looking at her. He stands at the window, arms crossed.

She resumes her careful tread across the room. Going diagonally now, toward the desk.

So what if it won't change anything? she says. You're still entitled to your feelings.

Can you be quiet? Can you—what are you doing? Why are you walking like an idiot?

She stops. I know you're scared, Nick, but don't be an asshole.

I'm not scared, he says.

She can't help it. She laughs.

I'm not, Jenny! I'm furious. This is—

> *It does appear from here on the ground that the fire, far from being contained at the twenty-fifth floor, is spreading upward.*

They both turn to the television, which is showing a wide shot of the building.

> *Counting the floors, we believe the highest level to be breached, where I'm seeing flames behind the windows on the left-hand side, is the thirty-third floor.*

Bye-bye, Barbara, he says.

Jesus, Nick!

> *Contrary to earlier reports, the FDNY has stated that no rooftop rescue plan is in the works. According to a department spokesperson, current weather conditions, specifically significant wind gusts, would make such an operation highly dangerous.*

Well, we're dead, he says. We're dead!

She crosses to the sofa and sits down. She feels sick.

No rescue from above. Fire creeping up from below. Nine floors away now.

Her mouth tastes sour. She swallows, forcing the nausea back down.

—insists there is at least one feasible route down what is still a structurally sound edifice, which will be available when—and if—the fire is contained and the smoke cleared.

Structurally sound, he says. That's what they called the World Trade Center.

Nick. Please.

Remember? They insisted on its *structural soundness.* Right up until the moment the South Tower went down.

She has pulled her legs up, wrapped her arms around them. She's rocking slightly.

We shouldn't have come, she says. We shouldn't have come. We should never have come.

He turns on her now. She can almost feel it, a whipping around of his body as he trains his rage and his fear on her.

What are you talking about? We did come. We're here. So, conditionals? Counterfactuals? They're pretty fucking pointless right now.

Listen to him. Her protector. Her savior. He's drawn close, he's looming over her. If she raises her head, she'll find him looking down at her with an expression that matches his contemptuous tone. So she doesn't raise her head.

We've been over this, Jenny. We had no choice. In coming here, or in anything we do.

He's not in control. She knows the feeling. But to think, as she did not so long ago, that he could keep her safe. Or that she could tend to him!

Talk about dumb. Talk about pointless.

They are alone here, each of them. They don't know each other. They don't know themselves. They're strangers.

They always have been.

Don't you get it? he says. This is always where we were going to end up, you and me.

She doesn't want to respond—she has warned herself not to—but she can't help it.

From birth? she says.

He throws his hands in the air with a look like, *Well, yeah, genius.*

She jumps up and crosses the room. This only agitates him further. She can feel him at her heels. She enters the bathroom and tries to shut the door, but he's already through it.

Taking a bath? he says. You're in luck. The tub's full!

Leave me alone, Nick.

You wanted to talk about this, Jenny. You kept coming back to it. Whether we can choose, or change. Whether we have any control. This is the perfect illustration! You wish you weren't here? Then *everything* would have to be different. You'd be a different person.

She leaves the bathroom. He follows.

No more books. No more famous authorhood. No more faking your fake orgasms with me for six years. That work for you?

Stop it, Nick. Stop talking.

You didn't have a choice, Jenny. Why can't you see that? We're here. We were always going to be here. And you should be glad about that.

She drags the duvet to the sofa and wraps herself in it, turning to the window. She won't let him upset her.

But he won't leave her alone.

Seriously, you should feel comforted. It relieves you of accountability. Your failings as a wife, a mother, a Catholic—not your problem! Your total lack of self-awareness, all your little lies and evasions? Not your fault!

Nick, I swear to God if you don't stop talking, I'll—

And the big lies, too. Cheating on your imbecile husband, for *years*. Fucking another woman's husband. Don't fret about that little bit of treachery against the sisterhood—you couldn't help yourself!

Shut up! she cries.

Why do I have to work so hard to convince you? He's standing over her again, voice raised, insistent. You already believe women are enslaved. That Feminism 101 insight makes sense to you, but you can't see that it applies across the board, that none of us are free, that we're all trapped in what is essentially one giant burning hotel room?

She looks up at him, glaring down at her.

We're not free, he says. We. Are. Not. Free. How do you not see that, Jenny? Tell me. How do you not see it?

And just like that, she does.

She sees it.

Not his *it*. A far more important one.

The answer to everything.

And it's in her hands!

She just has to do one thing.

Can she?

She looks up at him. Glaring down at her, hands on his hips, waiting.

She takes a deep breath.

nineteen

I fell in love with you, she says.

He stares at her.

I did, she says. I fell madly in love with you, and I loved you for a long time.

> *We're live at the site of an uncontrolled blaze in*
> *Midtown Manhattan, which has already claimed the*
> *lives of numerous firefighters and bystanders, while*
> *scores of guests remain trapped—*

What the fuck are you talking about? he demands.

Wow, she says. Her breath left her all in a whoosh when she spoke, and she's still trying to catch it. But not because she's scared. She's not nauseous anymore, either.

Jenny?

He's dumbfounded. Standing there, looking down at her, motionless. Hands dangling at his sides.

She reaches out and takes one. Examines it. Brushes her thumb over his knuckles, back and forth. He has such good hands.

It was years ago, she says. And I was never going to tell you. But I just did. I decided to tell you, and I said the words—the thing I thought I'd rather die than say. So I don't know, Nick.

Maybe you're right, maybe we're not free. We're not in control, we can't change. Maybe me blowing my huge secret wasn't a choice but a done deal, the inescapable result of every step I've ever taken and the person I am. But that's great! Because it means the person I am is one who can tell the truth. I've been lying my whole life, but I can stop.

I did stop. She laughs, still feeling a little stunned. I just did!

He has backed away. He lowers himself to the edge of the bed. Staring at her.

She untangles herself from the duvet and goes to the minibar.

Meanwhile, the mayor is urging—

He mutes the television.

You love me, he says.

Loved, she says, pushing bottles around in the fridge. Past tense.

She finds a miniature vodka in the way back, and a bottle of orange juice in the door. Screwdriver! Perfect. It's nearly morning.

He jumps up and starts to pace, swift strides across the room. Looking down at the floor, shaking his head. She mixes her drink and takes a seat on the sofa.

He stops in front of her.

All joking aside, he says. All . . . whatever. Anger. Recriminations. Are you telling me the truth?

She sips her screwdriver. Yep.

Yep! he says. You and your fucking yeps. When did this happen?

The first summer. Six or seven months after we started sleeping together.

And now it's over? How long did you . . . how long did it last?

A year, she says.

He is astonished. That long?

It was that long. Even in her own mind she minimizes it. But it lasted a full year.

And you're saying it stopped? How did it stop?

She takes another sip. I'm not crazy about your tone right now.

Well Jesus, Jenny! You can't drop something like this on me and not expect a few—

Stop interrogating me, she says. Sit down. Talk to me like I'm a human being.

He takes a seat on the bed.

You loved me, he says. Why?

Why? she repeats. A million reasons. And no reason. You read my books. It's all in there.

What?

That love you love? That swooning romance? It's all you, Nick. I never would have written those books if I hadn't fallen in love with you.

She can't believe how incredible it feels to say all this. And to think back to loving him. How totalizing it was.

She smiles now, remembering. Almost—*almost*—feeling it again.

It was fantastic, she says. Awful, too. It wasn't all rainbows and sunflowers. I felt this distance. From the real world, from my family.

She sips her drink, remembering how she would come home from being with Nick and sit in the chair in their foyer, that crappy yellow yard sale chair. She would take off her shoes and look down the hall into the kitchen, seeing Tom, the boys, all from a distance. She'd just had wrong sex, with the wrong man, whom she loved, wrongly. It made her an alien. A visitor in her own life.

Estranged from her friends, too. There was so much she couldn't tell them. So much, they didn't really know her. Nobody did. It was intensely lonely.

That's why you stopped? he asks. The distance?

He's not angry anymore. That's something. It's almost pleasant to be sitting here with him, discussing her great, dead passion.

Yes and no. That was nagging at me, for sure. But I realized I had to knock it off when you suggested we meet more often. Maybe you don't remember, I think we were in—

I remember, he says. I . . .

He stands abruptly. Then he sits down.

Why would that make you stop? he asks. Isn't that—wouldn't that have been what you wanted?

Oh no, she says. You just wanted more sex. But I was barely hanging on. To see you every week? I would have lost myself.

He's up again, walking to the window. Walking back.

None of this makes any fucking sense, he says. You kept sleeping with me, for *years*? Most people would have ended it.

I almost did. And I would have, if I couldn't have, you know, persuaded myself out of the emotional side of things.

Persuaded yourself, he repeats. Persuaded yourself to fall out of love with me. How?

I wrote, she says. A lot. Letters to myself. Letters to Tom, confessing what I'd done. Which I tore up, immediately. I made myself feel really bad about it. I explained to myself, over and over, that there was no way forward. That I didn't want to blow up my life, or yours. That we were too different. It took a long time. It was probably the hardest thing I've ever done.

He nods. Listening. But does he get it? Does he have any idea how she felt, loving him? He's read her books. Maybe he does. But even there, she didn't capture it.

Not even close.

He was in her bones.

Anyway! she says. Gradually I was able to detach myself from the big feelings, and go back to appreciating what we have.

How long did it take to, to stop?

Six months or so, she says. No, probably more like a year.

So, two years you were in love with me, he says. Not one.

I guess that's true, she says. Though the second year, when I was trying not to be in love, that felt different.

It's so easy to tell him these things. The thought of him finding out used to provoke shudders of horror. Terror! She didn't realize baring herself—*I bared my heart to you*—would feel so powerful.

She glances at the television. Brian is listening to something in his earpiece, nodding, looking grave. Powerful? She's delusional.

For all her fear, all the very bad news, she still can't believe they're going to die here.

Nick is pacing again, agitated.

What if—I mean, what if I'd loved you, too? he says. Loved you and been afraid to tell you? Wouldn't you have wanted to know?

You, afraid to say something? Come on.

He dismisses that with a wave of his hand.

Anyway, it didn't matter what you felt, she says. It was about how I felt.

About me! he cries, stopping in front of her. How you felt *about me*!

She rises now, coming to meet him. Don't be upset. She touches his arm. I—

He jerks away.

Don't be upset? You've dropped a bomb on me, Jenny! Out of fucking nowhere, while I'm dealing with—here he flails a hand toward the television—how am I supposed to . . .

He's all over the place. He needs to calm down.

He sits on the sofa. Grips his head in both hands and leans back, staring up at the ceiling.

What the fuck? he whispers. What the *fuck*?

How did he miss it? How did he not see it? Love? A year? A year she was . . .

Did it not occur to you, he says, addressing the ceiling, that I might want to know about this magnificent romantic experience you were having? Not telling me . . . that means we were having sex, dozens of times, over the course of years, and I didn't know you were in love with me. If I had known . . . I mean, you were sleeping with me under false pretenses.

Okay, well, I guess I'm a rapist, she says. Sorry.

That's not what I meant. Jesus, Jenny, I don't know what to think here! What am I supposed to do with this information?

Be flattered? she suggests. Touched? And maybe don't use it to attack me?

Why didn't you give me a chance to respond?

What, like, love me back? You didn't need to know how I felt to do that. I was right there, Nick. That was your chance.

No, he insists. Because that wasn't you! You were hiding your feelings. Hiding and lying.

You were hiding things, too. That didn't stop me. It never stops anyone. Insufficient information, remember? You didn't love me because you couldn't. Or wouldn't. And that's fine!

He walks to the window. Walks back. A few more lengths of the room and he feels calmer. Slightly. Because you can't survive at that pitch of aggravation for long.

He passes her again. Glances at her.

He always dismissed the thought of loving her, pushed it away, thinking only of himself, never wondering how she felt, whether she . . . and she did. Love him. And he didn't know it. When he made that suggestion, and she shot it down . . . what if he hadn't retreated? What if he'd asked a few more questions—actually tried to know what was in her head? What if he hadn't felt so rebuked, what if he'd risked . . .

Not me, obviously.

He knew it had been six years. But he didn't want her to know he knew. She didn't want him to know, he didn't want her to know . . .

Jesus Christ. What have they been *doing* all this time?

He stops at the door. Stands before it, in the low-lit foyer, still so elegant, unsullied by whatever the hell is going on downstairs, not to mention the turmoil between them. This fucking night. So longed for, so anticipated, so . . .

The door, he says.

He comes back to her. She's standing by the bed, eyes on the television.

They're saying one of the stairwells might be clear, she says. They have to check—

You said something to me. At the door.

What?

When you got here. I opened the door. What did you say?

Her expression changes. She looks guarded.

I greeted you, she says. I don't remember, it was—

Hello, you said. Hello something. It surprised me at the time.

She doesn't respond.

You know what I'm talking about, he says. I can tell.

It's embarrassing, Nick! I don't want to—

Jenny goddammit, what did you say?

Too loud. She winces. God, he's been a monster tonight. He was truly out of control there for a while. Now he doesn't know what to think.

Except that he needs to know this one thing.

He takes her hands. Jenny. Please tell me. What did you say?

She sighs. Looks down.

I said, hello, happiness.

Hello, happiness, he says.

She pulls away and covers her face. It was so corny! You opened the door, and I was so glad to see you, I just blurted out the dumbest . . . what?

He has taken a step back. He's gazing at her. Amazed by her.

You, he says. You.

She's so lovely. Even after everything, he's struck by it. She's got such a beautiful, lively, living face.

Youuuuuu, he says. Shaking a finger at her. You.

What?

You love me, he says.

I don't. I did—

And you still do.

Nick, no.

You do! You love the shit out of me, Jenny! Admit it. I'm your happiness.

Look, she says, taking his hands. I'm sorry about everything, okay? About not telling you, about springing it on you tonight, but I promise you, I got over it. I wish I had told you earlier. I've never felt so . . .

She keeps talking, and he watches her, letting her hold his

hands, look at him and speak. Watching her mouth form words of earnest denial.

Love falters, he knows. Love dies.

But he's her happiness.

Maybe not at this very moment. Or for considerable stretches tonight.

But recently. And for years.

People can't talk themselves out of love, Jenny. You can fall out, but you can't force it.

No? You tell me how it works, Nick.

I just think you're not being honest with yourself.

Often I'm not, she says. About this, I am. I care for you more than I should. But it isn't love anymore. I feel so lucky that it was. Like I tried to explain, loving you did a lot for me. I wouldn't give it up for anything. But the feeling itself? It's in the past.

She smiles at him, so sweetly. Smiles down at his hands, clasps them tightly in hers. Then she releases them and walks away.

He watches her pour juice into her glass. She's still so maddeningly calm.

You have no idea how I would have reacted, he says.

Oh, Nick. We both know you would have run as far and as fast as you could.

His chest is bothering him again. That pressure. He has to move, to loosen it. He starts pacing again, the endless pacing with nowhere to go.

He stops in front of her.

You didn't give me a chance! he cries.

My love was not an opportunity for you, Nick. It was *mine*. And it changed me. Don't believe me if you don't want, but I know it did. It made me . . .

She trails off.

Made you what? he says. Jenny? Made you what?

But before she can answer—if she even had an answer, if that sentence wasn't complete—it happens again.

Sound disappears. Like it's been sucked out of the room.

He turns to the window in time to see an orange bloom reflected in the building opposite. Just a few stories below them.

The silence. The bloom.

Then the roar.

It's louder this time. Or maybe it's just closer.

He rushes to her. They cling together, pulling each other to the ground.

The room shudders.

It shudders again.

He holds her tight, feeling her body beneath the thick robe. Her good, firm arms, her back.

She is real. She is here. Jenny.

The room shudders a third time.

The picture on the television freezes. Pixelates. Disappears.

The lights flicker.

The room goes dark.

part four

joy's bonfire

twenty

Hey, you've reached Tom. Sorry I missed your call. Leave a message and I'll get back to you as soon as I can. Thanks!

At the tone, please record your message. When you are finished recording, hang up or press pound for more options.

Hi, she says. It's me. I . . .

Sorry.

I'm . . . I should have planned what I was going to say.

Okay. I'm just, I'm just going to talk.

She takes a deep breath. She will not fall apart right now. Though hearing his voice, his chipper message, that was tough.

Doesn't matter. She will not fall apart.

So, I'm not upstate, she says. I'm in the city. I came back a day early, because . . .

Don't fall apart!

She's sitting on the floor, her back against the tub. It's almost completely dark in the bathroom.

When you wake up, she says, you're going to see there's been a big fire in Midtown. A new skyscraper that . . . maybe it won't even be here by then, maybe it . . .

She presses her fingers into her eyes. How is she supposed to do this?

Think about him.

Think about him having to listen to this.

I love you, Tom. And I am so sorry. This is not how . . . it is still *so hard* to believe this is happening! I never wanted to hurt you, but, boy, am I about to, and I am so, so sorry.

These words are useless. Useless!

But what's the alternative?

I want you to know, what I've been doing? The fact that I've . . . the fact that I've been cheating on you, for a while, with, with the one person you specifically asked me not to . . . it never meant anything. It . . .

No. No more of that.

You know better now.

That's not true, she says. It meant something. Means something. What I'm trying to say is it doesn't mean I don't love you. Because I do, Tommy! We . . . we had a sweet life, didn't we? You made me happy, you really did. I love you. I said that already . . . I'm sorry, I'm trying to keep it together, but I . . .

Don't let the boys listen to this, okay? I don't want them to hear me scared. I'm not scared, I have been but right now I'm okay. I just . . . I mean, who has to do this, who has to leave a fricking voicemail before they . . . don't let them hear it, okay? Ever? There's the book, the audiobook part I recorded, they have that when they need to hear my voice.

Also, I wrote to my parents. An email. Dad doesn't sleep so well anymore so I was afraid he might pick up if I called, and I couldn't . . . take care of them too okay?

I'm sorry I'm crying, I can't help it, but I'm okay. I really am.

I love you all so much. Tell my Ben and my Natey. My sweet boys.

Maybe we'll get out of this. There's still a chance. But it's bad. The smoke is . . . there's smoke in the room now. I don't know . . . the lights have gone out, so we can't see into the hall.

You're a good man, Tommy. I know you don't think so sometimes but you are. Take care of my boys. Take really really really

really really really really good care of them, okay? Tell them I love them. I said that already, I know, I just . . .

Okay. I'm going to go. I have to go.

I'm going to go.

Maybe I'll see you soon. I hope so. Or maybe . . . maybe later.

Maybe I'll see you later.

I love you, Tom.

Bye, baby.

She ends the call, lowers her head between her knees and sobs. Her tears drop down onto the soft bath mat.

She's not ready for this.

She told him the truth. She's not scared anymore.

But she is sad. So sad!

There's so much more she wanted to do. And her boys! She's fucked up their lives.

So she lets herself go for a while.

Eventually the tears slow, and her ragged breathing evens out. She is scoured and tranquil once more. She hauls herself up and finds the vanity, where she splashes her face with water from the full sink. All the towels are gone—she dries her face with a skimpy washcloth.

Her reflection in the mirror is pale, lit only by the dim light from the phone screen. It goes dark, and she taps it, checking the battery level. Nick needs the signal to send his emails.

Maybe I'll see you, she said to Tom. Not a lie, though she knows she's not going home. *You're never home,* Tom said, just last week, and it pissed her off, but he was right. Right without knowing why. She's been keeping some part of herself to herself, for herself, for a long time. She made a promise. She broke it, over and over again. She thought she'd have a chance to make it right.

But she won't.

She splashes her face again. The cool water is delicious.

It is what it is, she tells her ghostly reflection.

What it is.

What it was.

twenty one

All that illuminates the room now are the lights of Manhattan and the fire reflected off the building opposite. It's maybe four or five floors below them. He's not sure because he hasn't gone to the window to look. He needs to finish these emails.

Emails. Christ. Not how he would have chosen to say goodbye. But better something written than a phone call—a voicemail, for surely Jill and Caroline are both asleep. Writing, he can make sure he hasn't left anything unsaid. That he's included enough love and apologies.

He is a careful writer usually, judicious. But it's pouring out of him now. In a good way. He's in a confined space, a compartment the size of his laptop screen, and he can manage things nicely there. He can focus on the love, the apologies, for Caroline and especially for Jill, his sweet girl, his wonderful daughter, she has been his delight every single day, does she know that, did he tell her often enough? He's telling her, right now.

Anyway that's where he is, focused on them, which conveniently prevents him from thinking about the dark and the dire, the unbelievable unreality of what happened, is happening, might happen any minute now, which is why he needs to focus on the love, and the apologies.

So he does. Until he's said it all.

Jenny comes back into the room. He connects his laptop to the phone's signal, reads his emails one more time, then sends them. He closes the laptop.

Any news? he asks.

She's scrolling on the phone. They think there might be fire-fighters still alive in the building, but they aren't sure. If the sprinklers are functioning—they don't know that, either—there's a chance they could stop the spread. Otherwise . . .

He goes to the window. The exterior of the building across the street reflects an unfathomable sheet of orange flame, three or four stories down. An undulating mass of color, billows of smoke whipping away on the wind. It's weirdly gorgeous.

And close. So close.

They could make it quick. Leave the room and find a stairwell. It would take only a minute or two for the smoke to overwhelm them.

He turns the idea over in his head, even as he knows it's not an option. Not while there's still an infinitesimal chance they might get out of this. Not while there's still the boundless capacity of human delusion.

She's on the sofa, arms around her knees. He takes a seat in the chair across from her. He drums his fingers on the arm. Crosses his legs. Uncrosses them.

He stands up. Sits down. Stands up again and goes to the mini-bar. There's still so much booze left. Imagine being a recovering alcoholic and walking into this room. He takes a pint bottle of something—whiskey?—and returns to the chair. He cracks the cap and takes a swig.

My office at home looks down on the Parks' back porch, he says.

She lifts her chin. The light in the room is dim, but he can see her eyes shining.

I can't see it from my desk, he says. The place where we . . . I moved the desk, so I wouldn't . . . I didn't want to be looking down on it all the time.

He offers her the bottle. She shakes her head.

He walks to the window again, but comes right back, sits beside her and takes her hands.

How about this? he says. How about, if we get out of this? We be together.

She doesn't respond.

We go legit, he says. You and me. It'll be a shitshow, a scandal, but so what? Those can be fun. What are we here for but to provide entertainment for our friends and neighbors, right?

She is silent. Just looking at him with her big shining eyes.

How does that . . . what do you think? he says.

She raises their joined hands to her lips and kisses his.

Jenny kisses his hands!

I think it could be great, Nick. But we're not getting out of this.

He barely makes it to the bathroom. That the contents of his stomach end up in the toilet is a matter of sheer luck. On his knees in the darkness he clings to the porcelain and heaves. He hasn't vomited for years. Or cried, though he's crying now. He feels the tears on his face, tastes them even as he's spitting and spitting, trying to spit out that awful sour acid.

How is this happening?

He's wasted his life.

She follows him in, using the light of the phone to guide her. He senses her moving around, then she's kneeling beside him. He feels her hand on his back.

Take this, she says. She's brought him a glass of water. He rinses his mouth and spits into the toilet. She has a washcloth, too. She's thought of everything. She's so good, she's—

The glass slips from his fingers and smashes on the floor.

I'm sorry! he cries. Jenny, I'm so sorry!

Her eyes fill with tears. She can't help it—she always cries when someone else is crying.

But Nick? Nick weeping? She can't bear it.

I ruined everything! I've wasted my life, wrecked yours, I've—

Nick, no. It's okay. We need to get away from this broken glass.

What does that matter? Broken glass? What the fuck does that matter?

I know, but . . . let's scooch back so we don't stand in it. Here we go. Good. We're at the bath mat. Let me feel around and make sure . . . okay, we're good. Come with me.

She leads him out of the bathroom and tries to coax him onto the bed, but he cannot be still. He stalks the room, clawing his fingers through his hair. He is raging, raging.

Then he stops.

I need to call Jill, he says. I need to talk to her. Where's the phone?

Jenny lunges at the bed, feeling around until she finds it.

Here. But be careful. Try to . . . try to keep it together. For her sake.

He nods, already dialing. She returns to the sofa. When she hears his voice, she presses her ears closed, to give him some privacy.

Eventually he stops talking. He drops the phone on the bed and sits beside it.

We don't let her have her phone in her room at night, he says. So she's not up all hours, texting. She'll get it in the morning. My message.

He bends over suddenly. He covers his face with his hands.

I wasted it! he cries. My whole life.

Nick, no . . .

He jumps up, stands in front of her, shaking and wild.

Why didn't you come back? he cries. You said wait, and you went back inside and I waited, twenty minutes, thirty, I was freezing my ass off on that fucking porch but you never came back! Why, Jenny? Why would you do that?

I don't know. She's standing now, too, holding his hands. She would do anything to calm him. I don't remember, Nick. It's just what happened. I mean, wouldn't you say I didn't have a choice, going out on the porch was the inevitable outcome of—

Don't, he says. No no no. Stop that now. That's not relevant, it's not . . . I just think, if you had come back, maybe, maybe we would have . . . but it doesn't matter! You didn't, we didn't. We . . .

He tears away from her, rampaging around the room. Reaching a wall, he pounds on it with his fist.

You cheated me! he cries. You used me, to, to write your books, and change your life. And when I wasn't any use anymore you talked yourself out of it, and you never fucking told me!

She knows he's not trying to upset her this time. Even if he was, it wouldn't work. She's had the occasional wobble, like when she left the message for Tom, but she has been essentially calm since she told him the truth. Even when the building rocked and the lights went out, and she thought for a few seconds that this might really be it for them—even then, her heart didn't kick up. Her fear didn't rise to choke her. And it hasn't been back since.

I wish I'd told you, she says. I should have always told the truth.

Does he even hear her? He's off again, pacing to the window, pressing his forehead against it. Then banging his head on it, hard.

Nick! Stop!

She pulls him away and he sinks to the floor. Sobbing, shaking.

You got to love, he says. It was fantastic, you said, it changed your life. I didn't get to feel that. Don't you see how unfair that is, Jenny?

The poor man. The poor, poor man. She wraps her arms around him. Should she say it's going to be okay, they could still get out of this, there are miraculous rescues all the time, those Thai kids, the Indian road workers trapped for weeks in a tunnel, remember them? They're all fine! And we'll be fine. The entire world is watching, everyone rooting for a happy ending. Even now, great minds, daring adventurers are hatching a plan. It's crazy but it might just work! We'll emerge to cheers, swelling music, Ron Howard will snap up the movie rights. We'll live.

And Nick will have his chance to love. If he really wants it.

But she won't say any of that. She'll just hold him. Hold him and make hushing noises.

He cannot hush. He has not lived. If he had lived, he could hush, but he hasn't. He made rules, put up his goddamn bulwarks. Constantly pulled back. He could have loved. Again. He could have been in love! And he would have felt ridiculous, a middle-aged fool clambering once more aboard the merry-go-round, but he wouldn't have cared.

Because he'd be in love!

And there, in love with her, maybe that's where the yellow room was. Him in bed, Jenny walking away across the dark floor. But she would have come back. She would have come back to bed, in the yellow room, in the house where they lived, for as long as their love lived. Because maybe she was the answer. Not a sealed-off compartment but a whole life. Maybe he misunderstood every-thing. He was supposed to leave England because it was on the way to her. Maybe everything, even Caroline, even his malaise, was leading him to that kitchen, that porch, her, them. But he couldn't see it, couldn't accept it because he couldn't admit his mistakes. If he had . . . what if he had? He would have opened up to her. He would have been a pain in the ass about it but he would have shown her his true, full self. Been known by her, and known her in turn.

But he didn't. He didn't choose her when he could have chosen her and lived.

And now they're dead.

We could have had a life together, he says. We would have stopped sneaking around. We wouldn't be here.

She coaxes him up onto the bed, where he curls on his side. She curls around him.

We missed our chance, Jenny!

She strokes his hair. At what, happiness? It might not have worked, Nick. We might have only lasted a month. Anyway, we had a lot of happiness. You made me happy.

But—

Nick, stop. Okay? Stop. We're here now. We're together. This is what we have. It might not last for very long, but we have it. We're here.

He's still for a moment.

Did that work? Did she calm him?

No. Because now he jolts up, turning to face her, takes her hands and yanks her up, too.

He's kissing her hands. Threading his fingers in hers. He's smiling!

He looks so young all of a sudden.

She's never seen him look so young.

You're right! he says. We're here. Fuck the past! I feel . . . you know what? I think . . . I think I love you, Jenny.

Oh, Nick. No.

I do! I love you. In fact, I think I always have.

You care about me, she says. You think much more highly of me than I do. But you don't love me, and that's okay. It's enough.

You're wrong, Jenny! I get it. The way I think about you, the things you do to me . . . I couldn't want you as much as I do if I didn't love you. I just couldn't see it.

And now you do? she says. Isn't your timing a little suspicious?

Why are you being like this? he cries. All night you've been at me to talk about my feelings. Now I am, and you're disputing them!

She kisses him. Untangles their hands and holds his face in hers.

I'm trying to be honest, she says. I'm being the real me. I finally found her.

What the fuck does that mean? How can you be so calm? Don't you care at all?

She holds him tight, wishing she could lend him some of her calm. There's so much she wants to tell him. Because she understands now. She was afraid her whole life—not to die, but to tell the truth. So she hid and cringed and deflected and lied. And because she lied she didn't live. But that's over now. The lying. Maybe the living, too, but that matters less somehow. Because the lying is over. And he helped her get there. She needs to tell him, Nick, I get it! Everyone is unfaithful, all the time. To themselves, and the ones they love, and the world. We don't show our true selves, which means we don't live as our true selves, which means we don't live at all. We have to tell the truth. Terrifying as it is, awful, we have to! If we don't, we're not alive. I wasn't alive, until tonight. But now I am.

That's what she would tell him.

twenty two

Update: a growing chorus of state and national political leaders is demanding a full investigation into what is swiftly becoming the worst fire in the history of New York City.

Developing story: FDNY will shoot water into high-rise from roofs of nearby buildings as blaze continues to rage out of control.

Manhattan High-Rise Fire: Over 75 firefighters now dead or missing in action as fire continues its rapid vertical ascent.

@firechieftim: NYC Office of Emergency Management said to be contemplating evacuation of 3-block area around hotel, as possibility grows of total or partial building collapse.

Breaking: Hopes dim for dozens trapped in Midtown inferno as FDNY states fire is beyond their current ability to contain.

Where does #manhattanhotelfire rank in list of deadliest fires in NYC? Click to view slideshow!

twenty three

Let it not be said—ladies, gentlemen, let it never be said—that he gives up easily.

I love you goddammit Jenny, he says. And you love me.

Nick, honey, sit down. You're going to hurt yourself if you keep—

He stops in front of her.

He falls to his knees.

I'm your happiness, he says. You wrote books about your love for me! Don't you still love me? Can't you? Jenny? Can't you give me this one thing? Please?

He's breaking her heart.

I need you to love me, he says. I need you to feel it, and say it. Start again. Love me again. Don't look at me like that, goddammit, don't . . . I don't want to calm down, I . . .

He has jumped up again, he's pacing, clutching his head, shaking it as he clutches.

I wouldn't leave, he says. I wouldn't leave! I stayed in this room. I left England, but I stayed here. You left the porch. I didn't follow you. I have *always* made the wrong move, staying, going, always the wrong . . .

He sits down abruptly. Stares at nothing.

I am a stupid man, he says.

I am a stupid, stupid man.

She sits beside him. Leans into him.

Listen, she says.

But he can't, not yet. He grabs her hands.

I must love you, he says. I don't enjoy being with anyone as much as you. You're my happiness too, I just didn't see it, I didn't . . . this is where I've been alive for the past six years, this room, this . . . I knew it was six, Jenny, I always knew, I'm sorry, I . . .

He covers his face with his hands. I couldn't live!

They're both crying now.

I'm in love with you, he says. I'm so tremendously in love with you right now.

Nick, listen.

Jenny, please. Just say it back. I don't care if you mean it, if you're lying, I need to hear it. Don't look at me like that, don't . . . you've lied to me for years and you won't tell one more fucking lie to help me?

She places her hands on his shoulders and kisses him. Softly. Lingering there. She's always loved to kiss him.

It's only a word, Nick. Let's just feel, okay? What we have right now has to be good enough, because it's all we have. And it's good, isn't it? Whatever we call it? It's been so good. And it can be good for a little while longer, if you—

I'm so sorry, he whispers. Jenny, I'm sorry. I should have seen it, I should have—

Never mind, she says. Be with me now. You be you, and I'll be me, and we'll both just . . . feel what we feel. Right here. Together. Okay?

twenty four

It's time for them to get down on the floor.

The room is getting smokier. What was a light haze near the ceiling has grown thicker, visible in the light from the fire.

She takes off her robe. She reaches for the belt of his, unknots it, and slips the robe off his shoulders. The last time she'll undress him.

They embrace. He inhales the scent of her hair.

She brings the bottle of whiskey. They lie down beside the bed, on the window side. She pulls the sheet down so they're covered, like children in a blanket fort.

They lie face-to-face. She uncaps the bottle and takes a swig, dribbling some on the floor. She passes it to him.

I was looking forward to falling asleep with you, he says. We'll never get to do that. We'll never do a lot of . . . I'm sorry, I can't . . . I don't think I can . . .

He's gripped by overwhelming fear. Shaking, almost shaking to pieces. She holds him.

I've been so small, he whispers. So small!

So have I, she says. So has everyone. Small is what we are.

Breathe, okay? Breathe. We're still here.

twenty five

Later. Calm and quiet:

Jenny?

Yes, Nick?

I was loved?

Oh, yes. She kisses him. She holds his face and kisses his mouth, his forehead. His cheeks. His mouth again. Yes, Nick. You were loved.

Really loved? You loved me?

I did. She kisses him again.

God, I loved you, she says. I loved you so much.

She laughs a little, remembering how it felt.

It was crazy, how much I loved you.

twenty six

They're quiet for a while. Then it's her turn to break down. He holds her as she shivers and sobs, thinking about her little boys.

I love them! And I'm ruining them!

You're not, he says, hoping it's true. He thinks about Jill, and how bad it's going to be. But she's older. And she has Caroline. She'll get through it. Jenny's boys are still chaotic little force fields. So much could go wrong.

They're going to be okay, he says. They have Tom. Your parents, too, right? They have so many people who love them.

But they won't have me, Nick! They won't have their mom. Because I left them. I jumped out the window.

Honey, no, that's . . . come on.

And he strokes her head while she shakes with sobs.

This is it, she whispers. This is losing. I get it now.

twenty seven

Later. They're both calm again. A bit fuzzed by the whiskey. He's combing his fingers through her hair. It's warm in their little fort. Their foreheads are almost touching.

Jenny?

Yes, Nick?

What happens in the third book?

You don't want to know.

Now you have to tell me. You said Wilderkill burns down?

She nods.

And?

She doesn't answer. But the look on her face . . .

No fucking way, he whispers.

Well I didn't know this was going to happen!

Sophie dies? In a fire?

Yes, but she does it deliberately, she says. To be with Julian. It's okay, because they're together.

As ghosts?

As ghosts, yes. It's a happy ending. I promise.

Jesus Christ, woman!

They start laughing. They're drunk now.

You killed Sophie! he says. You're a monster.

I am. She strokes his hair. But I wrote an amazing ending.

twenty eight

The good cheer doesn't last. How could it? He starts shaking again. She holds him tight.

Just be here with me, she says. Be here now.

Now's not cutting it, Jenny. I need more than now.

How can I help you?

Tell me it's going to be okay. Tell me what happens next.

What happens next?

Our story, he says. From here on out.

You want me to . . . ?

Tell me everything. Don't leave anything out.

She strokes his head, his poor head. Their future. Can she do that? Should she?

It's not a lie. It's just a story.

Well, she says, we escape. Firefighters find us, they have oxygen and masks, and they lead us down a stairwell right before it collapses. It's a miraculous rescue, a real nailbiter. But then everybody finds out what we've been up to. They're happy we're alive—

But they hope we drop dead, he says.

Pretty much. Tom and Caroline dump us. The kids are upset, our friends are at war, it's gruesome. But after a while? Everybody calms down. They get over it.

Good. Then what?

We get married.

We do?

Sure, she says. Marriage is romantic. Stupid and romantic. Like us.

He finds her hands and kisses them. I love that. Is this the truth?

Well, she says, it's a story.

But a story could be true. Couldn't it?

Yes, she says. A story could be true.

So we get married. What then?

You quit the firm and go back to graduate school.

Oh fuck that, he says.

You do, Nick! You give it a shot. And I follow you. We live together in student housing.

Student housing? This is getting worse and worse.

We don't have much of a choice. Tom and Caroline cleaned us out.

Ah well, he says. They deserve it. How's the sex in student housing?

Phenomenal, she says. Barbaric.

I like the sound of that.

Our neighbors don't, she says. They're furious. We're exhausted. Your adviser is concerned. I keep missing my deadlines. But somehow? It all works out.

It does, doesn't it?

He kisses her, hard.

Jenny? I love you. I really do. I know it.

She holds him tighter. She doesn't say anything. But she scratches the nape of his neck.

Up and down, and up. And down.

He shudders. Here in the glow. Thick and orangey-pink.

Tell the rest of the story, he says. Don't stop. If you don't stop, we'll be okay.

She kisses him again. I think that's true.

It is, he says. I know it is. Keep talking. Tell the story. Don't stop.

I won't stop, she says. And she doesn't.

She tells the story.

twenty nine

It's late now. So fricking late! When have they ever been up this late together? That was the point of this night, their first whole long lucky night together. To stay up. To luxuriate in an abundance of time. They never have enough, what's that line? *Had we but world enough and time.* And now it's late. Well, early. Technically. Sorry, they're a little . . . how much have they had to drink tonight? They'll have a mother of a hangover tomorrow, if . . . right. Late. Early. Whatever. Point is, dawn is out there, somewhere, beyond the glow of the fire (oh Gad, Nick's glow!), beyond the black curtains of smoke outside, and the thick gray blanket of it inside, pressing down on them. But our intrepid lovers, Jenny and Nick, our lying, cheating, soaring and thudding, misguided, hapless, clueless humans (don't forget they're human, meaning they're flawed, failed, finite, just like you), they don't give a shit about the smoke. They're hidden in their fort. Huddled in there like a couple of passionate teenagers. Under white sheets, like a couple of ghosts. Jenny takes Nick's hand in hers and raises them, palm to palm. Tenting the sheet. She's telling their story. Whispering it to him. They're starting to cough. They may be ignoring the smoke, but the smoke isn't ignoring them, you know? So Jenny whispers. And coughs. And Nick kisses her. And coughs. I love you, he says. I always loved you, I just didn't know it. Because I'm a damned fool. Glad we got that straightened out, she says. He waits, watching her. Expectant. You really don't let up, do you? she says. Never, he says. She sighs. Well, fuck it. I love you, too. Do you? He takes her face in his hands. Don't lie! She laughs. I do. I do. And as she says it she knows it's true. Because it all comes surging back, the torrent, the ridiculous, the overwhelming . . . Love. It's fucking love! There's nothing like it. She smiles and kisses him. Now what? he says. Now you recite me some poetry, she says, and he bitches about it a little, but then he does. Little snippets, whatever comes to mind. *For God's sake hold your tongue and let me love,* he says. And she lets him love. He says, *So let us melt and make no noise.* And they both melt. *Busy old fool, unruly sun,* he says, *something something call on us.* He's whispering these things. Coughing. She's listening. Laughing. There's more kissing. And coughing. It's getting harder to breathe in the smoky room. Which is maybe why they don't hear it at first. The banging. Coming from the hallway. And the voices. Muffled at first. Getting louder.

Shouting. Then more banging.

Someone is at the door.

Acknowledgments

Suzanne Gluck is my agent, brilliant, indefatigable, and possibly a little spooky: she knew exactly when to drop me an email suggesting it was time I write another novel. I immediately thought of an idea I'd had ten years earlier, one I'd tried over and over again to write, only to quit in frustration and tears. This time, I tried again, and it worked. There were still tears—so many tears—but they were worth it. I would not have written this book without her. Thank you, Suzanne.

And then there's Amy Einhorn, who read the novel, loved it, and proceeded to improve it in a hundred ways with her tremendous editorial suggestions and innate grasp of what I was trying to say. I feel so fortunate to have her in my corner. Thanks also to the many other wonderful people at Crown who have shepherded this book into existence, including Lori Kusatzky, Austin Parks and Laurie McGee.

Many thanks also to my wonderful representatives in Hollywood, who read this novel and everything else I've written, cheering me on and helping to keep me employed for the last decade: Eryn Brown, Sylvie Rabineau, Justin Grey Stone and Hannah Davis. With respect to this book in particular, Eryn's deep and enthusiastic engagement with an early draft sharpened and clarified it. I am so grateful.

Many, many thanks to Professor Charles Jennings of the John Jay College of Criminal Justice at CUNY, who provided invaluable advice and guidance concerning high-rise fires. Thanks as well to Jerry Tracy for preliminary conversations and suggestions as I developed my catastrophe. Everything I got right concerning FDNY procedures, the management of emergencies in skyscrapers and the behavior of fire and smoke is thanks to these two experienced firefighters; all errors and exaggerations are mine.

Thanks also to Laura Kipnis, whose book *Against Love* changed how I think about love, sex, marriage . . . everything other than fire safety, basically. Though if she wrote a book on fire safety I'd read that, too.

To Brendan H. Kennedy: the fact that your daughter could put a novel like this in your hands, and you not only read it but praised it and read it again, shows what an extraordinary human being and father you are.

To Cooper Ferris: waob.

Finally, there's this guy I met one night—lo these many years ago—in the stairwell of a dorm at the University of Iowa. (Not escaping a fire; the elevators were slow.) As I got to know him, it became clear that he was headed for a shining literary career. I found this deeply annoying, because that's what I wanted, but I had zero belief that I deserved it. Nevertheless, we embarked on a friendship, and much later a relationship, and much later a marriage. He encouraged me to write and showed me what true discipline is. He is a generous, perceptive and endlessly patient teacher. He is my first reader, my last reader and the only person I ever want to impress.

Which means that the night I met Joshua Ferris was my lucky night.

ABOUT THE AUTHOR

Eliza Kennedy is the author of two previous novels, *I Take You* and *Do This for Me*. Her nonfiction has appeared in *The New York Times, Glamour, Real Simple,* and *Cosmopolitan*. A graduate of the University of Iowa and Harvard Law School, she lives in Hudson, New York.